K'TIA,

A SAVIOR

OF THE

JEWISH PEOPLE

ROBERTA KALECHOFSKY

MICAH PUBLICATIONS

K'tia, A Savior Of The Jewish People, (c) Roberta Kalechofsky, 1995

Printed in U.S.A. on Acid-Free Paper

Kalechofsky, Roberta.
K'tia, a savior of the Jewish people / Roberta Kalechofsky.
   p.   cm.
   ISBN 0-916288-41-2 $14.95
   1. Jews--History--Fiction. I. Title.
PS3561. A4165K75   1995
813'.54--dc20   94-26785
                               CIP

Acknowledgements:
The Ballad of 1095, Sou'Wester, Fall/Winter, 1980.
"1492," Quartet, Fall/Winter, 1974-75
"My Poor Prisoner, Phoenix Rising, Micah Publications, 1982
"Father Woytzski Leads a Jewish Youth Group To the Holocaust Memorial in Oswiecim, Poland," Phoenix Rising, Micah Publications, 1982
La Hoya, Micah Publications, 1976

Special acknowledgement to Professor Mario Materassi, who was kind enough to proofread and correct the blunders of anachronisms and spelling; and to my husband, who also proofread and corrected, and urged me to collect these stories.

micah publications, inc

To Mario Materassi

for your support, your kindness, for caring

The story I tell is a true story,
told with respect to chronology
--master of all things--
Conor Cruise O'Brien, The Siege

Other Titles

Fiction

Bodmin: 1349--An Epic Novel of
Christians and Jews in the Plague Years

Stephen's Passion

Solomon's Wisdom

Orestes in Progress

Justice, My Brother, My Sister

Poetry

The 6th Day of Creation

Haggadah For The Liberated Lamb

Non-Fiction

Autobiography of A Revolutionary:
Essays on Animal and Human Rights

George Orwell: A Monograph

Rejected Essays & Other Matters

Contents

K'tia, A Savior of The Jewish People

Rome for the ancient Romans was...
unbearably modern. Imagine the twen-
tieth century undergone by those not
yet fitted for or inured to it.

Elizabeth Bowen, *A Time in Rome*

Rome was not the first state of
organized gangsterdom, nor was it
the last, but it was the only one
that managed to bamboozle posterity into an almost universal
admiration.   Chester Starr,
The Roman Empire, 27 BC-AD 476

Four Centuries after Alexander's illuminating
conquests, the East cracked open like a bad egg. Refugees,
slaves and slave traders, merchants, missionaries, magicians,
travellers, soothsayers, prognosticators, fortune hunters and
fortune tellers came pouring out of the east, flowing westward
into Brindisi and everywhere else along the Mediterranean
littoral, as if a huge wind had sucked them up and sent them
flying willy-nilly like Dorothy in The Wizard of Oz, exchanging
homelands for glamor. After Alexander, boundaries collapsed,
and the earth stirred from the Euphrates to the Tiber, an
upheaval of organisms that overtakes life every so often and
whose cause remains buried in complexities of humus and

history. Everywhere the moving streams of people going westward confronted the Roman legionnaires, the Equestrians, the military classes and the usurers who went eastward on Roman highways marked with crosses and bodies hanging from them, decomposing in the Mediterranean sunlight.

A portion of the world is always rootless, but rootlessness was the soul and ferment of the times. It was climate and destiny. Everyone was moving somewhere and learning new things. The transition from republic to empire had created an interregnum, a religious vacuum, soon repaired by Augustine; nevertheless, the brief interruption in the religious rhythm when the vestal fires were left unattended had been sufficient: a crack in republican pieties opened: the sacrificial animals, the ox, the cow, the sheep and the pig were thereafter eaten.

Everyday a new idea and a new appetite were born. A new idea of freedom was born on the roads: that it was motion and inward, a state of mind and of movement, something that had no past, that was born every day, that made you and unmade you every morning and every night. Tertullian rejoiced: "The bare soul, just as it is from the road, the street, the weaver's shop!" The Roman road was a new thing in the world and set everybody free. It consummated Alexander's vision when he proclaimed at the banquet of Opis, the brotherhood of man. His influence was immense for millennia to come; his image haunted the Roman emperors and sucked them eastward. Trajan sacrificed in Babylon in the room in which Alexander had died. The idea of empire was transformed into the idea of universal monarchy, popularized into the idea of a universal God, into the idea of the universal spirit. People confessed that humanity was everywhere the same, except for minor differences of height and build and appetite and geography, history and color and gods or goddesses. Otherwise, the soul was the soul like water is water anywhere, whether a lake or an ocean or rainfall or a puddle. Voices of this wisdom came from everywhere. "Thou and I are but one," a certain Simon said. He declared desire to be wisdom and Helen his paramour to be the queen of heaven and the ruler of history. Some worshipped her, but others denounced her. Those who worshipped her opposed those who denounced her, but all declared themselves brothers in spirit. Others said that the good and the just cannot harmonize; and mercy and justice parted company. Some said that knowledge was power, more valuable than gold. Then knowledge and mercy parted company. It was also a revolution. But there was no road in or out of it. It was just condition and climate, no road, no markers, just fracture.

In between the cracks the soul was free, a new thing in the world, the essence of freedom. Only people who had a soul could be free. But everyone could possess one, and all souls were equal and in defiance of each other, searching for more soul, igniting each other to make a spiritual conflagration. The rubbing of so many bodies together in the slave markets and the slave ships, in the imperium emporium heated the air. The magnitude of the disorder stretched from the Tiber to the Euphrates like a unifying glue. Kindred spirits came together at night, at a juncture on the road, and parted in the morning, and everyone had a different tale to tell of where he had been, where he was going, what he had seen, why he was leaving. People suffered the anomaly of being kin and stranger to each other. A brother from Alexandria hailed a brother from Cilicia and hated him, but loved his soul. Blood ties were nothing. They were impediments to the soul. The body was nothing. The nation was nothing. What mattered was the soul, because with it and the road one could go anywhere. The world was Roman, and within the Imperium everyone who paid their tax could go anywhere and was free. The empire was a business. People invested in it like stocks, but everything was free and new and pneumatic. That was the important thing, and the empire did not care about that. It cared only about its taxes, so the knot of history was cut. The world of death was over. Everyone could divest himself of his body, except the crucified who marked the roads like milestones. Their bodies were real and they couldn't get rid of them. There was not enough spirit for that. They stank in the midday sun and spoiled your picnic. Decomposition was real. It spread like a smog in the air as you rode in your carriage and it drove the dogs crazy. Putrefaction was a world condition. The century quivered with slave rebellions: Ennus in Sicily, Athernion the Greek, Undart the German, Spartacus and Salvius the Thracians, Ben Joash and Bar Giora the Hebrews. It was a time of spectacular fires and collapsing cities and temples: Pompeii and Jerusalem, the Temple of Jupiter and the Temple of Jaweh. Sacrifices became problematic, done in hit and run fashion, hither and thither by small bands of people who made up their own rules and did the best they could under the circumstances, which was that the great rhythm of the world that had communicated daylight and night time, victory and defeat, accomplishment and failure, good and evil, guilt and requital, the tasks, rituals and states of mind immemorially and had been bonded to the spirit with blood sacrifice, was broken. The Romans ate their sacrificial animals and ingested their civilization.

Everyone perceived that if there were no world there would be no evil, if the body disappeared there would be no smell, and they contracted inside themselves into smaller and smaller human knots around the soul. They banded into smaller and smaller communities, knots of families and tribes called nations and had secret code words for each other, secret names for the Imperium, for the judge, for the spirit, for the smell. Everyone had a different system of signs by which to declare the universal sign of brotherhood. Everybody underwent gnosis, enlightenment, and perceived that by means of the soul they could escape the smell that clung to their clothes, to their hair, invaded the pores of their skin. A metaphysical opposition between spirit and matter was declared, war was declared upon matter, redemption was not redemption from sin but from creation, from the Imperium. It was the subtlest of strategies, and hazardous. They discovered nothingness and a new temptation was born, lusted for like ancient fleshpots. Terrifying winds filled them and emptied them out. They became space, souls dismembered from bodies which groped over continents searching for their parts. They sustained disorientation, anomie, ruthless attacks on their skin and organs. But bodily pain remained and they took it for a bride, for virtue; and disease and desire mated.

Into this interval stepped the four rabbis, Akiba, Gamliel ll, Joshua ben Hananiah and Eleazar ben Azariah, and the Roman Senator Flavius Clemens, nephew to the emperor Domitian, onto the marble wharf at Ostia. The rabbis had come on a diplomatic mission. Flavius Clemens had come, with other patricians and tradespeople, to buy a slave for his household. In dress and build and stature there was nothing to set him apart from the others, except his manner of choosing his slave. He dispensed with the examinations of teeth and mouth and limbs, and walked about, searching for something less tangible, staring into eyes rather than into mouths and ears. He was, by design, an indistinguishable man in a crowd, plump and bandy-legged, with a balding head lined with vertical wrinkles, which gave him an exaggeratedly grave expression, one which compelled attention or overwhelmed belief. Luckily, the latter reaction was customary. Few people took him seriously. His uncle, the emperor, decided that stupidity was the only explanation for his behavior, and for centuries afterwards his motives were scrutinized but never explained. Perhaps he intended to take them to his grave, for even his death was decorum itself, pious in spirit, however difficult it is to believe in the piety of a senator from the House of Flavius. Domitian, of course, never bought that motive and prayed that death, one way or the other, would overtake his nephew before his seedy alliances destroyed the empire. He sat on a throne in a vast room made wholly of marble polished like mirrors and thought about the problem of his nephew. His advisors advised against assassination. "You exaggerate his importance," they said, a remark of no consequence since no one knows the future and, at any rate, Domitian dismissed this advice because he knew that as emperor he did not have to suffer the inconvenience of a hangnail. He plotted his nephew's demise, if for no other reason than to have one less thing to worry about.

His advisors took a dim view of this impolitic itch for revenge, and reminded him that his order for the expulsion of the Jews would be voided for a year if a senator died during the transmission of the law. "You can either get rid of Flavius or the Jews, but you can't have it both ways." The dilemma stimulated Domitian like an emetic. It moved his imagination.

Not unmindful of this, Clemens strolled from slave to slave, among the bales of wheat and corn, the casks of oil and wine, the marble, the gold, the jewelry and pearls, ivory, coral, lions, glass, amber, elephants, arms and armor, silk and spices, that were being unloaded from ships from everywhere, and poured out of the warehouses that surrounded the marble wharf. To be in Rome, or at least to be in one of its harbors, was to be in the marketplace of the world and all marketplaces, in spite of greed and ambition are redolent of human ingenuity, things lovingly wrought, grown, carved, woven, and sold for pittance, the sweaty trader bent beneath his wife's rugs, her life and burnt-out eyes on his back. The air was hot and lively, the wharf dense with humans of every kind, but mostly with slaves and traders, for Rome was the world's emporium. She bought everything, and everyone came here to sell or to predict the future which, next to war and usury, was the favorite occupation of the day. Prostitutes and female slaves, who knew the value of beauty, walked about with bared breasts. Freed male slaves, with the avaricious glint of fortune hunters, competed with them for a foot of space and attention. In Rome, everybody lived off someone else, particularly the informers who invaded the city in swarms and feasted on dribbles of information left lying about in a temple, a marketplace, or a vomitorium: who was buying, who was selling, who was going into exile or returning from exile, bits of conversation snapped up and regorged out at a senator's table or his wife's closet. Slaves from every nation, Judeans, Parthians, Germans, Gauls, Celts, paraded shoulder to shoulder with merchants and moneylenders, returning soldiers, world travellers, women of fashion and prostitutes, and the ever ominous invisible army of informers and conspirators. The atmosphere was cosmopolitan and predatory, the way Romans liked it: hectic and edgy.

Clemens quickened his step as if he recognized someone and approached an unlikely slave specimen, one whom everyone else would know better than to purchase. The man had desert eyes, desert skin, each follicle of the hairs on his arms distinct in its mooring, vengeful, probably dangerous, more than a hint of the revolutionary and the outlaw in him. He was one in whom criminal behavior and political action had coalesced, unkempt, aged, battered. The slavetrader was lucky to get a denarium for him.

"What's your name?" Clemens asked him in Greek, and when the slave didn't answer, pretending not to know the language, repeated the question in Aramaic.

The slave's face still registered nothing, as if he were deaf, but Clemens knew better, he knew the type. "Come, come," he repeated in Aramaic, "what's your name? I know you understand me and you might as well answer." But he would not. Clemens pressed on. He was sure he knew his man. "I'll give you a name," he said, lowering his voice. "We'll call you Judah Simon bar Giora." The slave's eyes flicked like a snake's tongue, hungry with poison. Clemens grunted, "You like that name, do you? But I shall call you Judah bar Simon. Where are you from? Galilee? Capernaum? No matter." He signalled to the slavetrader to take the chains off the slave and remove his numbers.

The journey back to Rome from Ostia was uncomfortable. Clemens was not above desiring gratitude. He would have thought his benevolence was obvious as they passed, now and then, a dessicated form hanging from its cross in the landscape of the hills where other slaves prepared the ground for planting. But Judah's eyes looked at nothing. They were gloomy, ferocious, insane with hurt, nothing accommodating to present circumstances. "I might as well be taking a tiger into my house," Clemens thought.

So did his servant and amanuensis, Marcus, who was wary of his master's proclivities. Flattered by Clemens' interest in Jews, he was also made anxious by it, and for good reason: it was illogical and, perforce, illicit. It excited curiosity, it was contrary to human surmise. Clemens understood, had no friends, and trusted only his wife, who had been subdued by his obsessions and followed him, fatally. Domitilla was conventional in all ways except two. She loved her house, her garden, vacations in their villa, times spent listening to the drone of insects with her children in her lap. But she could display an unexpected willpower, and she had a regard for her husband which was contrary to public opinion. She regretted the loss of privacy--the garden violated by sly footsteps--the house watched constantly. "Which house is not?" Clemens asked. True, but other houses, other citizens had causes of common concern. Theirs was eccentric and she had no one to share it with. They were isolated by ridicule.

Even the Jews in the Trastevere were amused by Clemens, or feigned amusement as camouflage or bravado. They privately nicknamed him K'tia, the circumcised one, though Hera the whore said she could not testify to it. They reacted to Domitian's decree, the death penalty for circumcision, with the cynical glee of the underclass. The brothels went wild with amusement. Hera brawled, "The emperor will have to come to us to find out who's been cut and who hasn't. We'll become his advisors."

"Marcos," his uncle roared, "the decree will make honest Jews of us. We'll have to stay out of the bordellos."

"It will put us out of business," Hera yelled back.

Her girls, Cara, Regina, Minerva and Julia, sang consolingly, "Not as long as they have six inches left."

The rabbis arrived, predictably, to request a reversal of the decree. Bets were placed on the outcome.

"They'll only make things worse by coming," one said.

"Worse!" a woman spat, "what can be worse?"

"Wait and see," someone else said. "You don't know what worse is yet."

The neighborhood tensed as if for an earthquake. Some said it would have been better if the rabbis hadn't come. Others asked, "Can they ignore our plight?" Warnings about their fate were everywhere--a shaking of the ground, a mysterious rising of dust, a decline in Jewish visitors from elsewhere, a new column built to celebrate the emperor, another arch, another circus, another tax.

"What else?" the barber asked. "They already tax the urinals."

"And the prostitutes and the pimps," Hera added.

"We can't screw and we can't pee free anymore," Julia said.

"Down with taxes," someone scrawled on a wall. It

brought shivers to the neighborhood, and someone else erased it at night.

For decades now nothing could settle down in the Trastevere. A port area on the Tiber, home to dockers, porters, carpenters, polyglot whores and soothsayers, everyone and everything came there, and everything was always at extremes, very funny or very menacing. The neighborhood got drunk at night when they heard the news that Bar Giora had cut off Cestius' baggage train at Beth Horon and had taken it back to Jerusalem, but in public they kept their eyes shut and enjoyed nothing. Every night graffiti went up on the walls in the language of sedition. In the daytime, miracle workers walked with winks and passed doctrines in a handshake. Nazarenes were everywhere, Ophites, Sicari, Salvationists, Sons of Light and Sons of Darkness, Yir'i adhonay, God-fearers and ger-toshuva, those who preached the end of the Law, and those who preached its eternity. Burial societies flourished--other forms of gathering were illegal. People socialized in cemeteries; they brought wine and bread and plots. Subterranean figures, refugees and exiles, lived in the tunnels and the pipes.

Prophets prowled through the alleyways and preached the communion of matter through common love, or the communion of blood, milk and semen in the body of woman. Promiscuity and asceticism were equally valid roads to salvation. Astrologers took up their posts on the bridges over the Tiber and threw down missiles of judgment to the passing barges. In the distant Forum a procession of the vestal virgins wound down from the Palatine Hill, chaste, delicate, dedicated, to join the emperor in his box at the circus and watch the gladiators die.

One saw everything in the Trastevere, or saw it written on the walls: "Death to those who pay the tax," and "Death to those who do not pay the tax": plots, counter-plots, and make-believe plots. Jews paled in the morning and by night were chuckling. "A cut and a coin is the whole issue," Hera said.

"But no different than in the real Rome," her girls sang. Knights came to them for a nap, with a steel corselet beneath their togas. The bordellos were the only safe place in the city, refuge extended by the exiled to the anxious. "Never mind,

Hera," a knight said to her the other day, "just take off my armor and my breastplate and let me sleep a while. I'll pay you just the same." She hung a sign out, "Rest cures available here."

In the day time, the streets were filled with artisans, cobblers, jewelers, cabinet-makers, bookstalls, barbers, vintners, and the omnipresent fortune tellers scurrying between the tenement buildings, the warehouses and granaries along the banks of the Tiber. In the night, the streets filled up with pimps and knights, chariots and wagons, the ferocious wheeled traffic permitted to move only after dark to keep the streets passable by day and everyone awake at night. Prostitutes prowled with the cats, and gazed up the legs of their patrons. Hera brawled her power to passing pedestrians: "Since Domitian's decree, the whole world hangs on a piece of flesh. What would you like to know?" In the morning the dust rose from collapsed buildings and smoke from the fires set at night. Margaretta, the neighborhood's demented mascot, sat in her fourth story window and sang, "My brother juggles, my mother sells flowers, and I tell fortunes."

Marcos, an orphan, was plucked from this neighborhood by Clemens when he was fourteen. "Mazel tov," his uncle said, "we need a Jew in the house of a Roman senator." But Marcos grew up morose and wily, in the shadow of things, and had to make the best of it with a morbid intelligence. Caius, his uncle, was a stone-cutter and lived above a shop in a single room overwhelmed by marble and slabs of stone, sarcophagi, chisels and effigies of emperors which Marcos--humiliated by the trade--he knew what his uncle thought of these--sold for him in the Forum. His uncle worked in marble for the Romans--busts, columns, gods and goddesses; in stone for the Jews and the proselytes for whom he made secret sarcophagi for the catacombs and carved their Roman names in Greek letters with a tree of life, a menorah, Shalom in Hebrew.

Marcos had no sympathy for his uncle's politics, but joined the mourners and secret participants whenever a body was interred, out of a loyalty without fondness. They went by night, without candles, silently through the countryside, in a comradeship held together by secrecy. Each knew what was to be done--groping over rocks and brush until, communicated by a stealthy signal, an opening in the landscape was found and they slipped into it like a column of ants, swallowed up beneath a cypress tree.

The secrecy solemnized the revolution, but in the daytime, in the synagogue, faces were watched for betrayers. There was no password for "friend" or "foe," no way to tell except by what was between the legs. "Can you ask a man to lift up his shirt when he comes to pray with you?" Caius asked. On the day Bar Giora was strangled, the Jews vanished from the streets. Every window in the Trastevere was shuttered except for Margaretta's, who sat in her window and sang her song. No Jews in the Aventine, their shops shut, the Forum empty except for Bar Giora and the Romans who had come to kill him and celebrate their salvation from another slave. The air swelled with imminent elation, Roman heads thrust forward, waiting for the snap of the slave's neck, the signal that they were safe again from a slave's rebellion. A roar of victory swept through the city. Bar Giora was gone, he was done, he was finished. Really finished, strangled, dead, his body dragged away by horses. He was dead, he was gone, he was finished. Rome was safe again.

The fortune tellers along the Tiber vanished like flies. Margaretta paused in her song. Marcos, sitting alone in Clemens' house, shuddered. Suffering from insomnia--like everyone else in Rome--he went later to a tavern. Temperate by day, at night he lived in dark places, among strangers, sailors and freed slaves from Pontus and Ephesus who passed cryptic messages which he viewed with distaste and obsessive curiosity.

His uncle was amused by revolution; he was not. His uncle enjoyed being sly with the Romans; he did not. He was sly with his uncle, crafty for the sake of Domitilla and Clemens. His uncle accepted Bar Giora's death untragically, "unavoidable in a revolution." Marcos trembled at the deed. He was dispossessed of the household of faith, that community which presumed, without assurances, comfort, diagrams or plans, that God would destroy the Kingdom of the Wicked. He sat in the back of the Synagogue of Freed Slaves where the proselyte, Breturia Paulina, mother of Two Synagogues, had walked publicly with her entire household through the deserted streets of the Trastevere and rent her clothes. He sat in the back, alone, and wept with them. He cared nothing for the revolution and everything for its martyrs. The next day the shops opened, the fortune tellers flooded back over the streets. The day was wickedly ordinary.

"Marcos, my amanuensis," Clemens said to Judah when they arrived. It was his smooth skin that enraged Judah. The rabbis, however, a few days later, were not disconcerted. Once one left the sacred land what could not befall a Jew besides shaving? In fact, they were heartened by what they found in the Kingdom of the Wicked--four functioning synagogues, and much quarreling. For the most part--that is, discounting human frailty--the communities of faith held firm, like nests in a storm. The rabbis made their way from the poor of the Trastevere to the prosperous of the Aventine Hill, inspected pots and listened to tales. Everyone had advice about their interview with the emperor.

"You should have come ten years ago. He was a reasonable man then."

"Beware of his smile. If he smiles, things will go badly."

"Read his book. He wrote a book on the care of the hair. Enter, carrying it."

"Do not comment upon his ruddy complexion. Or his eyes. Or his toes."

"Remember, he hates Jews," the head of the Jewish community cautioned.

"Unduly?" Gamaliel asked.

"For political reasons. He built the Arch of Titus to laugh at his brother's affair with Berenice and to remind him of the Roman conquest."

"You should have come ten years ago. Maybe ten years ago something could have been done. He was not so bad then. Now he sits alone and stabs flies with a stiletto."

"If you wish to conciliate him, flatter him, but not too

much. He is very suspicious. Flatter him exactly enough, not too much and not too little."

"One last piece of advice. He is very contrary. If you remember this, all will go well."

Advised, they were pirated into Clemens' house in black capes, huddled together. The danger of coming there made them giddy, yet who else was there to trust so close to the emperor who had sons who might succeed him, and also a Jewish amanuensis.

"God is good," Rabbi Gamaliel said.

Marcos was not flattered by the rabbis' attention: they saw him as an ingredient in God's plans, a bridge between the two worlds, the divine and the wicked, and were prepared to live with the fact that he shaved. They were affable and able, cautious, appropriately worried. A sword of death hung over the Jews in Rome, but they had precedent and proceeded historically. There had been other intransigent emperors. Gamaliel ll, descendant of Hillel, had served diplomatic missions in Syria and spoke Greek with the great Nasi of the Sanhedrin in Judea. Eleazar ben Azariah was one of the sages of Javneh and came of aristocratic lineage, a priest and a descendant of Ezra. Joshua ben Hananiah, true, was a plebeian and a blacksmith, "a maker of needles," but together with Eliezer ben Hyrcanus had carried ben Zakkai out of the flames of Jerusalem in a coffin and had delivered him to Vespasian, whereupon he had miraculously sprung to life with plans for a school--so outlandish a tale of resurrection that later generations consigned the story to the category of legend--though Vespasian believed him. And Rabbi Akiva, the shepherd-scholar, illiterate to the age of forty, whose wife had sold her hair to buy him books, he was the novice in the group, agreeably amazed by Rome, always prey to unruly delights.

These then were the inheritors of ben Zakkai's fabulous strategy, members of the peace party and members of the war party, liberals and conservatives on issues of proselytes, women's rights, accommodation to Rome, open admission to the academy, the calendar, the meaning of repentance. Much was on their minds that day. Rabbi ben Azariah said that God forgives transgression on the Day of Atonement, but man never does. Rabbi ben Hananiah, the last of the peace party, had lived through the revolt under Trajan, and said that only God could forgive the Romans, but he was prepared to negotiate. They argued and hovered between piety and strategy, eating little of Domitilla's offerings, and probed for workable policies in the lineage of Domitian's antipathy to the Jews--a family quarrel with his brother over the affair with Berenice--revulsion to a foreign queen, a conquered queen, on the Roman throne. Should Titus do what Julius Caesar had been forbidden to do? And Domitian's fears over inchoate forces in trends and fashions.

"He sees conversion as treason," Clemens said.

"So it is, from his point of view," Marcos added. "He is prepared to live with Jews as Jews. He is not prepared to live with Romans as Jews."

"Shall we refuse to take converts?" Rabbi Joshua asked.

Marcos affected to retire from the discussion with the comment, "I do not advise, I only explain."

Clemens said, "All the omens at his birth predicted that he would rule the world."

"Did they predict his policies?" Gamaliel asked.

"Or his death, perhaps?" Eleazer asked.

Clemens sidestepped. "Each nation to its own fate. Ours is to betray ourselves. Even Virgil blessed the empire."

Marcos interrupted in spite of himself, not wanting to listen to another recitation of the century's evils. History needed managing, not regrets. "The Jews can worship as they please in their hearts. Domitian wants only a public gesture." The rabbis smiled. Marcos detested their expressions. His soul rose in protest, against his better judgment, to protect the jugglers and the flower sellers.

"These Roman Jews perplex me," Rabbi Joshua said later as they walked back in the dark to their lodgings in the Trastevere, avoiding potholes and broken steps. "A difficult city to live in," Rabbi Gamaliel concurred. "Do you think Clemens can be trusted?"

They stopped walking. Rabbi Akiva looked at the night shadows in the corners of buildings. "I believe so. He has the grace of a true patriot."

"And courage?"

"Yes."

"And what do you make of his household?"Joshua asked.

"His wife worships him. They are an island and have no one else to rely on."

"Neither Marcos nor Judah?"

"Marcos resents his involvement."

"How curious," Rabbi Gamaliel said testily.

Marcos was glad to see them go, secreted out as they had been secreted in. Afterwards, he went to a tavern. It was better than staying at home, trying to fall asleep. Judah lay awake, in a bed near his, separated by a curtain, and muttered throughout the night. Overwhelmed by homesickness, he was continually awakened by his displaced body and complained cantankerously against governments and officiousness and the complexity of simple matters, like desert stars and freedom. Awake, in the morning, his companionship was equally futile. Marcos was annoyed with histrionics, but polite. One has to put up with the suffering of others.

"Are you homesick?" he asked.

Judah looked at him maliciously.

Marcos tried another approach. "What do you dream about--so violently?"

"My wife."

She must be dead, Marcos thought, but Judah said, "She used to be a perfect wife, silent as the desert night, but she became a Greek harpie and licks my ear with her tongue." He smiled ferociously. Further conversation was dangerous. Advice was aberrant. Marcos went his way and Judah his. Ambiguity settled on their doings. Nights Marcos spent in taverns, compulsively listening to the heckling complaints of Greek drunkards: "We built your civilization and you made slaves of us," while Judah kept to his room and listened to his wife's voice. Fastening his imagination on her silence, he filled it with the voice of a fishwife, skilled in mockery. She persecuted him, and he plotted how to forget her. Eventually Marcos did what was expected of him and piloted Judah to his uncle's house, where he could join the revolution.

The rabbis paused on a bridge over the Tiber. They were grateful, very grateful for the courteous and dangerous hospitality of Clemens and Domitilla. Spray from the river wet Rabbi Gamaliel's face. He wiped his lips, of nothing. They were dry. "Are there no lights in Rome?" he asked irritably. "The bridge is wet. I cannot see my way." Buildings collapsed, at least three, as they struggled through the traffic and down alleyways, avoiding flying bricks and marauders. With relief they heard Margaretta's voice and knew they were near their lodgings. "My brother juggles, my mother sells flowers, and I tell fortunes," she sang. A Roman knight threw her a bag of coins. "I'm coming up," he said.
"I only tell fortunes," she sang.
"It doesn't matter," he said. "I only want to rest. This armor is killing my back."
"I only tell fortunes," she sang.
"I'll only stay a while."
"I only tell fortunes," she sang.
"You're mad," he said.
She paused and cocked a serious eye at him, but no one could see it in the dark. "Only slightly," she said, and continued her song.
"We are struggling with omens," Rabbi Akiva said. They slept badly and felt like Romans. The morning dawned only slightly better than the night. It was overcast and rained intermittently. They retraced their steps from the Trastevere and reclimbed the Palatine Hill, this time to Domitian's palace. Sheets of rain covered the streets, the marble houses, the gardens, the oleander bushes. But from time to time, the sun burst out and they took heart. People thronged through the streets, hurrying to shops and clients, or to spread a rumor and inform on a plot hatched during the night. Then an immense cloud rolled back over the sun and rain fell again, in a sheet, without warning, exactly like the Day of Wrath is predicted to come, unscheduled, as people scurry for cover, holding their wet togas aloft from puddles.
"These Romans confuse me," Rabbi Eleazar said again. The remark was a sign that he felt unprepared for this meeting with Domitian. The palace was icy cold. Outside the rain

wrapped the hills. Everything was dreary, wet and mammoth. Domitian sat on a throne in a vast room made of phengite marble which reflected everything, the minutia of dust, insects, the rabbis, the hundred slaves fluttering along the walls, his beloved deformed child on a throne next to his, the flies which waited to be hunted, and his figure contradictorily both dwarfed and magnified in endless replications.

It was hard at first to locate him, ensconsed as he was in images of himself. Luckily, his voice gave him away. It darted out from a corner with a cackle, "What's that you have in your hand?"

"Your book," Gamaliel said. "What a delight to have read it."

"Spread it out on the floor. Flutter the pages open, and spread it out on the floor. Then kick it in a corner. You're not supposed to carry anything in here. Don't you know that? Where are your ambassadors, your diplomats to advise you of correct procedure?"

Gamaliel took up the burden of response. "The fault is mine. I was so carried away by the wisdom in this book, that I could not be parted from it."

"Not bad," Domitian said. "I could test you to see if you did read it, and have you put to death for lying."

Gamaliel was undaunted by this threat. Learning was his forté. "Try me," he said. "I can recite the book by heart."

"Cunning," Domitian said, "but it doesn't matter, because when you go back everything will be exactly the same. But now you know that I am literate and determined. I also want you to remember that we conquered you. You forget it from time to time. I am a fair and a reasonable man and only want what's due me, which is the acknowledgement that you are dead and finished. There is a logic to history in the rules of victory and defeat.

"Presumably," Rabbi Akiva said, "but we do not believe in logic. That's a Greek invention."

Domitian snorted, "I've heard that rumor." He bent his morbid eyes on them, watching them like exotic beasts. "So you are the wise men from the East. Let me put some riddles to you. Here in Rome we suffer from insomnia, dyspepsia, traffic, noise, anxiety, informers, conspirators, falling birthrate, assassination plots, indolent senators, corrupt rich, and an ambitious Greek bureaucracy. Can your religion cure me of these?"

"Eventually," Rabbi Akiva said, "but only one at a time. Which disease would you pick first?"

Domitian smirked. "An evasion. I need relief from all of them immediately, all of them and all at once. You're imposters. But do not be alarmed. I will not reveal your inadequacies. I am temperate, wise, polite and generous, though you probably weren't told this. It is very good that you believe that when you die you are reborn into a glorious world. That's wonderful, exactly as you should believe, since you clearly can do nothing about this world. But I can." He clicked his fingers and aquatic music filled the room, rivulets and streams ran down the polished walls, fountains opened up in the middle of the marble floor, rivers gushed along the polished sides of the walls, and mist enveloped the room from floor to ceiling. Domitian flicked his tongue over his lips, "Enchanting, isn't it?"

"Amazing," Rabbi Akiva concurred.

"Do you really think so?"

"Absolutely."

"You're not trying to flatter me?" He eyed them scrupulously. "I detest flatterers. No doubt you've been told that about me by your elders or your sages, or whatever you call them. They advised you to read my book, which you detested but memorized. I could have written a book on how to void the bowels and you would have done the same. Everyone reads everything I write. What author does not envy me?" He jumped from his throne and beckoned them to follow him. "Come, come, don't be afraid." He slid across the marble floor like a child on skates and his slaves fluttered after him. He threw open another door onto a terrace overlooking the city. The rain had passed. The sun was out and washed the temples in gold and carried the song of the vestal virgins into the warm air like golden notes as they wound down the hill to view the circus. "I am so glad the sun is shining again," Domitian said. "Bad weather spoils everything. It's terrible to take a trip and not to be able to enjoy the sights. Come, come, from here you can see the whole of Rome spread out beneath you, the Circus Maximum, the sacrifices in the temples, you can hear the prayers of my people. I had my palace extended just so that I could have this terrace overlooking the circus and have this view of the city and hear its prayers. I never have to leave my palace to hear men pray or to watch them die." He pulled the drapes to a side and wrapped himself in them and bid them move closer to the window. His insistence was imperial, but they hung back. "We have come on a mission concerning your decree with respect to the Jews here in Rome," Gamaliel said.

"No missions, please. Missions are detestable. They come and go all day long. Come, come, I insist. I know I can't feed you or I would invite you to dine with me." He twittered with abhorrence and delight at their discomfort. It was exhilarating. "I insist," he shrieked. "I want you to see my innovations. I added several new colors to the combats, purple and gold. I want you to see the effect of this. I can order any color uniform or weapon." He pulled the drapes further back for their convenience and curled himself tighter into them. Diplomatically, the rabbis stretched their necks like hesitant cranes. Domitian's eyes clouded over with bliss. "There are many forms of entertainment, and I can order others. Watch." He snapped his fingers and the circus became a Teutonic zoological garden filled with falcons, monkeys, rhinoceros, wolves, wild boar, prisoners thrown into cages of bears for the entertainment of commandants. A new wave of hatred made him breathless. "You think we Romans are so bestial! The idiot Clemens does not grasp the danger. Conversion is treason. Rome knows better--I know better-- than to allow a union of national and religious interests. We learned that lesson from the Druids." He enveloped them with his bulging eyes and twisted himself tighter into the drapery and giggled. Their bafflement was complete, arousing. A trickle of semen ran down his thigh. "I am finished," he said, "now you may leave."

Outside, Rome stood at attention. The sun was out again, the air warm again, the sky Roman, cast in intense blue. Gold limned the marble temples, the marble columns, the marble porticos, while Roman senators ascended the Via Sacra in measured tread. The rabbis reflected on the scenery from their boat anchored in Ostia, as they prepared to depart. The sky was brilliant, metallic, malicious with heat. They sat in silence for days and only changed their posture when the shoreline of Jaffa came in sight.

"The Jews of Rome are on the brink of annihilation," Rabbi Eleazar said fatally.

"Ssshhh," Rabbi Joshua said.

Eleazar wrapped his cloak sullenly about himself. "What is the good of ssshhh? Let us say it and gather it into ourselves. Let us suck the poison of this knowledge."

"What is the use of advertising their demise?" Rabbi Joshua said.

"God, as I see Him," Rabbi Akiva said, "is a political necessity." He took this long view of things when he was flayed alive half a century later by Hadrian's soldiers. For the moment, he added phlegmatically, "Let us pray for Domitian's death and for a good emperor to succeed him."

Domitian, in his palace, clapped his hands at his success and called for his advisors, three on this occasion. "I smelled Clemens on them," he said. "My closest living relatives, his sons heirs to the throne of Rome and he can't think of anything better to do with his life than to lick the feet of Jews. I do not understand him, or these people. Everything reasonable is Roman, everything generous, just, lawful, is Roman." His voice rose to a shriek. "I want Clemens dead. I want him dead immediately."

It fell to his chief advisor to clarify the problem. He cleared his throat in anticipation. "To kill him is easy. To give the senate a reason would be hard. It will cause a fuss if they have no good reason. They can swallow assassination if they see a logic to it."

Domitian settled back in his throne and picked out a stiletto from its box and aimed it with preternatural accuracy at a fly. "Tell them Clemens fancied he had become the messiah of the Jews."

The advisors did not applaud Domitian's joke. One

said carefully, "Some, even in the senate, might not doubt it. What if they turn him into a god?"

"Let them. I don't give a fart what becomes of him in the next world."

"And the decree to banish the Jews?"

Domitian put his arm around the shoulders of the boy companion on the throne next to him, content with the future. "We'll re-introduce it next year. Let the rabble fortune tellers have an extra year. What does it matter?"

Clemens perceived that there had been a change in Domitian's plans. The footsteps behind him became more omnipresent. "Do not leave the house," Domitilla pleaded.

"As long as he hates the Jews more than me, I'm safe," he lied to her.

She warned him, "Domitian has made a bargain with time."

A nervous depression settled over the Trastevere after the rabbis left. It was known that nothing had been accomplished by their visit. Everything was the same, and that made matters worse. Marcos sat, unrepentantly critical, in his uncle's studio, while Caius chiseled and polished a figure. "Clemens will take his life," Marcos said bitterly. Grief assaulted him as if he were already in mourning. The Roman ritual passed before his eyes--the cup of poison or the sword--the choice of death--the chosen moment--Roman honor vested in the final freedom. He rehearsed the scene, bracing himself for it, punishing himself, retracing arguments, hounding arguments into their dead-end corners. Affection for Clemens was his last argument. Domitilla would be with him to the end. He would choose poison for her sake.

"Why should I fall by a stranger's hand?" Clemens said. Here I am in my bed, with my Domitilla, who will stay with me until the end. Do not weep, sweet wife. So many times I have thought it out. How I would die, who would bring you the news, how you would receive it. My fear was always that I would be alone, on a deserted street, clutching the arm of a loveless assassin. Now, let me go to sleep and sit with me. No unkind breezes. Lower the lights. Let me hold your hand, and I will go to sleep."

Domitian had planned a state funeral for his nephew, to demonstrate his sorrow, but Clemens' body disappeared. Those who buried him, the mourners from the Trastevere, the jugglers, flower-sellers, prostitutes, salvationists, slaves, gladiators, fortune tellers--crossed the Via Portuense late one night in the Roman darkness, and made their way to the south slope of the Janiculum. Caius led the line, carrying a large slab of stone on his shoulder, upon which he had carved the word, K'tia. They came to a mole's hole at the bottom of the hill and one by one slipped into a secret passage in the earth. Caius stayed outside and ushered them down. "He has paid the price," he said to each, "now go and live your lives." They slipped down into the ground like burrowing animals and the earth closed over them.

The Trastevere was rocked first with grief for K'tia's death, then with the consolation of reprieve when Domitian was assassinated. They went drunk on the wine of miracles. Wrapped in flames half a century later, Akiva reflected on the unpredictability of salvation.

Domitilla's Mirror

AFTER the death of her husband, Domitilla fell into a hole in history and disappeared from public knowledge. Like other women yoked to an electric moment in history because of their husbands, she had a left-over life to kill. Ensconsed in sober propriety , she could not shake her Republican style in an age of imperial flamboyance. Time and behavior passed her by. She was a daughter of the past, of Virgil and Cincinnatus. Corruption and asceticism gripped Rome with equal compulsion. No one seemed simply to live anymore, to raise children, keep a garden, honor the panetes. Of her four grandchildren, one she had disinherited for unspeakable behavior, one had disappeared with a band of foreign soothsayers, one had gone to Egypt, and one sat in the senate and pared his nails. The future was useless to her.

She wandered through her lovely home and was unbearably lonely. Memories plagued her like flies. They buzzed through her brain and hatched unseemly eggs wherever she looked, at the golden frescoes on her walls, at her furniture, at her mirror, where she searched for clues to how she had disappeared. If she held the mirror one way, it showed a face slightly different than when she turned the mirror around, like the masks of comedy and tragedy, one face with one feature gone awry, a mouth pulled down or pulled up. Both images were recognizably hers, but she could not say how. She studied her face and saw the same nose, the same ludicrously intense eyes, the same once-fashionable ringlets. The features were hers, but a shift had taken place. She had metamorphosed into something of a Janus, with no one to explain the problem to her. It was not even clear that it was her face which had changed, but rather the background which had become transformed. Perhaps it was an optical illusion, a calumny produced by how the light struck the mirror, but she could not ignore it or solve it, or dispose of the problem, or explain it. It terrified her into inarticulateness. She could not tell anyone about it, because she did not know what the problem was.

Her lovely house became a morbid place to her, haunted at night by riddles and in the daytime by her mirror. No one came to visit her. Even the footsteps in her garden had departed a long time ago. Little by little she curled up into a tight ball and squeezed herself into a corner of the garden where she became a snail and let the earth cover her up.

The Emperor's Statue

IT took about three weeks for Caligula's request to reach his Syrian legate in Antioch. Petronius read the letter with dismay and was about to crush it in his hand. Recalling, however, that he would probably be observed by informers and enemies who already knew what the letter said, he exclaimed: "Ah, a request from the emperor to have a statue of himself built in Antioch. In the courtyard of the synagogue." The posture of the guards shifted; they braced themselves for the future. The messenger waited unnecessarily for an answer, for the answer was predictable . Petronius responded in a pleasurable voice as if wine were running through his mouth: "The emperor's request is my mission." As soon as the messenger left he went to his concubine's room where he spit epithets and spewed gloomy prognostications.

It took three weeks for the letter to reach Petronius, but a few days for the news to go from Antioch to Alexandria. Petronius' enemies were thrilled: either way, the career of the wily bureaucrat was over. If he built the statue, some Jew would killed him. If he didn't build it, Caligula would kill him. Spite ran in people's mouths. The Greeks in Alexandria rioted in anticipation that the city would soon be theirs again, never to dispute it with others. Jews armed themselves with knives. Caligula prayed they would kill each other, and that he would live to kill whoever survived the battle between them. The aging Jewish philosopher, Philo, came from Alexandria to plead with him to rescind the order. Even Herod Agrippa, the fetchit Jew, said, "That is the one thing calculated to start war.

Restrain yourself. You know you can have anything you want but that."

Caligula knew. That's what being emperor of Rome meant. He had warned his grandmother, "Bear in mind that I can treat anyone exactly as I please." Mostly the senate. Their capacity for acquiescence at first amused him, then astonished him, then drove him into furies. The obsequiousness of humans was unending. Their appetite for status and respectability was inexhaustible. He could compel a senator to run alongside his chariot dressed only in his nightshirt. He could order a senator to stand naked and tweak his organ with his sword. "And guess what?" he said to Herod Agrippa, "the idiot stood his ground and was grateful I didn't castrate him. I know how he felt, for I served in this role myself once, toady to an emperor. That's how I learned to be a good actor. The empire is the greatest theater in the world, and the urge to be an actor in it is enormous. It commands the largest stage in the world because the imperial appetite is enormous. You cannot feed it enough. As much as you feed it, you need to feed it more. Its appetite cannot come to an end, even though it swallows up empires and vomits them out again. What actor does not want the world for his stage, and a world in which the best role in it is his. Only mortality limits my power, only mortality builds a hedge around the Imperium. That's the thought that curdles my stomach. It's infuriating to see human beings worship people as immortals, no matter what else they are or were. The capacity of human beings to worship anything or anyone, good or bad, ugly or beautiful, revolting or otherwise, is infinite. You cannot put it to the test or find the end of it. Human beings are by nature idolaters. That is their most ancient instinct. They will worship anything on any pretext: a handsome man, a chicken, a goat, the stars, a tree, a crazed old woman, virgins, whores, athletes, soldiers. Why not me? Why not me, Agrippa? It's absurd to argue that my credentials for being worshipped are not as good as a wrestler's or a virgin's."

He had the heads of Greek statues removed and replaced with copies of his own. No one complained. But his request for a statue of himself in Antioch sent up dark murmurs. He was thrilled. Muscles flexed. He was intoxicated by the fuss he created. It was more fun to play with the Jews than with the senate. He tapped the tips of his fingertips together merrily. "Precisely," he said to Herod Agrippa, "I've had you several times, but that doesn't work anymore." Corrupting Agrippa was like stepping on a bug, which went to show that the Jews too could produce a Roman monster. But they couldn't produce a Roman god. At least the Greeks could do that, they could produce Roman monsters and Roman gods. Some alliance was possible with them in mourning the fading pantheon, the semi-gods, the half-gods, the divine humans, the human divinities. The thought that he might be administering to a dying empire and a dying pantheon at the same time was terrible. That would make him a lame duck emperor and perhaps a lame duck god. He felt a coming chill. There were so many foreigners in Rome these days, people from anywhere. The streets were filled with languages he did not understand. One day he went out walking among them, trying to figure them out. They didn't even know he was their emperor. He was an alien in his own city. He attributed his impotence to their presence. The only thing one could count on to stay the same was marble. Everything else apparently was mud, mud in flux, people, ideas, foods. Even his tastebuds had gone inert. The first time he ate partridge from Paphlagonia and pâté from Gaul, he had swooned at their succulent tastes, like a caress upon the tongue felt all the way down through the gullet. The spoils of war were marble, meat, wall painting, gold, slaves and corruption. But only marble remained to be enjoyed. Paintings faded, meat spoiled, slaves rebelled, corruption bored. His organ was more and more flaccid. Little pleased it anymore. "Surprise me," it said to him, but nothing did. When he had been a youth, it had surprised him, it had often shocked him, tumbled him over, whacked his brains out, did its own bidding, humiliated him. Now that he was the master of it, it was a limp slave, a bad slave, a sluggish slave. Sex had lost its context. Being free to fornicate whenever, sitting, standing, walking, in the senate, in the theater, behind any bush, with anybody, with anything, with any animal, in any way, in any posture, with any number, it had become dull. His organ was constantly flaccid and it took greater and greater effort to make it sparkle. He had slaves kiss it, caress it, whip it, sting it, massage it, pull it, push it, flip it, twist it, and put the slaves to death for failure. Sometimes that helped. Cruelty was a reliable strategy, though he was in terror of the slaves. What Roman wasn't, when it came right down to it, though the trick was to reverse the impression. The enemy fed him, bathed him, dressed him, knew all his secrets, every mole on his body, and they had such powers of revenge. A month ago three hundred slaves on a latifundia had committed suicide just to plunge their owner into debt. Was that reasonable? The old solutions didn't work anymore. Only war worked. Except for that, nothing else worked. The senate had become a bunch of asslickers and the thrill of that was gone. Only new things were really interesting, and then only for a short while. He wept at the thought that he could not keep things from going stale or from fading. Change crazed him. Like everyone else, he wanted the world he knew to be eternally fresh. He had bouts of nostalgia where he wandered about the streets of Rome in the dead of night when it was relatively free of people, only some thieves whom he enjoyed terrifying with his revelation that he was the emperor and would put them to death if they touched him, or put them to death if they didn't touch him. They didn't know what to make of him, whether to believe him or not, whether to steal from him or not, whether to murder him or not. Was he worth the risk? Their calculations amused him. They could go down in history forever if they killed him. He tempted them, but thieves didn't care about glory, they were so practical-minded. He could not even tempt a murderer to murder him or disease to destroy him. He walked about naked in storms, but woke in the morning with health shining in his cheeks. Not even nature would touch a Roman emperor. Friends stuffed their gullets, puked in the streets and lay groaning with bellyaches. But nothing made him sick. Maybe his body was dead, maybe he was a god. Either way he was invulnerable. There must be a reason for that. He had found this message one night when he was walking about in a rainstorm. It was marvellous how it had come into his possession. It had floated down the street in the storm while he was out walking. His wet toga was pasted to his body. A pebble lodged in his sandal and he bent down to dislodge it. The message swirled past him in the dirty rainwater. He caught it just before it would have sailed down the street. He was amazed at what it said, it was his thoughts as they had been struggling to express themselves. He looked about to see who could possibly have dropped this divine message at his feet. But there was no one else about, not even thieves. Everyone else was at home, cozy and dry, waiting for the storm to pass. He laughed. They thought he was crazy, walking about in a rainstorm late at night, but he had been anointed by the rains of heaven. He took the message back to his palace and by the light of a torch read the breathtaking words: "If you do not make yourself equal to God, you cannot apprehend God, for like is apprehended by like. Outleap all body and expand yourself to the unmeasured greatness; outstrip all time and become Eternity; so shall you apprehend God."

The fools, the courtiers, the senate, the knights, the diplomats, the Greeks, the fools of realpolitik, thought he had ordered the statue just for fun, one more whimsy from the whimsical emperor. He sent messengers monthly to inspect the progress on the statue. Work was continuing apace. The feet and ankles had been built. Each foot was two feet long. It was obvious to everyone that this was going to be a very big statue. The toe nails measured six inches. The Greeks in Antioch came to inspect and were amused by their size. They gathered in the courtyard of the synagogue and, to taunt the Jews, climbed over Caligula's feet and sucked the toes. The Jews watched from a distance. They would no longer go into the synagogue. The Greeks were hilarious at this. They beckoned to them with whining voices to move closer and inspect the statue, but the Jews kept their distance and watched.

Three hundred slaves and a dozen master sculptors labored on the project. Yet the work proceeded slowly, very slowly. After a year's time, the legs were only as high as the kneecaps, though they alone were already six feet tall and stood athwart the yard like a colossus-to-come. They alone already took up the entire courtyard. The Greeks shouted, "Higher, higher." Petronius obliged. It took another year to reach the crotch.

Caligula became impatient and sent another messenger: "Why is the project taking so long? I'll be dead before you finish it."

Petronius flattered: "This will be the highest statue in the east. Already the crotch overlooks the Arabian deserts. It will reach twenty feet--and more--most likely--more in height when it will be finished. It will be higher than the Pyramids. Only the mountains will be higher than your statue. When your royal head is set atop it will look out over your eastern empire for a hundred miles and people everywhere in the east will see it."

The slaves built scaffolds and pulleys to reach the place where the hips would sit on the thighs. Each thigh was forty inches in circumference. They crawled about on scaffolds under the pelvis to set the hips in place. The torso weighed two tons. Three slaves fell to their death from a fold in the toga. Two others were crushed to death on the ground when they fell on top of them. But the work went on. The Greeks kissed their fingertips. Soon, soon the head would be put in place on top of the shoulders. Soon, soon, hell would break loose. The entire empire waited for the coup de grâce. But it was taking ages to come to it. Caligula tapped his fingertips together. He was losing patience. He was getting bored. Of all the boring things one could do in this world, waiting was by far the most boring thing. Anticipation wore thin. He sent another letter to Petronius who saw, by its contents, that flattery was also wearing thin. "I'm not interested in waiting until I'm dead to be worshipped. How much longer?" Petronius replied, "Art can't be hurried."

"True," Caligula answered back, "but you can be."

The Greeks whispered suspicions. Now they distrusted the delay, the size, the complications, the endless details, the need for more slaves, the dismissal of sculptors, the search for other sculptors. Folds in the drapes were redone four times. Caligula's sandals were redone three times. The straps were tied and retied. A big toe was recast twice. Some whispered, "He means it to take Caligula's lifetime."

"Impossible," others said gleefully, "Caligula is only twenty-nine. He might reign for another fifty years. No statue can take that long. Petronius will be dead by then by imperial decree if not from old age." The Jews stood on a hill and watched. "It's very big," one said, "but it's still headless."

The Greeks started rumors. "Why so big?" they queried each other aloud. "It's never good enough."

Their queries reached Caligula's ears. He wrote again to Petronius, "Why so big?"

"Size is power," Petronius wrote back. The Greeks winked at this. Caligula thought, and tapped his fingertips together. He had a dozen Greeks killed for being smarter than himself and wrote another letter to Petronius: "Make preparations to take your life." The messenger, an Illyrian slave, had trouble delivering the message. Pebbles got in his sandals time and again. Once he fell asleep for two days on a hill in Illyrium and dreamed that he was free again. It was so balmy and new buds were just beginning to emerge. It was his favorite season. Once he stopped in Tarsus to hear the new preachers from Judea and was overtaken by another messenger to the east. This messenger did not procrastinate, the season spurred his zeal. He stopped in every port and town to give the message that the emperor had been assassinated. It was taken up by relays and reached Petronius while the first messenger was still dallying in a village outside Syria. Petronius paid the master sculptors and sent them back to wherever they had come from. The slaves climbed down from the scaffolds, glad to be on terra firma again. When the first messenger finally arrived, Petronius crushed the letter, threw it into a fire and watched it burn merrily. He mourned with the mourners and, after a respectable delay, gave orders for the statue to be disassembled. The Greeks were disappointed, but said nothing. The Romans and the Jews were relieved, but kept silent. No one expressed an opinion about the matter, one way or the other. Certainly not Petronius.

The Ballad of 1095

"It is stiffely canvassed betwixt learned men ,whether this warre was lawfull or not."
Thomas Fuller, <u>Historie of the Holy Warre</u>

"Not all of them, indeed, were there in behalf of the Lord...."
William of Tyre, <u>History of Deeds Done Beyond The Sea</u>

Mes enfants: Célestine, Adeline, Madeleine, Josephine, Caroline, Jeanne,
    et les autres: Gilbert, Robert, Roger, Raymond, Simon, Jean. Les soeurs et les frères. Faites attention.
    Sister Catherine came into the draughty west hallway of the museum.
    "Mes enfants," she said. A dozen heads straightened up. "Regardez," she said. Twelve pairs of eyes rolled upwards to the Gothic ceiling. Ah!
    Sister Catherine tucked her hands into the pockets of her skirt. "Maintenant," she said to the ticketseller. He was a man with broken teeth who was semi-retired, and he felt graceless transacting business with a nun, although the museum was not his business. Sister Catherine was patient while he considered his position. She had been educated in a convent and had gone, without pause, from convent to nunnery. She was the middle sister in a family of five children and had been regarded by the

others as the one least likely to succeed. She could not play piano like her sister, Josépha. And Monique, le bébé de la famille, had taken all the beauty to herself. Sister Catherine had an indefinite body, breasts of neutral ampleness and hips of well meaning fullness. Her body was companionable and it accompanied her companionable temperament and her companionable complexion. Sister Catherine was always equitable. She was unpresuming. She was modest, pious and equitable, but she was not likely to succeed in the world of worldliness. So Bernard, her brother, and man of precise judgments, accompanied her the day she went from the Convent of The Immaculate Mother to the Convent of the Sisters of The Sacred Heart.

Bernard paused under the sculptured archway of angels fluttering in flight towards heaven. Catherine (née Colette) looked up at him trustingly from under the brim of her black straw hat. Points of sunlight filtered through the straw and fell on her inoffensive cheeks. Bernard bit his moustache. But the angelus rang and Catherine's body was motherly. Bernard kissed his sister on her forehead and she passed in under the stone archway while, overhead, the angels continued their flight.

The years proved him right. Catherine inclined in age towards what she had always been: modest and equitable, pious and content. Her skin aged well, gently and softly. Her hair whitened; her voice acquired a musical tone. She wore a pair of inoffensive glasses. She was unattractive and serviceable and everybody respected her. Bernard, on the other hand, became immensely wealthy and very thin and everyone respected him. He supported two mistresses, one with a baby grand piano atop of which sat a Louis Quatorze clock of Apollo in his chariot which rang a delicate chime every half hour. Josépha had six children and became fat. Monique went on the stage, married a basketball player from America, and was disinherited. Raoul gambled. They saw him once a year at Christmas time, along with Catherine. She, not Raoul, was invited to stay the night, to shower influence on Bernard's children. At matins, on Christmas day, the clock struck the hour between the sacred and the profane and Raoul went home to a sparse flat while

Catherine stayed on amid a flutter of Louise Quatorze demigods. It was Catherine, not Josépha, who sat in the center of the table under the crystal chandelier, flanked by Bernard's children to whom she told in her musical voice Christmas tales of bygone days. Josépha played the piano and bored the children, but Sister Catherine, with a cupboard full of stories, was prosaic and serviceable, but not boring. She could refer to Charlemagne as an intimate and imitate Roland blowing his horn. Toot! She cupped her hands to her mouth. Even Bernard found it quaint. But only at Christmas time. For the rest, he found such phrases as "God's truce," and "the Christian king," serviceable only in defense of his children's faith. The girls he sent to the Convent of The Immaculate Mother and the boys to St. Joseph's Academy. But when they grew up he found husbands for the girls and positions for the boys, and asked Sister Catherine to remember them in her prayers.

So Sister Catherine understood the ticketseller, who, in turn, rang up twelve sales for the children and beckoned with an arthritic finger that she should pass through the turnstile with them. And the turnstile clicked thirteen times: Célestine, Adeline, Madeleine, Josephine, Caroline, Jeanne. Sister Catherine held up her hand. "Encore six," she said. Gilbert, Robert, Roger, Raymond, Simon, Jean passed through. "Et moi."

"Mes enfants. Regardez." She looked up at the stained glass panels so high. Ah! Two hundred feet high. Madeleine's hat slipped off her head. Ah! It could be God looking down at them. In that blue hexagon. It was God looking down at them. Might as well be. It was St. Peter in a brown smock with a sturdy brown cross on his shoulder. Standing next to the sky. With a gray Holy Ghost on his head. And in the next panel the noble Gottfried de Bouillon kneeling on his sword in front of Christ. Madeleine rescued her hat. Célestine squinted her nearsighted eyes. "Mon enfant, do not squint," Sister Catherine said, out of respect for Célestine's parents who had asked of the sisters that they keep a special eye out for this trait in their child. "Célestine, do not squint," Sister Catherine said and tucked her hands into the pockets of her dress beneath her pleated bosom. The children lined up in proper places: Célestine, Adeline, Madeleine, Josphine, Jeanne. Sister Catherine looked at Caroline with reproach. Caroline took out a wad of gum from her mouth. Adeline was glad she had been caught. But Sister Catherine only said, "Très bien, encore six. Gilbert, Robert, Roger, Raymond, Simon, Jean." They presented the coat lady with their raincoats and jackets and she presented them each with a ticket. And they proceeded in size place, girls first and then the boys, around the large room, following Sister Catherine and the trail of the blue velvet rope over the polished bricks under the unglad eye of the guide who did not like children. They went from le salon des modernes to le salon des impressionistes, thence to a writing room used by Louis XIV, a toilette de Marie Antoinette, a salon of the Princesse de Soubise, wood carving by Herpin, unapologetically rich. Sister Catherine consulted a floor plan. Caroline retrieved her gum from a secret place and in view of Adeline popped it back into her mouth. Sister Catherine tucked the floor plan into her pocket and proceeded. The children proceeded too, one by one in size place, through the salon des modernes, et le salon des impressionistes and came into a room more suitable for the defense of the children's faith: Uccello, Mantegna, Sassetta, Giotto, Masaccio, Piero della Francesca, Botticelli, Raphael, Perugino, Pisano, the Annunciation by Spagna, a Madonna by Pisanello, a nativity scene by Piero, a crucifixion from fourteenth-century Cologne, the Descent by Grunewald, a Pietà from the school of Avignon. And paused in front of a large brown painting of God handing the Law to Moses and Moses handing the Law to Peter. Peter was in a brown smock again with a hempen belt and a halo. Moses did not have a halo. Neither did God.

Robert passed a dirty note to Simon and Simon passed it to Raymond. Raymond passed the Pietà and genuflected and passed the note to Robert, and Sister Catherine was pleased with Raymond. So Roger passed the note back to Robert and Robert froze as Sister Catherine's eye fell on him, and he stuffed the note in his mouth and his tongue turned blue.

Ensuite, Sister Catherine studied the floor plan and proceeded to the room of her choice. Ensuite, in size place the children proceeded too. The young ladies carried their straw hats in their hands and the young gentlemen wore white handkerchiefs in their breast pockets, and all behaved as expected and came at last, through a meandering of art and ages, to the medieval rooms, the armor, the reliquaries, the crusader's sword, the crown of thorns set with jewels and gold, the crucifixion in mahogany, and the tapestries, three to a wall, those grand architectural features of woven fantasies and even, here and here, of reality.

And the topic matter of those colossal cloths: the Acts of The Apostles and The Loves of The Gods, the Deeds of The Heroes and The Dance of the Hours, The Labours of Hercules and The Triumph of Petrarch, Apollo In His Chariot and Christ on His Throne. Ah! Ladies and gentlemen who lived so passionately in your age: The Army of Clovis looks like The Army of Caesar, and all look like the army in The Capture of Jerusalem. The race of knights is constant. La gloire de l'histoire et de l'art et du Catholicisme, l'esthetique de l'histoire et de la religion. The patrimony of art. Twelve chairs had been placed in advance in three rows for Sister Catherine's students by a guard in a blue uniform who did not mind children.

The young bucks, Roger, Robert, Gilbert, Raymond, Simon and Jean threatened the knights in armor. Simon, avant de s'asseoir, put up his fists and clobbered a knight on his visor. The metal rang out and a guard came running. Sister Catherine wrung her hands and apologized and pinched Simon very hard in the muscle of his right arm. The young ladies, Adeline, Madeline, Josephine, Caroline and Jeanne, held their straw hats in their hands and offered him a snooty sympathy. "Maintenant," Sister Catherine said and took out a textbook. "This is not a park. Here you must be still, look and listen. That is all. Faites attention." And held them with a look of warning in her eyes. And the children, Célestine, Adeline, Madeleine, Josephine, Caroline, Jeanne, Gilbert, Robert, Roger, Raymond, Simon, Jean, understood this and gave her thirty seconds of respect before they unbuckled again. They moved, step by step, behind her back, over the polished brick floor, around the formidable four-poster bed and paused at the table of reliquaries: a tooth of St. Andrew, blood in a vial from St. Gregory, a hip bone from St. Jerome. Josephine was humbled, and shuddered. The young men passed it over with manly smirks.

And came to their places in front of their seats in front of the wall of tapestries in front of the French doors that swung half a foot each, open onto a little balcony upon which splashed a warm rain. Sister Catherine counted their heads as they took their places.

"Célestine."

"Oui."

"Adeline."

"Oui."

"Madeleine."

"Oui."

"Josephine."

"Oui."

"Caroline."

"Oui."

"Jeanne."

"Oui, ma soeur."

Silly laughter. Sister Catherine gave Jeanne a very good glance for that one. Et les autres:

"Gilbert."

He hesitated. The code called for him to follow Jeanne's daring with something of his own. To merely imitate was fatuous. To go a step further would be dangerous. He wavered and Sister Catherine looked past the head of les autres to see what was delaying Gilbert's answer. Gilbert looked up at the turrets of Jerusalem for a tricky response. Sly Raymond stuck his finger in Gilbert's ribs. "Oui, oui," Gilbert said and dissolved into giggles. Sister Catherine fingered her cross. Under the circumstances discipline was limited. There was the inevitable one thousand "I Shall Not Giggle In A Museum Standing Under The Crusader's Cross" to be written. Then she continued, pronouncing the rest of the names with an emphasis that would not be misunderstood.

"Robert."

"Oui"

"Roger."

"Oui."

"Raymond."

A cowlick of hair hanging over his forehead gave a hint of possibilities, but he only looked sly and said,

"Oui."

"Simon."

'Oui."

"Jean."

"Oui."

And Sister Catherine disposed of the rest of their nonsense by reminding them of their history and their future rewards, their duty as Christian children, the struggle in Spain against the Infidel, and their responsibility to their parents and their teachers, and threatening to levy on each the tax of one thousand sentences of "I Must Be Respectful In A Museum Which Houses God's Gifts," and concluded with, "Asseyez-vous."

The response was not bad. The girls placed their straw hats in their laps, the boys sat down behind them morose in high-polished shoes. Miraculously a pointer appeared in Sister Catherine's hand. She tapped a tapestry behind her and said, "Regardez," and Madeleine found the unicorn sitting in a blue field flanked by the French doors, behind which fell an uncertain rain. "Regardez," Sister Catherine repeated, "comment s'appelle la bête, Madeleine?"

"La licorne."

"Oui, très bien."

"There's no such thing as a unicorn," Jean said behind her. Madeleine turned the brim of her hat in her hands. If there was one thing she could not tolerate it was twelve year old boys, and among the twelve year old boys fat Jean was the worst. Madeleine said, turning her head only enough so that her voice dropped over her shoulder on to fat Jean's lap. "I read in a book that there were unicorns."

Jean snickered. "What happened to them?"

"They became extinct." Her voice fell like a rock into his lap. Her aggressive stupidity was threatening. He said with feigned cleverness, "I read in the encyclopedia there was never such things as unicorns."

Madeleine's sense of status, her vrai twelve-year-old-dom and slim figure took command. She said with chilly sophistication, "What did you look it up under?" Jean would have clobbered her on the shoulder blade, but Sister Catherine directed a question at him. "Jean, comment s'appelle la plus fameuse école de tapisserie?"

"Arras," Jean said, and believed he had vindicated himself, but Madeleine kept her eye on the unicorn and, to spite him, swore eternal love to it. Oui. And the unicorn received her devotion. Peace in a woolen eye crouched in a cruciferous field in gentle majesty. As well as in limitless suggestibility. The lamb crossed with the goat. And about were the unthreatening hunters, lads in embroidered hosiery and woolen tunics, and the ladies with plaited hair and velvet kirtles that fell in winey drapes about their bodies and the unicorn in their midst, at peace, gazing with guileless eye because the arrow is only woven.

"Vraiment, Arras," Sister Catherine said. "Fil fin d'Arras." Her pointer traveled up the turrets in The Conquest of Jerusalem. "Gilbert, what is the thread used in tapestry?"

Gilbert crumpled. He had no recollection of ever having studied the subject, but under the watchful eye of Sister Catherine an answer came to him.

"La laine."

Sister Catherine was suspicious, but in the absence of particularities there was nothing to do but to continue. "Vraiment, la laine. Wool ést l'indispensable material in the warp, but il est possible d'employer silk et quelquefois les filaments de l'or et de l'argent, n'est-ce pas? Threads of gold and silver. Thread from Cyprus. Thread bought with crusader's blood."

Eyes floated to The Capture of Jerusalem and looked for the blood. "Yech," Jeanne said, spotting it on a wall.

"Splash," Roger said behind her.

"Mais non," Sister Catherine said and used her pointer. "C'est la vraie laine rouge, ce n'est pas la soie." She minced her fingers in the air. "La soie est un filament délicat. Dis-nous, Josephine, comment la soie est employée."

Josephine looked bland. She looked at the rain outside. She looked at the sleepy guard. She looked at the tapestry and looked bland. Sister Catherine ignored her look as best she could. She let her pointer drift over the tapestry while Josphine sank or swam or was rescued by someone.

Nothing happened. Josephine went on looking bland. Sister Catherine came to the end of her reserve. Her pointer stopped on the beard of a knight. "Faites attention. Il est employé pour les cheveux, le ciel, la toile, les fleurs. Pour couleurs, jamais le noir. Pour les détails fins." And gave Josephine her due disgust and went back to the tapestry with a sense of moral investment. "Clairobscur." Wool and silk, light and dark, the warp and the woof. "Vraiment?" And since morality inevitably leads to allegory, to symbols and to signs and to signatures, all was woven of the devil and God. And since it was Sister Catherine's way to go from a technique to an insight, from a lesson to a story, she said with élan. "And do you know, mes enfants, how all this came to be, this great tapestry and all the great tapestries that hung in the great halls of the barons? The crusaders brought back the secret of it from the Egyptians. Each thread you see is a drop of martyr's blood."

Adeline, Madeleine, Raymond and Roger saw it, but Célestine said, "I don't see a thing."

"Squint," Roger whispered.

"Célestine, do not squint," Sister Catherine said.

"I do not see the blood," Célestine complained.

"It is martyr's blood," Sister Catherine said. "It stays in heaven."

"How does it get into the tapestry?" Célestine asked.

The young bucks laughed. Jean said, "They carry it down by unicorn express." Raymond thought that was wonderfully brilliant and he was jealous and became an atheist. But Sister Catherine did not shrink from the challenge. It is the nature of the spiritual world to survive on the rim of disaster. A single question can dissolve it. She said enthusiastically, "Do you not see how the crusaders sacrificed everything they had to deliver Jerusalem? Comment! Because they bend the knee and the will to do God's work. Do you not know what it was Pope Urbain ii said to them to make them so courageous? Qu'est-ce qu'Urbain leur a dit?"

The young bucks and the young ladies bowed their heads under their ignorance. Simon took possession of Madeleine's hat and passed it to the others. One by one, Gilbert, Robert, Roger, Raymond, Jean, passed Madeleine's hat behind their backs. The young ladies, Célestine, Adeline, Josephine, Caroline and Jeanne did not betray their knowledge of this activity. Madeleine turned blue with anger. Sister Catherine pretended not to know what was happening. "Qu'est-ce qu'Urbain leur a dit?" she repeated. The unicorn's eye looked down, mild and believing. Madeleine could have died with vexation and would have liked to have been a lady in a kirtle in that cloth of blue field upon that cloth of fleurs de lis.

Said Caroline, pointing to a beak on the helmet of a soldier, "Qu'est-ce que-c'est?" And Roger told her in a whisper. Caroline blushed and dropped her gum. Sister Catherine adjusted her glasses to look at the tapestry where Caroline pointed. "Vraiment! That is a nose guard." Out of loyalty to Sister Catherine's answer, not a single eye looked diverted. Her innocence held them. The guard turned away respectfully and drummed on the window sill and watched the rain fall coldly onto the little balcony.

Sister Catherine was still waiting for an answer. Her students looked at her as students will who haven't got the answer and know they should have it: innocently. With good pedagogy, Sister Catherine clicked her teeth to shame them and told them how it began: "Mes enfants, regardez l'oeil du croisé." The pointer moved. Their eyes followed. It was a very good eye she pointed to, woven in robin's egg blue with ochre creases in the lids, with a tawny beard and an ice-blue helmet and a blue iron shield, and all about crusaders woven in red and blue with the head of an infidel looking at Gilbert who had never seen an infidel before. And the rest, thousands with swords and horses and armor and rivets and nails and metal and mail and iron and bells and banners and pennons and lance tilted à Jerusalem, pushing through the gate of the city. Mes enfants:

Stephen of Blois
Robert of Flanders
Robert of Normandy   et
That young buck, Bohemond
          Who stayed in Antioch   et
          Gaston de Bearns   et
 Gerard de Roussillon   and
Tancred the colorful
Who boasted he was the new
                              Ninus
Who would smash the walls of
                              Babylon

The Ballad of 1095/42

Which he did   et
Les autres: Baldwin
Who burned a cross into his
                              forehead
                                                et
Godfrey de Bouillon et son épouse   et
L'épouse de Baldwin du Lorrain   et
Raymond of Toulouse   et
Les enfants, oh! beaucoup des enfants   et
Les paupères, beaucoup de paupères   et
Les hommes des lettres:
Fulcher du Chartres
Raymond d'Agile
Alexander, amanuensis
Les prêtres: Sannardes,
                Priest à Robert du Normandy;
        Gerhard
Abbot d'Allerheiligen;
Adalbreron,
Archdeacon of Metz; Norman-Odo,
Bishop of Bayeaux; Bonfilius,
Bishop of Foligno
Peter of Narbonne, charged
        with despoiling
the tombs d'Avraham, Isaac et Jacob   plus tard
                Bishop d'Albara   and
                Adhemar of Le Puy,
the Pope's legate   died too soon in Antioch
                God find a place for Adhemar
                        Jerusalem did not
                Clop! Gilbert thought the gate
                of Jerusalem

looked like the guillotine   Clop!   Clop!

                Urbain,   he said
                "Mes enfants,
                I beseech you as Christ's heralds
                to publish this everywhere and to

                                        The Ballad of 1095/43

persuade men of all rank, knights
as well as foot soldiers, rich as well
as poor, to bring aid promptly to
all Christians in the East and to
destroy the infidel race from the
lands of your brothers. Mes enfants,
Christ commands it."

He turned in his golden robe in the
green field under a French sun on
the afternoon of November 7, 1095
it happened in Clermont

"Qu'est-ce qu'a dit le consul à Urbain?" Sister Catherine did
not expect an answer. She was becoming hardened. "Deus le
volt," she said. It was a glorious motto and she repeated it.
"Deus le volt. Oui."

Célestine, Adeline, Madeleine, Josephine, Caroline, Jeanne,
et mes enfants, les autres, Gilbert, Robert, Roger, Raymond,
Simon and Jean, they followed the pointer to Jerusalem. The
guard turned from the window and supported his back against
the wall and warmed his derriere on the radiator beneath the sill
and daydreamed that his children went to the school where
Sister Catherine taught instead of to the dirty school they did
attend where the girls did not carry straw hats. Madeleine
retrieved her hat, and her complexion returned and her spirit
was pacified and she thought about the unicorn and how she
longed to have lived then when men said things like "Deus le
volt" and fought for His Truth and clasped chastity belts on
their women and the unicorn ran wild on a field of blue.

"Et Pierre l'Ermite," Sister Catherine said. And Roger, he
looked at the tapestry and wondered which one was Peter the
Hermit, but Jean stepped on Robert's toe and Robert looked
around to see if anyone was watching him and stepped on
Simon's toe. And Simon, he smiled. The offense was not an
offense. It was a call to brotherhood. Simon passed the
message to Raymond. Raymond ruminated. He could not
afford any more trouble with his family or school. His eyes,
ruminating, caught the tops of the turrets of Jerusalem. The call

to brotherhood was stronger than fear of parental punishment
or scolding or conscience or love of peace.   Raymond passed
the message to Roger,

So they came the men of God in four armies
the men of Lorraine and the men of Provençal
and the men of France and one thing you had
to say about them they were tough fighters
you could cut skin from them and leave them
laughing the men of Lorraine and the other kind
too the conquistadors la gloire de leur
martyrdom in the lands of the Aztecs, Incas,
and the Indians et les crusaders those
younger sons cut off from the lands of Europe
claimed Jerusalem in recompense for not being
                                             the

                    chosen

                              loin

                                   fruit

And Sister Catherine despaired for their souls because they
were ignorant of their past and Simon slept. Saliva sparkled on
his lips. His dog, appellé Roi, trotted through his dreams and
he, Simon, called to him and Roi, good Roi, came and licked
his hand. Sister Catherine tapped Simon on the shoulder with
the pointer and said sternly, "Simon, dis-nous qui était Pierre
l'Ermite?"
     Simon's eyes swam on his dream. "Roi," he said, "le roi de
paupères." The answer took Sister Catherine aback, for it was
neither right nor wrong. It fell into the valley of ambiguity.
And the rain fell in large gray drops onto the red tile floor. And
French pigeons sat outside beneath the eaves of the roof, at eye
level, and cooed into their wet wings. And Sister Catherine
decided that the answer contained no improper intention. "Oui,"
she said, "Peter, he said the least of these shall enter Jerusalem
with you."

                                        The Ballad of 1095/45

And they did, God's poor enter Jerusalem with
them in the rear where famine and ambush strike
and other things too tafurs they were not
like other poor they were really poor they
died of famine in Nicaea and they died of famine
in Antioch and they ate roots and smeared their
bodies with animal fat to keep warm and they sank
in the scale of human things and became not quite
human and not unlike humans   nobody could say
what they became   but they were serviceable as
the toughest among the tough the stoneslingers
and the bonecrushers and no one would leave them
out when they took Jerusalem   they fought with
clubs and with hatchets and with shovels
and with ugly ugly maces even their weapons
were ungodly to say nothing of their ideas   they
caught the infidel by his legs and
twisted his ankles like a goat's and tore his flesh
from his body and some say they ate it in the fields
uncooked for the way to the spirit was through
the flesh yours and mine mes enfants while up
ahead the knights marched in mail or rode with tilted
lances a-jousting in Jerusalem   but Bohemond that
young buck he stayed in Antioch and laughed and
roasted the heads of his enemies and put them up on spikes
while king tarfon he growled with famine and
dysentery and howled at the moon because he was
sunk in the scale of human things with massacre
and rape and famine and disease and when he
howled everyone could see that his teeth were
broken and brown with indigestible matter

And Sister Catherine said, "Oui, Peter, he said the least of
these shall enter Jerusalem with you." And Madeleine liked the
speech very much, but she knew she would rather be the lady
with her hand on the unicorn's neck than the nun holding the
pointer in her hand. And Caroline curled the gum around her
tongue and Célestine's eyes drifted out the window and floated
out into the rain. She looked far but she did not squint and did

not see anything either but the gray, cold rain. And Jeanne had to pass water, but how does one say it in French, and suffered silently the humility of the flesh. And Sister Catherine stopped in the middle of the lesson and looked shocked and said to Robert, "Pourquoi est-ce que ta langue est bleue?" But Robert would not explain and the others, Raymond and Roger, would not help him but gazed with great interest at the tapestry. And Sister Catherine repeated the question, "Robert, pourque est-ce que ta langue est bleue?" And Robert maintained silence and Sister Catherine could not force him to talk, so she said, "Go wash it out." and Robert rose and left the room and Adeline and Madeleine kept their hats on their laps and showed him no sympathy. Robert deserved a blue tongue. "I hope he dies of it," Adeline thought. Just like that. But Sister Catherine returned to the tapestry and renewed her efforts to redeem the lesson. "Mes enfants, we see here a great and heroic action. Byzantium was in trouble. Attacked on all sides by the infidel. Byzantium called for help to her Christian brothers. And the great heart of Christendom responded. Oui. And Urbain addressed them in Clermont in French. And they went, aussi les enfants to Jerusalem. Carrying the cross and the sword."

Robert came back. He hesitated whether to sit or to stand or stick out his tongue for inspection. Sister Catherine could not bear the silly problem. "Robert, have you never seen a crusader's sword?" she said, just to give him a question to think about while he stood there oafish and already too big for his age. Robert thought. He thought about all the swords he had seen in all the museums he had been to. But he could not say which one was a crusader's sword and he remained standing, oafish and too big for his age. Sister Catherine clicked her teeth with exasperation. And this was his punishment for his blue tongue. "Have you not read Roland?"

"Oui."

"Oui?"

"Oui."

"Can you not describe Roland's sword?"

Robert thought again, deeply, and this time he had an answer. "It was very big and very long and very heavy."

"Oui."

"Oui."

"Très bien, continue." But Roland could not continue and Sister Catherine had to, and she said, "And the handle was shaped like a cross and in the handle were precious stones and more precious than the stones were the relics from the saints. Quelles reliques?" Robert was struck dumb again and his eyes rolled everywhere. They rolled towards the ceiling and out the window and at the guard and into Josephine's hair and over the tapestry and around his right thumbnail. But there was no help in any of these places. And Sister Catherine had to answer for him again, "A tooth of St. Peter, blood of St. Basil, hairs from the head of St. Denis, and a piece of garment of the Virgin. Oui?"

"Oui," Robert said.

"Assied-toi."

"Merci." And Robert slid gratefully into his seat. At the first opportunity he stuck out his tongue at Gilbert. It was still blue. Gilbert smirked approval. Sister Catherine did not see this. "Maintenant," she said as she looked at the great scene before her which hung from the ceiling to the floor. "Regardez le croisé. Martyrs. As is Christ, aussi le croisé. Always the infidel has threatened the Christian. First came the infidel from the north. Alaric et Attila. Alors l'infidèle de l'est est venu. Comment s'appelle le barbare de l'est, Jean?"

"Ghengis Khan."

"Oui. Ghengis Khan. Et comment s'appelle le barbare de l'Afrique, Jean?"

"Le mahométan."

"C'est vrai. Oui. Les Chrétiens étaient entourés par le barbare du nord, alors par le barbare de l'est, et bientôt par le barbare de l'Afrique et toujours les juives dans le centre." And the head of the infidel gazed at Gilbert and the French pigeons sat on the small balcony and soon the rain turned to sleet for it was only a day before Christmas and Sister Catherine said, "Mais toute la terre est du Dieu. Nést-ce pas?"

"Oui," Celestine said in her heart and wept for the gray, wet, drab pigeons sitting on the balcony rail in the cold rain.

"Alors aussi Jérusalem, n'est-ce-pas?"

"Oui," Madeleine said.

"Oui," Sister Catherine said, "and when le croisé came into Jérusalem and le mahométan mocked him from the towers his heart turned to stone to be in his spiritual home and to be mocked as le Christ was mocked. Oui, his heart turned to stone." Her pointer traveled over the tapestry and searched for a detail to give drama to the text. In the distance, in the very far distance through the French doors, over the red rooftops of the city, smoke curled from a chimney. And the rain fell, sometimes nicely, only wetting the air, and sometimes aggressively in big drops swollen with snow, for it was wintertime. But either way Célestine had mournful thoughts. And the guard's eyes fell sleepily. He kept his arms folded on his chest and his eyes fell inside himself and he dreamed about an exotic woman he saw in the cinema who played a mandolin and seduced men with her music.

Then Roger did an acrobatic trick. He wrapped his ankles around the legs of his chair and leaned forward perpendicularly. Gilbert, Raymond, Simon, Robert and Jean were impressed. They did the same. All succeeded but Simon. He fell off his chair and chipped a tooth. Sister Catherine was mortified. The noise and the clatter woke the guard and transformed him into a roaring animal. "Qu'est-ce que the hell is going on here." He apologized to Sister Catherine. She apologized for Simon's behavior. Simon apologized for disturbing the lesson. Raymond snickered cynically. Simon sat down. A trickle of blood from his gumline fell on his tongue.

"I see it," Célestine said.

"Mademoiselle, do not speak out of turn," Sister Catherine said. "Regardez la tapisserie. Comment s'appelle le croisé qui était le premier à Jérusalem?"

Célestine regarded the tapestry as she was told to do, but she could not find the name of the crusader who was the first to enter Jerusalem. The others laughed. Without any reason.

"Mademoiselle, comment s'appelle le croisé qui était le premier à Jérusalem?" It did no good to repeat the question. It did not make Célestine intelligent. Ignorance tortured her and she was one of those children who feel remorseful and guilty when they do not know something. Unlike some others who think it is clever not to know. "Celui-là," Roger whispered

behind her, "the one with the big hook on his helmet."
Laughter swept through the seats. Discipline threatened to break
down altogether. Sister Catherine clapped her hands for order.
The rain commenced in earnest, now gray, now white, now
gray and white. A covey of pigeons took flight in the wet air to
seek shelter while they came the men of God came in four
armies

The men of Lorraine under Godfrey and the
Normans from Italy under the young buck
and the knights of Provençal under Raymond and
Adhemar who died too soon and even the king of
France's own vassals came under the duke of Normandy
and the counts of Flanders and of Blois came the
flowers of Europe her younger sons and the poor
under Peter and the chroniclers and the poets
and the campfollowers and some whores and a lot
of priests and some bishops and it was the Pope's
own army so they wore red crosses on their sleeves
and the others burned the cross into their foreheads
and they walked across Europe to Heaven and they
all arrived together the poets and the priests and
the children and the knights and the foot soldiers
and the tafurs and the ones that wore the red
cross on their sleeves and the other kind who
burned the cross into their foreheads all arrived
together beneath the wall of Jerusalem
with gratitude to Christ that they had all arrived
together with siege engines and flame throwers
and lances and swords and helmets and mangonels
and mangons and the other kind who arrived with
clubs and hatchets and stoneslingers and ugly ugly
maces

"God grant Godfrey of Bouillon eternal rest," Sister
Catherine said. Madeleine would have liked to have said such
words herself: God grant Godfrey of Bouillon eternal rest. He
was the first to enter Jerusalem. Across a footbridge he had
slung from his moveable tower to the wall near Herod's gate.

And later, Sister Catherine told them, William of Tyre wrote it up in a book called History of Deeds Done Beyond The Sea, how they went barefoot the knights and the priests through the streets of Jerusalem and kissed each stone along the way where the Savior had trod and wept and shed tears upon entering the Holy Sepulchre even though and because the cries of the dying were left outside and felt, even though and because the dying were dying, that they had entered Paradise and stood where He stood and Raymond said, Sister Catherine told them, in words carved each like a jewel, that he would not wear a crown of gold where Christ had worn a crown of thorns and Madeleine took the words and wore them like a necklace because they could not find a crusader to be King of Jerusalem because Bohemond he became Prince of Antioch and Tancred he became Prince of Galilee and there were no more princes left, so Godfrey agreed to be king and when he died, because he humbly agreed, they buried him with Christ in the Church of the Holy Sepulchre to which came the soldiers of Christ in victory through the streets of Jerusalem, streets so narrow, blood so high the horses slipped and fell and children too, they fell in the narrow streets where the blood oh! famous blood rose to Godfrey's stirrups as the knights came and les infidèles, les Musulmans et les Juives they came and hid in crevices and shadows and bit their children's tongues out so they would not cry in the famous famous streets they scattered down the alleyways and into the mosques and synagogues and the young bucks they came like saintly soldiers like St. George like St. Theodore St. Maurice St. Mercury St. John and St. Michael they came into Jerusalem down the little streets into the narrow alleyways into the crevices and the shadows into the mosques and the synagogues because as younger sons of Europe

                   they

                       knew

                           the

                             value

                               of

                                 holy

                                   property

The Ballad of 1095/51

I wish, Madeleine thought,
I could have been a lady-in-waiting in King Louis' court or
maybe, she looked at the tapestry for a clue to her longings, a
nobleman's wife who followed him à Jérusalem

Raymond of Toulouse
Tancred
Baldwin of Le Bourg
Gaston de Béarn
Gerard de Roussillon
Robert of Flanders
Robert of Normandy
Godfrey of Bouillon   the flowers of knighthood
And the others,
The priests and the chaplains
The bishops and their servants   they all went
into the empty houses to wash themselves   of blood
and marched with lit candles to
the Holy Sepulchre   reliquary   of reliquaries
and burned incense   and received the blessings
of the priests   and bowed the knee to Jesus
Christ   and gave thanks   for this holy victory
which was fifty thousand slain in fifteen hours
of Moslem and Jew   not a creature stirred
and   took the city   and chose themselves a king
                        it happened on July 15, 1099
                        in Jerusalem

    The guard who hated children came into the room and
flipped out his wrist. He did not look at his watch, he did not
even look at the guard who was dozing. He merely flipped out
his wrist and so accurate was the flip that a factory whistle in
the distance blew just then and vespers rang and a pigeon flew
off the ledge of the balcony and the guard who was dozing
woke up and became very busy. "Time to leave," he said, "five
o'clock. Time to leave. The museum closes in five minutes."

The Ballad of 1095/52

The guard who did not like children liked this very much. He nodded approval and left the room.

"Maintenant," Sister Catherine said, "make sure you have your hats and your handkerchiefs. Leave the chairs alone. Do not diddle with them. Remember to turn in your little ticket to get your coat. Maintenant, size places." And they lined up behind her, in front of the French doors decorated in plum-colored drapes with gold-braided tie-backs. In the courtyard the cold rain fell and Madeleine said adieu to the unicorn in the tapestry and the unicorn kept his eye on her and Madeleine felt ineffable longings and tears as big as the raindrops fell on her cheeks. I wish, she thought, I just wish I could have been the wife of Godfrey of Bouillon and gone with his men of Lorraine through the fields of Byzantium. It was in the unicorn's eye the

blood of heroism
blood of dreams
blood of ecstasy

The gates of Jerusalem rolled open to let in the crusaders. Madeleine's heart skipped a beat. I wish I could have been there, she thought, and blood dropped from her mouth. "I see it," Célestine shrieked. Smoke from a factory in the distance went up in blue billows.

"Célestine, do not shriek," Sister Catherine said, "do not raise your voice in a museum. Regard it as a church. It houses God's gifts."

Et mes enfants, Célestine, Adeline, Madeleine, Josephine, Caroline, Jeanne et les autres, Gilbert, Robert, Roger, Raymond, Simon, Jean, lined up in size place and followed Sister Catherine into le salon de la princesse de Soubise and into la toilette de Marie Antoinette, into the writing room used by Louis XIV with the gilded desk and the feathered pen, dans le salon des impressionistes et finalment au salon des modernes

too late   the news of victory reached

Europe too late in August. Urbain he died

on July 29 and did not know and could not

give thanks, or anything

and mes enfants: Célestine, Caroline, Jeanne, Simon, Josephine, Gilbert, Jean, Robert et les autres, Madeleine, Raymond, Adeline et Roger presented their coat tickets to the coat lady and the coat lady gave the raincoats to the young ladies and the jackets to the young gentlemen and the guard who did not like children accompanied them into the damp hallway under the Gothic ceiling to make sure that nothing went wrong. Nothing did go wrong. Les enfants followed Sister Catherine out in size place and behaved as they were expected to. Mon enfant, Célestine, she shivered et les autres, Adeline, Madeleine, Josephine, Caroline, Jeanne, Gilbert, Robert, Roger, Raymond, Jean went through the turnstile and the turnstile clicked thirteen times and the ticketseller with the broken teeth bid them good day. "Bon soir," he said to Sister Catherine. He even felt noble saying it, though he was not a religious man.

The Ballad of 1095/54

1492

Micaele Jerónima, unforgiveable Jewess, I beg you to read this letter with your soul and I warn you, as one who trafficks in dangerous thoughts and lives so deeply in Hell that I fear God has lost sight of me, judge me not. Judge me not, Micaele Jerónima, for I have been through revolutions of pain and would hardly falter now at the thought of revenge. Reserve your female scorn for your own kind who cannot affect your life one way or the other and who scarcely have control over their own destinies these days.

I saw you pass outside the wall of our monastery the other day. Do you go by deliberately to remind me? Because I know, Micaele, what dwells beneath your clothes. It will not do anymore to cover up, to walk with your shawl across your bosom, though my eyes are old and I do not pretend to be worldly. Had I wished for worldliness I would not be a priest. I did not become a priest for a piece of bread. My family owns lands. Nor am I innocent. I know there have been worldly priests, but I am not be to confused with the Archpriest of Hita. No doubt he had compensatory virtues, but I have only scholarship and my chastity. The virtues of patience and humility have escaped me and, it seems, all talent for martyrdom as well. I count my sins, but if I were not to count my virtues too I would have despaired long ago and left the priesthood, I have so little else to offer to be deserving of Heaven. But from an early age I was predisposed to chastity and book-learning, and I have tried to excel in these virtues. Why, then, now, when old age should have disaffected my unused passions must I be stricken like a boy of fifteen? When your God wished to test Job he whipped him with the death of his children, the loss of his properties and his worldly position. There is dignity in such chastisement, but there is no dignity in an old man who shakes like a pubescent boy at the sight of a woman. It is a disaster to be young and old at the same time. Micaele, I covet old age. I would be decrepit tomorrow, yet my bones have been filled with youth and my hell is irresistible. Let me then say it and be done with it: if you came to me, Jerónima, I could save you.

I am not to be cured like Ramon Lully who saw his mistress' breasts disfigured with cancer. A thousand times I tried to see your breasts like that, swollen with disease, flaccid with age like my Aunt Rima's, whose house I had been sent to when I was a boy of twelve. The poor woman had an attack of stones and was in great torment. For days she groaned and passed stones. I nursed her because my mother was in childbirth and my father and brothers were in Cordoba fighting the Moors. The doctor and I helped the old woman sit on the bowl. She was of immense size and in such agony she lost all control. She seized me by the wrist when the fit of passage struck her and screaming to our Blessed Jesus to rescue her, straddled the bowl between her thighs, thrashing and moaning so that we were in terror she would miss the bowl, and to our horror, rose up like an ox with her chemise twisted around her waist. She cursed and the stones were dislodged. We helped her back to her bed. The doctor said the stones were invaluable and, being a Jew, gathered them into a cloth. May he receive the same welcome abroad as here. I say this only because of his lecherous soul. When he left, he said I was to forgive my aunt for cursing because the woman was in great pain and that I could forgive her best by forgetting what I had heard--and--he brought his forehead next to mine--seen.

God knows I have absolved myself of that sin. Am I now to sacrifice a lifetime of sacrifice? The disproportion of giving up Eternity in exchange for a few hours of pleasure plagues me. Who would not say that this is the worst bargain a man can make? How is it that the thought of losing Heaven is not enough to destroy my memory of you? How is it that the sight of your breasts can creep between me and God like the interposition of the Devil? Thus, your people thrust Abishag between David and God when David was dying. Instead of absolution you gave David Abishag--and to no avail. "For they that are after the flesh do mind the things of the flesh; but they that are after the Spirit the things of the Spirit." And is it not a portent that David was too old, a thing of spirit already beyond the reach of Abishag? Should I then love such breasts that will rob me of Heaven? I despise them. In time they will rot with disease like the breasts of Ramon Lully's mistress, for it cannot be but true, as St.Paul said, that the flesh is death and enmity against God. In time, your belly and private parts will wobble like my Aunt Rima's. But by then you will be gone. If I say not a word, you and your family will be gone in a week. And do not blame this on me. I am not responsible for Ferdinand. Bitterly, I am not responsible for myself these days. I cannot believe fate has thrown me into this contortion. What is so loathsome as a lecherous priest? I have been wrenched from every prediction of myself. If I died tomorrow would God know who I am, this lonely man, this beggared priest who for forty years was chaste without a qualm? Do you wonder if I curse you? I have eleven hairs on my head and my bowels are enflamed like a youth's. I look at the fire in the grate and want to thrust my hand into it to distract myself with greater pain, but your powers are stronger than my prayers, my fasting, my acts of devotion which have become puerile.. You are a disease which has disfigured me and made me unfit for worship. Into the house of God I went at the very first sight of you. As I stood praying on bended knee before the altar, I saw your breasts raised in the air, the water glistening in your armpits. I saw birds perched there. On your sacred hair, I saw water hang like jewels. Jerónima, I am tied to you forever by this vision. I am more married to you than a fisherman to his wife whom he has bedded for forty years with the bedclothes down to her knees. Indeed, I know now that there is a different law in my member, warring against the law of my mind, and bringing me into captivity under the law of sin, which is in my member.

Not a lifetime of sacrifice weighs on me, but fifteen hundred years of struggle to free ourselves from the earth-bound flesh. It is the privilege of priests to burn. Believe me, Micaele, I would no more run away with you than with a mad stallion. Last week I was ready to give up Heaven for you, this week I must give up Spain too? I give up nothing. Fifteen hundred years of spiritual pressure weighs on me. Even if I have lost Eternity, I will not mock our martyrs. I saw you but I will forget. Moreover, I will not let you pass stories among your people about the old priest who watched you bathe in the river. I saw that you saw me standing behind the tree. I was gathering herbs. So persistent is grass it covered the markings I had made only the week before. For all that I know you waited deliberately for the moment when I was befuddled and my eyes became transfixed by the beam of sun on the water as you emerged, your arms raised as one in prayer, but with you in lewdness, for who comes forth naked in prayer? Is it not known everywhere that among your people so guarded are you in your approach to God that your men must cover their heads? Whom were you trying to deceive? Did someone tell you, Micaele, go, seduce that old priest, maybe he will intervene on your family's behalf? If I had such power, I would still send you flying from this land, and not with your goods and jewels, but with the whip on your back. Then would I say with Eulogias: "Time was when thou dids't vouchsafe to show me thy neck all torn with the lashes, bereft of the lovely and abundant tresses which once veiled it." Micaele, listen, if it could be so, I would lay my hands upon such wounds with great tenderness. I could come to you in my priesthood and find salvation. Your wounds would be my cure. Your flesh would be holier than my vestments. It is not impossible that a mixed blood flows in your veins. There have been those with only a few drops of Christianity who have travelled the road to spiritual fame. Your family makes preparations to leave, but for you, Micaele, there may still be an open door to Heaven's wealth through the accidents of history.

I ramble. I am a man who has lived on the hard bread of chastity for forty years and whose habits of restraint have suddenly been destroyed. Do you wonder that I ramble? Did not your own Sarah falter and mock God's word when he told her she would bear a child in her old age? How are we to live through such reversals of fate? I should have been struck blind before my eyes looked upon my Aunt Rima, but I was struck blind afterwards and by the malevolence of this earth you have restored my sight. Can you deny, then, that you are bound to me, responsible for me? Micaele, I know that I am a starving man. In my pride, I thought I had conquered my carnal nature, but it was not true, I had never wrestled with the devil. These passions were dormant and, now aroused in my late hour, they have sprung on me like tigers and I have not the strength to fight them. The other day I saw a female dog in the street whose teats had been pulled by her pups. My nerves jumped as if I were looking upon the nipples that rose from your breasts as you left the water. I am so far gone in iniquitous thoughts my soul only listens for the key that will shut me into hell forever.

Rescue me, Micaele, I am dying of thirst. Let me place my hand beneath your breast like a cup and drink. I see the glisten of water in your armpits, my nose hides there and my mouth tastes the wine of your body. I have given up Heaven. That is surely a sacrifice. Can you not match it and give me one night? There is a precedent for everything, even for fallen priests. I will petition Ferdinand on your behalf, for fate has tied me to you and you cannot desert me now. This edict has crushed my joints. Come, Micaele Jerónima. The syllables of your name bring sweat to my brow. My bones are shaking. If what is hell is what cannot be mastered, never was a man so far into hell as I am. I cannot struggle. I have no name for what has deprived me of hope, except it be called the Jewess, Micaele. Come, remove your shawl. Do not cross your arms on your bosom with modesty. Lift them up once more and let me look. I am in such pain I cannot breathe. Come, little daughter of Abraham, do not leave me in this fire. Do not depart. Go slowly, slowly, fate.

LA HOYA

Which means a grave, hole, or ditch

ARTISTS take their initial inspiration from a revulsion to human nature. They then spend their careers crawling away from that origin. Some succeed, others don't. In "View of Toledo" everything is falling down. El Greco spent a lifetime painting up, making his human beings less human as he went along. Even in "El Entierro," which is about a man going down into his grave, the spiritual movement is up. Heaven exists and exerts a magnetic pull on the earth's tomb. Success was almost El Greco's; then everything came tumbling down. In "View of Toledo" the whole town slides into the Tagus. There is no counterforce. The view is not so much of the town of Toledo, which lies huddled in a corner of the canvas, as it is of the bullock-like hills and clouds swollen with an overwrought omnipresence. There is light in these clouds over Toledo, but it is not the light of spiritual heaven. Everyone knows, just to look at the painting, that that light is not the same as the light in "El Espolio," or in "El Entierro." These pictures were painted before the grand auto da fé of 1600 given in honor of Philip lll's visit to Toledo.

The connection between El Greco's development as a painter and such an event as the grand auto da fé of 1600 is implied for the sake of establishing the principle that there is a gravitational pull exerted by history on the psyche of artists. In "View of Toledo" we cannot see beyond the clouds. They suggest nothing but themselves, not even the wrath of Jehovah, that anthropomorphic staple of a thunderous sky. In this somber and portentous painting the light lights up nothing but the clouds. We see that the town lies in the grip of a force which is quite of this world, suggested by the massive hills and the storm that seems capable of pulling Toledo from its moorings. All is in descent, a fury of descent to some point below the Tagus River, behind the house at the bottom of the picture, or just to the right of the canvas. It is as if the world were being sucked down some hole behind a bush, probably where the town's cesspool is kept.

Instead of God or heaven, there's the Alcazar in the background, bureaucratically squatty, and the insubstantial-looking Gothic steeple shaggily rising up like one of those castles built on the seashore out of the drippings of moist sand. There appear to be some figures along the shore of the river, probably children with fishing poles and a few stories under their belts. The year is 1608 or '09 or '10, but they talk like children have always talked, cosmically, trading their knowledge of the world and examining each other's secrets. One, Tomé, has a great deal to say this afternoon, for he had an adventure that morning. He regards Rafael, six months younger than himself, as a stupido or dolt, and dominates him. Rafael allows this because he knows that Tomé is more knowledgeable about the world than he is. A third boy, Alejo, enjoys the same seniority rights as Tomé. For one thing, Rafael's mother and aunt are regarded as half-wits, which already gives Rafael less leverage with his peers. For another thing, he has ears which stick out from the sides of his head, and for the last thing, he is the youngest of the three, and there is no overcoming the stumbling-block of his innocence in their eyes.

This story is about Rafael, and the subject is torture. Through Tomé's uncle, who is a torturer for the Inquisition, Tomé has discovered a spot where he can watch the secret proceedings. As soon as he had verified for himself that such a secret spot did exist, he ran straight for Rafael's house to tell him. As usual, Rafael's mother, Belita, stuck out her tongue when Tomé came through the door. She was jealous of Tomé's friendship with Rafael and kept up a perpetual battle with her son about his friend, hissing with venom that Tomé was maléfico. Although it was supposed to be a secret everyone knew that his uncle was a torturer for the Inquisition. For Belita this made Tomé an unholy child. "Let him be," Rafael's father said. "A qué? Your company is better?"

Actually Rafael loved his mother and the aunt who lived with them better than he loved Tomé, but he often found his mother and aunt boring and without sympathy for his ideas, so he kept his distance from them. Something warned him that they were not trustworthy and he fought the frequent impulse he had to confide in them, small matters and big matters, like the stories the older boys told him of the brothels in Barcelona, or the bad dreams he so often had where he saw a Moor's head on a platter, like the head of St.John with Salome. He knew his aunt and his mother would not deceive him, but they always took his confidences in an unexpected way. Once he told his aunt about his dream of the Moor's head, and she cackled and said, "That was as it should be." She was very pleased that this had been revealed to Rafael, for it was a sign of God's mercy when horror was revealed in a dream instead of in life, and she said that Rafael was a holy vessel of God's prophecy. She was a firm believer in the faith, but she had a horror of the auto da fé, this business of scourging the flesh. Indeed, she feared the sight of anything she considered painful. If she passed a crippled man in the street she put her hands over her eyes. If she heard a troubled child crying she stopped her ears from hearing. She was forever covering one organ or the other, her eyes or her nose or her ears and crossing herself, babbling that God was merciful and that cruelty was a conspiracy against the innocence of her soul. She even pretended to be blind if the Grand Inquisitor passed her on the street. She would shuffle past him in her broken shoes and tap her cane vociferously. Since she did the same when a funeral passed her or a lame dog or a deformed child, people let her have her way. Both she and Belita were regarded as a pair of hysterical birds who became unhinged at the mention of pain and fled anywhere, Aunt to her favorite hill, Belita under the table or under the cow.

"Take care," Rafael's father would laugh at Aunt,

"someone will report you."

Her invariable response to this was to cross herself, clasp her hands in front of her lips, roll her eyes upward, and whisper fifteen denunciations on her brother's head. Aunt felt she had the authority of St. Bernard and Gregory and who knew who else, authorities better than Roxas. But if she hated the thought of anyone or anything being in pain, the thought of herself suffering surpassed reflection. She stabbed the air with her terrible hooked nose and cursed her brother for mentioning such a possibility.

Sebastián was known by his neighbors as "un buen hombre con mala suerte," a good man with bad luck. He knew himself to be surrounded by a household of half-wits, except for Rafael. He would go to see the auto da fé when it was being given and could not resist baiting his sister with a description of it.

Aunt would grab her crucifix and hold it in front of him as if she were disinfecting the air. "Mercy to sufferers," she would cry.

"Spare us," Belita would cry too.

"Justice to blasphemers," Sebastián would say, to heat them up a bit. "Take care, solterona," he would say to Aunt, "the fire will tickle your toes. Welcome it, woman. God knows, it's the only warm embrace you'll get this side of the grave."

As usual, Aunt picked up her skirts and fled from the house, as much insulted at the mention of her spinster state as terrified of the vision of herself burning. "It's a sin, it's a sin," she would cackle over her shoulder, departing on a pious note. "The sin of pride, to win men's souls that would not be won. Forgive them, forgive them, Jesus cried. Vengeance is mine, saith the Lord. Forgive them, Jesus cried, for they know not what they do." Throwing the whole lot together, she would pick up her skirts and run out of the house.

Rafael was always sent to bring her back. Sebastián would not go, for everyone knew that would do no good. In such a state, Aunt would throw herself into the river before she did Sebastián the favor of returning to his house. Rafael was sent because Aunt believed he was a holy child, clean without corruption. At any rate, it was he who could always mollify her hurt feelings and who knew in which hill it was that Aunt hid herself. Once, when she refused even his entreaties to return, he walked all the way back to the house to get one of her birds and brought it back to her hiding place so that she would not be lonely. Aunt burst into tears, made the sign of the cross over Rafael and fell on her knees to kiss his feet. Rafael was so startled he began to cry himself. Aunt hastily got up off her knees and wiped his eyes with her dirty skirt. "Holy child, sweet Rafael, don't cry over your goodness."

Rafael wanted to confess his dreams to a priest, but Aunt persuaded him that they were not a sin, though to him they felt like a sin. It was she who mainly ministered to his education, and even Sebastián had respect for Aunt's learning. She stuffed Rafael with cakes, carried him on her shoulders while he held one of her birds, sang hymns to him, taught him Latin and took him to see the great churches in Toledo, Santa Maria la Blanca and the San Juan de los Reyes where the iron chains brought home by the Christians who had been taken from the Moorish dungeons by Isabel and Ferdinand during their conquests still hung from the ceiling. Aunt knew a great deal about the history of the city and could remember the great auto da fé given in honor of Felipe Tercero when he came through Toledo. Of course she did not go to see the celebration, but she said that she could not escape the smell though she had put a clamp on her nose. Sebastián said Aunt's nose was so large she should put a saddle on it. Fifty Moors had been burnt in honor of Felipe. Aunt could also remember when Toledo was the capital of Spain and of the world, before Felipe Secundo moved the capital to Madrid. "That was the beginning of all Spain's troubles," she told Rafael, "because God had put his finger on Toledo to be the center of his religion." She never tired of pointing out that Toledo was built high on a bluff because God was drawing it up to Heaven.

Rafael was an only child, the apple of his family's eye. He never for a moment thought that any of them would deceive him about anything, yet they remained untrustworthy, beyond the pale of his soul's consolation. His mother had been a half-wit from the second year of her marriage. She knew some hymns, but no letters at all, or if she had ever known she had forgotten them. Rafael could not tell her anything he was troubled about. He certainly would not tell her where Tomé had been that morning. That would only give her another reason for her enmity. And if Rafael described to her what Tomé had seen, Belita would break into an idiotic dance or whinny like a horse or baa like the sheep or whistle through her nose or tinkle a bell in his ear. If that didn't cheer him, she got down on her hands and knees and charged him like a bull, goring him in his stomach with her head until he screamed, "Basta, basta." She would do anything to make him laugh and her efforts threw him into dreadful pain. If he screamed for her to stop, she sat down on a stool and started to cry. Like Aunt, she could not bear it if he was unhappy. She was a dumb animal who wanted to keep him under her wing and lick him all day long. Belita could spend hours sitting with Rafael, if he let her, looking into his eyes or holding his hand. Rafael understood why only he and his father could love her.

From his father Rafael got trust in endurance, but little conversation. Sebastián was a tilemaker, and in spite of the incompetence of his wife and sister who sometimes helped him, he had a good trade. Rafael would follow it. He loved to be in his father's shop, a shed behind the two rooms that was their home. Often he went down to the banks of the Tagus and dug up huge pots of reddish clay and brought them back for his father to bake into tiles. Frequently he was allowed to paint the designs on them, and Rafael knew he was good at this. Tomé and Alejo had nothing to match the talent he had. It was serenity to sit on a stool with a tile in his hand, and the sun on his neck and go to work. The workshed backed their garden where they kept a cow for Belita, a lamb for Rafael, and birds for Aunt. No sooner would Rafael mount the stool when Lástima, the cow, would put her head into the window and Gentileza, the lamb, would take up her place at Lástima's tail. Sometimes Rafael signed his name on the back of a tile and sometimes he inscribed Ciudad Imperial y Coronado, for he was proud of his work and if his father was not looking, he held up the tile for Lástima to see, who swished her tail in recognition of his art.

Sebastián was not a man who wasted words on compliments, unfortunately more often on criticism, but Rafael knew when his father stood looking over his shoulder in silence that he was doing good work. If he were not, his father silently took the tile away from him. Between them, most of Rafael's conversation was "Sí, Padre," or "No, Padre" or "Inmediatamente." "Rafael, you draw the scroll too wide. Estrecho, estrecho, mal fragile." "Sí, sí, Padre," whether Rafael liked his scroll that way or not.

His mother and his aunt were loquacious, tearful, soulful, prayerful, twittering or silly, but his father was never any of these things, so Rafael never told him anything except the information he asked for, that the cow had given milk, what he had sold the tiles for, and so on.

Even at night, if Aunt who slept with him, didn't hold his ears shut, he heard his mother chattering and whistling through her teeth, but never his father. Sometimes Belita jabbered like a bird and hummed, "Lentament, Sebastián," or "Rapidamente," or sometimes she would cry, "Por qué no me quieres?"

There was no one Rafael could ask why his mother cried like that at night. Aunt's eyes would have rolled with horror, she would have rattled the crucifix over him and immediately he would know that what he had heard had been a sin. Already he had formed the idea that his mother cried in her lucid moments and whistled and cackled when she was insane. That was why she had to be "una poca loca," because when she was sane she was always in sorrow. Tomé knew a great deal about what went on between men and women at night, but Rafael knew he had heard something he should not have heard and he knew, as well as he knew that he had a soul, that to tell Tomé or anyone else was to shame his mother. Sorrow in her was so monumental when she was sane. That was why she was una poca loca.

Sometimes, in the morning, Belita would sit with Rafael at the table, swollen-eyed and hiccoughing. "Tell me the truth,

Rafael," she would say, "do I look like una poca loca to you?" He always said no, but as if the words came from a frozen statue. He was ashamed when she asked him this question. He wanted to comfort her, but he could not. Mamadulce. He was wrung with pain for her. "Ah," she would say, "would you believe it, Rafael, I am not yet thirty." A bitter look would pinch her lips. She would take up a mirror, comb her hair, braid it, set her face in order as if she were resolving an idea, as if sanity were something she could make her mind up about. Rafael could read her thoughts: "I will not be una poca loca anymore. Before I was married, I was the envy of my friends for my beauty. Come, I will put shoes on my feet and walk with my head high." Then lucidity would vanish. She would throw her arms around Rafael and, weeping, whistling, laughing, tell him that he was recompense for everything. What woman had such a gift from God? Pity the women who had never borne children and whose wombs flapped like empty bladders. Pity the women who had ugly children and could not bear the sight of them. Pity, pity the women with wicked children and crippled children and niños locos. She, Belita, had a jewel and that was recompense for everything. She would grow gayer by the moment. "Belita," she would sing, "Belita, put your jewel away before someone robs it." Rafael wished he could be a saint and deserve his mother's love. He knew that the demented were in the special care of God.

"Vamos," his father said to Rafael if he were in the house when Belita was in such a mood. He could not stand to hear her mad talk. Rafael felt his tension. He always accepted his father's invitation to escape. It made him feel both guilty and grown up as if they were two men joined in a conspiracy against his mother's madness.

That morning Tomé called for him before Rafael went out with his father, and he got permission to go off for the day. Rafael saw right away that Tomé had something important to tell him. They flew down the stone streets until they came to an appointed spot on the Tagus, where they joined Alejo who was fishing. Already the sun scorched the rooftops and the hills looked as barren as shorn lambs. They went past the great cathedral and past the house of El Greco, the artist in Santo

Tomé, and past el Transito and down the streets of the homes of the rich and the powerful that overlooked the Tagus. Down in a bend of the river a group of women were washing clothes.

At first, Rafael thought Tomé had caught his sister naked or had gone down to watch the Judaizers scourged in the morning. Tomé came from a family with six sisters and was always catching one or the other naked, at least he would tell Rafael and Alejo that.

Alejo nudged Rafael to tell him that he had a bite on his line. Rafael grew tense, for he wanted to catch a fish for his mother. Tomé was disgusted with his luck that morning. He threw down his pole and went behind a bush to urinate. Alejo's fish got away, and as soon as Tomé left he threw stones in the water to annoy Rafael. Tomé came back, sat down again and wiped his brow. When he picked up his fishing pole, Alejo stopped casting stones, but by that time Rafael's fish had taken off too.

"Well?" Alejo said. He was waiting to hear Tomé's story. He said it without eagerness, for he would not let Tomé enjoy the knowledge that he was interested.

"Did you ever think how they do it?" Tomé asked.

Rafael stiffened unpleasantly. He imagined whips or men chained to the wall, and since he had heard stories like this from birth, his imagination had sorted out and absorbed some of the details, a few at a time. He understood that a man chained to a wall could not feed himself when chained or scratch an itch or claim ownership of his body. If thirsty he had to be given water by a guard, a disgusting thing for a grown up man. But he could not handle the problem of how the man passed water or eliminated his waste. Once the problem did come to mind and some necessary details floated into his imagination, he crossed them out from his consciousness. "Jesudulce," he whispered to himself, "perdoname," and crossed himself. It was a sin to think such things.

Tomé gave his little laugh of superiority over Rafael's stupidity. "Have you never seen an auto da fé?" Rafael knew that Tomé knew that he never had and that he would tease him about his innocence. It was Tomé's way, and Rafael had no choice but to surrender to the baiting. It was a ritual between them. "Not even the auto da fé given in honor of Felipe when he came to Toledo?" Tomé asked.

"No, and neither did you," Rafael said.

"Sí, I did. I was only a baby, but my father took me." Rafael had a sensation of envy, yet he had no wish to see an auto da fé. But he would never tell that to Tomé.

"My father will take me the next time," he said.

"Ha," Alejo said, "you hide under your aunt's skirts." He and Tomé laughed, for they knew the joke was not only on Rafael's innocence, but on his aunt's decrepit spinsterhood. They drew in their poles, for the fish had gone for good. They linked arms and walked down to the Puente Alcántara.

Alejo would not say "Well?" again, for that would tip his hand, but Tomé felt that another note of solicitous interest was due him. They locked horns and walked in silence. Rafael was content to let the fate of battle be decided by them. They passed the cesspool at the bottom of the town. As usual, Alejo and Tomé threatened to throw each other in. They stood for some minutes throwing stones and watching them sink, leaving a sucking hole in the muck. Tomé winked to Alejo. Quick as lightning they flipped Rafael over, head down, feet up, and threatened to duck him. Rafael shrieked with fear and sportsmanship, for he knew that they wouldn't do it, though there was always a lurking possibility. He was so much lighter than they, they had flipped him a thousand times by now with no harm, but still there was the possibility he could slip.

"Decid qué sois Judio," Alejo said.

"No," Rafael said.

"Decid qué sois Judio," Alejo said.

Upside down, Rafael folded his arms on his chest and sealed his lips. Mild clouds floated overhead and Rafael looked at the upside down sky. Tomé and Alejo lowered him an inch. Rafael could smell the cesspool beneath him.

"Decid qué sois Judio," Alejo said.

"No," Rafael said.

Tomé tickled the sole of his foot. Rafael started to jerk and yelped rapidly, "Sí, soy Judio, soy Judio." Immediately Tomé and Alejo flipped him back and set him on his feet.

"Confesion, confesion," they shouted. "Now we can report you. Vamos, vamos," they laughed and ran down the street. They reached the Puente Alcántara and sat down to listen to Tomé, for Alejo had finally conceded Tomé's superiority by throwing his arms up and saying that the body of a Moor could rot faster than Tomé could tell a story.

Rafael tried to tell Aunt what Tomé had told them, but as soon as he opened his mouth she fled to her crucifix and held it aloft like someone with a candle trying to shed light. Bedraggled like a wet hen with her black skirts falling about her, she croaked fiercely, "Debes olvidarlo, Rafael. Debes olvidarlo. You must forget what you have heard. You must think only good, cheerful thoughts, Rafael, for your soul is the mirror of your thoughts, and your thoughts, your thoughts feed your soul like a river feeds the land. Sometimes circumstances force one to sin but a thought is in your head, possessed entirely by you and free of circumstances. You cannot blame your thoughts on fate. Clean them, Rafael, scrub them. Better to scourge your thoughts than your flesh." She rattled the crucifix at him like a witch doctor. "My child, my child, you have become tainted. Your ear, your ear, which you thought was innocent, has been corrupted. A snake has crawled into your ear and into the passageway and up through the side of your skull and it now lies coiled around your brain."

Rafael started to cry.

"Aha," Aunt said, "see if you can tear it out." She pulled Rafael's head down and searched his skull as if she were looking for lice. "Where is that snake, Rafael? Give me that snake. You see you cannot find it because it is now part of your soul. You have heard a terrible tale and it is part of your soul because you cannot unhear it now. Innocence!" She threw her arms up. "How can I make you innocent again? Rafael, niño, niño, child, lamb, how can I clean you?"

Rafael was shuddering and crying as if a worm had crawled into his belly, unsavory and foreign to his system, a thing he rejected and yet it was inside him. Aunt could not bear to see him cry. "Ssshhh, ssshhhh, ssshhh," she said. "Courage, Rafael. Fight. We are struggling for innocence. God will not let a putrid soul into His heaven. Fight, Rafael.

Bad thoughts drive out good ones, like gangrene, if unattended, possesses the whole body, like a wind that carries a foul odor drives out even the smell of a garden."

It was true, it was true! Rafael could not drive out from his head what Tomé had told him. He struggled to forget, but the thought breathed in his skull. It is easier to kill oneself than to kill a thought. That night Rafael had a bad dream. He had known all day that he would, and at night he saw the man as Tomé had described him, hanging from a beam like a slaughtered calf. The white scarf he wore around his neck had caught fire and burned till it made its way through the man's neck. His head came loose and rolled into Rafael's lap. There was a terrible noise in his dream. Soldiers with shields and swords stood in front of the man and laughed and in the center of their laughter was a terrible sound, a tap, tap, tapping like the sound of a bird in a tree or like the sound of Aunt's cane tapping in the street. The men wore helmets and on their breastplates the imperial design of Rome, and Rafael knew that the tap, tap, tapping was the sound of the nails being hammered into Jesus' body. The sound of the knocking woke him up.

As soon as his eyes opened Aunt's eyes flew open too, as if she had been waiting for him, and immediately she put her hands over his ears. "Debes olvidarlo, Rafael, debes olvidarlo." Rafael gritted his teeth and knew he must concentrate on not remembering. He heard Gentileza baaing under his window and Aunt's birds fluttering like souls in the dark. He took his silver cross that hung above his bed and went to the window to pray. In the moony garden he could make out the form of Lástima standing in a shadow with her everlasting patience. His mother's cow! He loved her for Belita's sake, but also for the cow's sake because she never caused anyone trouble, but just stood wherever it was cool in the summer and warm in the winter. They had bought her for the milk and for Belita to have someone to talk to all day, for Belita could not do without chattering. No one but a cow could stand to hear so much talk. His father's words, and true. Not even Rafael could listen to his mother all day long.

"Come to bed, Rafael," his aunt said.

Rafael stiffened. The more his aunt said, "Debes

olvidarlo," the worse the memory gripped him. "Go to sleep, Aunt," he said, "I am praying."

"At this hour?"

Sí, sí."

"You have had a dream again."

"No, Aunt, I am only keeping Gentileza company. She is here under the window and wants someone to pat her." There was a moment of perplexed silence, then Aunt said, "Very well, Rafael. But come to bed soon. A tired body cannot fight for its soul."

That was too terribly true, for Tomé had told them he knew a window where they could see what went on inside and Alejo had said "yes" and Rafael could not say "no". They were going to confess the same man again, and when he had confessed they were going to take him up in the auto da fé that week's end.

Rafael's cross fell to the floor. It clattered in the dark night. Gentileza jumped with fear.

"Rafael," Aunt called, "how can you be praying if your cross is on the floor?"

"Pronto, Aunt," Rafael said. He picked up the cross and kissed it and placed it on the window sill. He put his hand out to pat Gentileza, but her nerves had been shaken by the clatter and she shied away. Rafael crawled back into bed and prayed that the man would die during the night so that he would not have to be confessed again. But it is a sin to pray for someone's death and Rafael felt a constriction in his throat as if it had become paralyzed. He had a sudden terror that he would never be able to talk again. He prayed that his father would require his services all day long so that he could say to Tomé and Alejo that he had work to do, he prayed that he would be too sick to leave his bed in the morning. He thought of pretending to Tomé and Alejo that he had an order of tiles to deliver. But in the morning Sebastián said he would go to the Calle Tornerias that day to deliver the tiles himself, and when Tomé and Alejo appeared in the doorway he told Rafael he could go with them and play until noon. Belita put her hands on her hips and stuck out her tongue until it touched her chin. Alejo stuck his tongue out at her.

Rafael was hurt, but it wasn't clear what he could say about this. His mother had done the same. Alejo saw that he was hurt and punched him playfully in the belly. "Come on, Rafael, I am only fooling." He and Tomé began to jostle one another. Tomé stuck out his tongue at Alejo and Alejo pulled his ears out donkey-style. Tomé found a broad stick with a point and brandished it like a sword. "I am Santiago Matamoros he bellowed. "Come, I will fight you to the death. Muerte, Moros," he shrieked and charged at them. They scattered and ran down the steep street. Tomé twirled the sword over his head like a baton. "Hiuup," he bellowed and came down the street slashing at the houses and the trees. "I am Santiago Matamoros," he bellowed to the sky, "Santo y conquistador por Dios."

"Chirp, chirp, chirp," Alejo teased him from behind a fence. Tomé slashed at him. Alejo skipped out of reach. He plunged to the bottom of the street and jumped into a deep ditch. Rafael followed after him. Tomé made a leap with one yell. "Hiuuup!"

"Now I have you," Alejo said. "This is my dungeon. Do you know how the Moors torture their prisoners?"

""Neither do you," Tomé said. "You have never even seen a Moor."

"Sí, but my uncle was taken prisoner in the Battle of Lepanto, and one time he told me. It is worse than the fire or the rack."

Tomé wiped his nose on his arm and caught his breath. "Worse than the fire or the rack?"

"Sí, sí."

"There can be nothing worse than the fire," Rafael said. But he wasn't sure, and immediately he felt his body stiffen in anticipation of something unpleasant, something that Alejo knew that was worse than the fire.

Alejo crouched down on his knees and beckoned to them to get down low so that he could tell them. The ditch was filled with refuse. A dog, attracted by the smell, poked about. Tomé threw his stick at him and the dog ran off. Alejo beckoned with his hand for them to crouch lower. "You know how they chain a man to the wall," he said.

"Sí, sí, sí," Tomé said.

"Well, the Moors do not chain their feet together but apart as far as they will go, and his arms the same way. Then they take a long feather from a bird and between his legs they tickle him."

Tomé stuck out his lower lip. "That does not sound so bad."

"Sí, it is. They tickle him under the arms and on his feet as well, and after a while it makes him crazy."

"But he does not die," Rafael said.

They heard footsteps above them. Alejo popped his head up and saw a priest walk by. He crossed himself respectfully, then popped his head back down again. "No," he said, "they do not die, but they are crazy forever after that."

Alejo was right. Rafael felt something attack his human nature. He sensed a torment of indulgence that was worse than pain, a mockery of the susceptibilities of the flesh. He knew how prone his own body was to sensations and he felt a corrupting liaison with Alejo's victim. He was right. It was worse than the fire. Rafael felt wretchedly ill. "The Moors are very wicked people," he said.

"Sí," Alejo said, "my uncle killed many in the Battle of Lepanto and he said their blood was not red but black." Tomé shrugged his shoulders. He contested this information, not because he did not think it was true but because he did not want Alejo to know something he did not know. He decided it was time to get down to the Castillo. "Vamos," he said, and they climbed out of the ditch.

They walked with their hands wrapped around each other's waists and Rafael forgot how wretched he felt in the satisfaction of their consolidarity. The stones on the street were a torment to his feet, but Tomé and Alejo wore no shoes and neither would he. Aunt said that the stones were slowly whittling Alejo's feet away and that he had already lost an inch. Belita said Tomé's feet, like his soul, were rotten with callouses. "But you, Rafael, have feet like Gentileza," she said, "and must have protection." When he had to, he wore the shoes she gave him, but took them off as soon as he was a distance from the house.

If Belita could have had her way, she would have glued Rafael to the stool in Sebastián's shed, for she liked nothing better than to sit under Lástima and watch Rafael at his work. Aunt too. She had twenty-two cages of birds in the garden and was forever re-arranging them, putting them into the sun and putting them back in the shade, letting them loose one at a time and caging them up again. They were named for the twelve apostles and other characters in the Bible whom she liked, Rachel and Leah, and Isaac who was her favorite. Sometimes she had a secret falling out with a character and took the name away from the bird that bore his name. Peter had been changed three times, and Jonah had gone back and forth with Noah. Aunt couldn't make up her mind which was worse, a fanatic or a drunkard, or a man who denied his God. Only Isaac's name was never hanged.

That was serenity for everyone except Sebastián, when Rafael sat on the stool painting, Belita sat under Lástima, and Aunt cackled to her birds, using them as a sermon for Rafael or as a story to tell to herself. For Sebastián, life had been at first excruciating, and then merely plodding, ever since his wife had gone witless and he had brought his equally witless sister to care for his witless wife. He had an incoherent affection for Belita. He had loved her since he was fourteen, but had never dreamed of marrying her. Her father was a rich merchant and he was a peasant then. She had sinned with him and married him against her family's wishes. Now he felt responsible for her, however taxing he found her. The face which Rafael loved tormented Sebastián with its shaggy pieces of beauty in the uncombed hair and dirty skin, the dead black eyes and the deader lips he felt forced to kiss at night sometimes, never sure if he wished life in them or not. He almost never spoke to Belita, as if he could not bear to look at her. He kept his face in his food when he ate, his eyes on his work when he worked. He never looked out the window. Rafael knew him as a withdrawn man and, of course, what his father was he assumed he always had been. Sebastián occupied a place in his mind as fixed as God's, no childhood, no running down the steep stone streets with bare feet, no fishing in the Tagus. Childhood belonged to Rafael. Manhood, eternal manhood, belonged to his father. The only way Sebastián expressed a human trait was in teasing Aunt.

"Be careful, solterona, you they will string up by your nose, not your arms."

They had come to the Puente Alcántara and Tomé put his hands on his lips for them to follow him quietly. There was no need, but it added to the adventure. They crossed the bridge and crawled down to a spot near the castle. Here the ground sloped up and a sliver of basement window was visible. The space available for viewing was so low to the ground they had to stretch themselves out and press their eyes to the window.

They looked down into a room which was round, all brick, walls and ceiling, and almost forty feet in height. Rafael felt he was looking into a chimney, except that against the wall was a table with candlesticks on it and against another part of the wall were chairs for spectators. Their eyes were level with the ceiling from which partly hung the apparatus for torture. The other part of the apparatus was stationed in the floor beneath them.

"La garrucha," Tomé said.

Alejo gave his head a smart nod and whistled low. "What do you think is worse, la garrucha or el potro?"

"La garrucha," Rafael whispered.

Alejo clicked his teeth. "I don't think either is so bad. Surely they only mean to scare him."

Rafael felt relieved. "Sí, sí," he said. He jabbed Alejo with his elbow and stuck out his lip. "Sí, that was why they took him away yesterday. They only mean to scare him."

"Sí," Alejo said. "It is only," he shrugged his shoulders smartly, "to scare him a little to loosen his tongue."

A door opened in the round room and several gentlemen entered. One who was the notary or secretary to record the proceedings, put pen and paper on the table. Two inquisitors entered with the Grand Inquisitor, Roxas, who was Cardinal and Archbishop of Toledo, and then the prisoner, two guards, and the torturer who was masked.

"Your uncle," Alejo sneered.

"No," Tomé said.

"Sí," Alejo said. "Everyone knows your uncle is a torturer for the Inquisition."

Tomé denied it. The Archbishop put the Bible on the table and lit the candles. Everyone in the room, the prisoner too, bowed their heads and prayed. Then Roxas turned to the prisoner with polite impatience, for it was the third day of this inquisition and there was, in truth, nothing further but confession to be said. The issue had had ample exegesis by now. All that was left was the ritual of pressure. But Cardinal Roxas restrained his impatience. He asked the prisoner, courteously, for the love of God, to tell the truth. The notary picked up his pen and waited for the prisoner's answer. There was none, and he recorded the silence.

"Por Dios," Roxas said. "Tell the truth for the love of God." Each word was pronounced evenly, without a shade of tonal difference, uttered like the cry of a bailiff in court, calling everyone to attention, neither more nor less than bodily respect being asked for, uttered like the atonal sentence of a deaf man who has never heard human speech. "Tell the truth for the love of God." The sentence was a formula and the prisoner did not register reaction. No one expected him to respond at first, but everyone expected him to learn from experience sooner or later. So Roxas waited to give the prisoner time to reflect on his punishment. The prisoner reflected nothing. Roxas had to decide whether he was being impertinent or whether he had not comprehended. He did not think the latter was probable, for the prisoner had parried arguments with him well enough on the first day. Roxas rubbed his lip with his thumb nail. The prisoner kept his face averted from him. Roxas turned away and raised his hands to the crucifix that hung above the table.

The torturer knew this to be his signal. A guard took off the sheet that covered the prisoner. He was naked except for a loin cloth which covered what belonged to God, put in its usual way, "for decency's sake." Without clothes it was difficult to tell what kind of man the prisoner was, what station of life he had come from. He had the black eyes of a gitano and the beard of an hidalgo. The torture belt was slipped around his waist, cords were tied around his thighs, under his armpits and around his shoulders. The prisoner was familiar with the routine. Today he could encompass, without feeling violated, the touch of the guard undressing him. Trussed like a chicken, he stood while the torturer slipped sticks though the cords on his body and slowly turned each one. The prisoner's body jerked involuntarily.

An inquisitor said to him, "Tell the truth." Roxas kept his back turned. The notary paused, pen in hand. The inquisitor repeated, "Tell the truth for the love of God." Silence. The torturer pulled on a cord with his weight and the prisoner rose upward about a foot. He hung, twirling in the air, looking inconsequential, inanimate as a book or a chair or a pot hanging in the air. For a grown man to be tied, lifted, and carried into the air against his will, to be rendered inanimate is sufficient, without pain, to destroy him.

"Tell the truth for the love of God," the inquisitor said. He looked up at the prisoner. The notary, pen in hand, ready to record any reply, looked up at the prisoner too. Roxas paused in his prayers, his hands stretched to the crucifix, and waited. The notary waited, pen in hand, waited. He sighed at the inevitable. The torturer put weights on the cords and the prisoner jerked up another foot. The cords in his armpits cut to the bones. His fingers, tied behind his back, went spastic. The inquisitor repeated the command to tell the truth for the love of God, the torturer pulled the cords, the prisoner jerked up another foot. The cords split the skin in the hollows of his armpits. He registered the pain silently.

Roxas felt that something was wrong. He felt the concern and self consciousness of one whose position is new to him. He had been appointed only a few months ago, and inexperience will rob anyone of confidence. The torturer gazed at him for instructions, but Roxas kept an impassive stance, determined to find willpower in prayer and in the consciousness of his position, newly appointed or not. The torturer picked up a whip. With a pause between each stroke, to give the prisoner time to confess and to save himself from the next stroke, he began to beat him. The notary gazed up at the prisoner hopefully, that he would break his silence. He had no desire to see him suffer. His lashes fluttered with sympathy.

The organs on the prisoner's face lost connection to each other and went in different directions. His tongue hung out first from the right corner of his mouth, then from the left corner. His eyeballs rotated slowly like flowers on a pool of water. His skin broke at a hundred points and blood flowed from all of them. His body crumpled and then twirled like dead weight.

"Tell the truth, tell the truth, tell the truth, tell the truth," the second inquisitor said. An air of impatience filled the room, discomfort, thwarted expectations, mild desire for it to end. The notary, pen in hand, put his head on a side and waited hopefully. "Tell the truth, tell the truth, tell the truth," the second inquisitor repeated. His voice bristled with impatience. Roxas kept his back turned and read his Bible. His ecclesiastical robes, perfect in tailoring, conveyed in fold and drape not only majesty and tradition and lawfulness, but the triumph of the idea of man. He turned a page. His eyes wandered and searched here and there over the text for comfort and confirmation. Christ on Calvary had suffered for ignoble humanity. Should not ignoble humanity suffer for His sake?

The laws of torture are certain. Tears fell from the prisoner's eyes. A guard took a long pole with a dab of cotton at the end and wiped them away. Roxas suppressed the difficult admission about the man's discomfort. It was no use to sympathize. The schemata for spiritual survival demanded continual struggle against heresy, faith of martyrs in the victory of the spirit. The punishment of the flesh must not distress. A spiritual kingdom was no small reward for occasional agony. Europe retained its balance in the foundation of a pax Catolica. This hour in late September, 1608 or '09 reaffirmed the boundaries of her religious assumptions. Beyond these borders: spiritual disorder, metaphysical chaos.

"Tell the truth," the inquistor said. He repeated it after each descent of the whip. The weights were applied and the prisoner's body ascended. The whip fell on his back, on his buttocks, on his thighs, on his calves. "Tell the truth," the inquisitor shouted up to him. The whip caught the prisoner on the sole of his foot. He stirred. He was brought back from a cave of memories he had crawled into for shelter, a sweet bed of dreams he had found for himself in the moss under a tree. He opened his eyes reluctantly and discovered his irrelevant body twisting from a rope. This swinging body caused him pain and he rejected it. It was, surprisingly, the object of Roxas's desires. It could be had for a torturer's fees. He gave it to them freely and ascended in silence.

He hung and twirled and bled and his eyes, like moons moving slowly in the sky, rotated without further reflection or content. It was difficult to know if there was consciousness, or personality, or history left in them. So much had been emptied from them. They came to rest upon the crucifix, the tortured lids of the Christ wrinkled in black folds. Like the prisoner's, the eyeballs floated on the bottom lids, detached from seeing, no longer concerned with the concatentation of events that had brought him to this spot, swinging fifteen feet in the air, surrounded by strangers. The prisoner looked at the Christ figure with a universe of expressions, incredulity, bitterness, aversion, irony, a history of hatred. The belly of the Christ bellowed out to him in pain. His hands were tied behind his back, the muscles in his arms stretched with pain. The head lay on the chest, the tongue hung out in the idiotic stance of agony, the eyeballs swam along the lower lids.

The prisoner drank knowledge from the wooden eyes. Dead, carved, a sculptor's idea of ideal martyrdom, they no longer made connection between events. The eyes gazed downward with paradoxical peace. For the prisoner, pain destroyed the way back to life. He did not wish to return to the living, to be a man among men. He twirled past the Christ figure and their eyes locked in recognition.

Below, Roxas turned pages in a book, reading passages of beatitude and justification and high poetry.

The prisoner ascended. Blood poured from his mouth. He licked the dripping beads of sweat from his face. He kept his eyes on the Christ. In the crustaceous, tortured lids he searched for a response, that he might not die alone in this round room under the eyes of seven strangers, not a compassionate witness among them, not a soul to tell the world that his was a particular agony. He knew the Christ figure. They knew each other. They were the past and the present, participants in each other's agony. They were both spirit and matter, witnesses to the same event. They were the event. The prisoner ascended. The name of the man whose suffering saved Europe on that afternoon is not known. He ascended in silence. When he felt the pain threaten his resolve not to talk, he drank unconsciousness as he had once drunk wine at his wedding, as he had once drunk water from a cup that an old woman living in the hills had given him.

"Gracias, Señora," he had said.

"De nada," she protested, "water is a gift from God, not from me." She did a little dance, shuffling in her broken shoes and bowed low, hiding her uncomely features.

"Sí," he said, "but you are the one who brought it."

She was overcome by the remark, as if the compliment was too much for her. She bowed, put her hand to her mouth and shuffled away.

He drank the water and went to rest in the shade of a tree. He lay down in its monumental coolness and found there a box of precious jewels. It was his silence rioting in the sunlight. He whistled for his son to give him the gift. "Jorge." Two black eyes looked down at him. He was almost on a level with the window. Light struck his face. Children were staring at him. He struggled to slip back into darkness. Someone's terror brought him back from his journey again. He opened his eyes and tried to understand what he was looking at. Ah! children. He ascended.

Rafael did a terrible thing. He stood up to run, but his legs buckled and he could not move. He lost control of his body and flattened his head and his arms against the building. He screamed to the man to save himself. "Stop it," he shrieked, "stop it." Alejo put his arms around his waist and tried to pull him away, but Rafael clung to a bar on the window and screamed for them to stop it. "Stop it, stop it, stop it," he shrieked. Tomé tried to muffle him. Rafael bit his fingers. "Stop it," he shrieked again. He kicked the building. "Somebody stop it." They heard guards running. Alejo and Tomé ran. Rafael knew he had to run too. But he had a terrible feeling that he was deserting the prisoner. Fantasy and hope made him think he could run to someone's house and ask for help, he could run to Aunt or to his father. Someone would come in time. Someone would surely come in time. But he knew the man was dead. His guards had forgotten about him when they had seen Rafael and Alejo at the window. Roxas stood amazed at the interruption. Incapable of registering what he saw, his eyes squinted at the light near the ceiling. A score of unfortunate speculations ran across his mind, perhaps as Darius might have thought, that ancient Daniel had found a way of playing a trick on the universe. Roxas snapped his fingers for a guard to go immediately and investigate. Alejo ran. Tomé ran. Rafael smashed his fist against the wall. "Be dead," he screamed to the prisoner, and ran too, downhill all the way, without stopping until he got to the bridge. He jumped into the river without thought of what he was doing. His body jerked around without control. He swam until his arms were leaden with exhaustion. When he could not move them anymore, he let the river carry him, he didn't care where. He wanted to go anywhere to escape the sickness he felt. But he could not. The sickness stayed in his body, no matter how hard he swam or where he floated to. He crawled on to the bank of the river and lay there. He tried to push the sight from his eyes, but he could not. "Debes olvidarlo," his aunt's voice said. Rafael turned over on his arms and wept.

"Niño," someone sneered.

Rafael scrambled to his feet and peered through the bushes.

"Chirrp, chirp, chirp. Niño, nene, nene, nene."

Rafael crouched down and searched the bushes. A pair of legs was standing in the middle of them. He picked up a branch and crawled to the legs. "Aha," Alejo pounced out at him. "Nene, nene, nene."

"Liar," Rafael screamed, "you said they would not kill him."

"Sí," Alejo said, "but he did not confess. They did not kill him. He killed himself. You saw how he did that."

Rafael covered his ears with his hands. He did not wish to hear anything. Tears were in his eyes and he did not want Alejo to see that either. He plunged through the bushes and ran in the direction of his home.

Without Tomé, the sport of baiting Rafael was dull. Indeed, at that moment, Alejo might even have preferred Rafael's company to being alone, but he could not resist demonstrating that he was in command of himself. "Nene," he teased him and flung a handful of sand at Rafael's legs. The sand did not hurt Rafael, but it stung him with insult and with perplexity at being insulted for feelings he could not help. His mother could not stand the sight of pain and she was a lunatic. His aunt could not bear the subject of torture and she was a disreputable spinster. His father could look upon pain with the same silence that he looked upon his work or his food, and he was manly. When Rafael came into the house Aunt said right away she could tell by the look in Rafael's eyes that something bad had happened.

"Sí, Aunt," he said to mock her, "I know where they torture the heretics. Tomé took me and Alejo there this morning and we watched a man being tortured with la garrucha and then whipped."

Aunt began to tremble. The dry skin on her face slid up and down for seconds before she could talk. "Cristodulce," she said, "what have your little eyes seen?"

Rafael burst into tears and buried his face in his arms. Belita crawled under the table and began to whimper. "Rafael," she called to him, "come, sit here with me. If you sit under the table no one will hurt you." Rafael wept. He knew that something irretrievable had happened to him. He would never be the same again. A terrible feeling threatened his life. Yet the sound of his mother trying to comfort him filled him with loathing. She circled her arms around his legs and tried to console him. He wrenched his legs away. He struck his head on the end of the table because he wanted to kick his mother and could not do that. "Niño querido," she pleaded with him. If she could not soothe him she would go utterly mad. But when she tried to touch him he screamed so loudly she crawled away into a corner and buried her head against the wall.

Sebastián came flying in from the shed. "What is all the screaming about? Is it you, solterona, frightening the boy again with your babble? Leave him alone. Do you hear." For once

Rafael was glad to have his father shut Aunt up. He flung himself into Sebastián's arms. The events of the morning seemed to lose their force in his father's presence as if they were absorbed into his practical ability to get on with life, no matter what its terms. Rafael knew that was the truth about it all. His aunt and his mother were broken stems on a river. But it was beyond Rafael to decide in what way Sebastián's survival was worth more, or to know that if he told his father what he had seen that morning it would have reminded Sebastián of similar experiences in his childhood. But this confession would not have gotten them far. Sebastián would have spit and have said cursorily, "Sí, so what? If the man deserved it, who are we to question?" He knew how many doors one had to shut behind oneself in order to grow up, and that it was very dangerous, having arrived at adulthood, to open one of these doors again. He knew that Belita would never be well because she kept all the doors to her past open and constantly walked in and out of them. She remembered once having seen a dog tortured by some boys and then flung into the river to drown. She was six at the time, and still would crawl under the table and talk to the dog as it were alive. She remembered the time she had sinned with Sebastián in a field near the river and then had spent the night weeping on the church floor. She could not bring herself to confess this sin, but she confessed it to Sebastián time after time, how she had not wanted to go into the field, how he had tricked her by saying he would do her no harm, and so on. She only did not remember when she took leave of her senses. And that was the one door Sebastián could not close for himself. "Go into the shed and do some work," he said to Rafael. Whatever the trouble was that was the remedy.

"Sí," Rafael said, glad to escape from Aunt and his mother. He wiped his running nose on his hand and climbed up on a stool, but it was no use. Grimly he painted designs on some tiles. Lástima came and stood by the window and Gentileza took her place at Lástima's tail, but it was no use. Rafael could not rid himself of the scenes in his head. There was an unaccustomed silence in the courtyard. Only after a while did Rafael realize it was because Aunt was not there, talking to the birds. He looked at them with dread, their black eyes, their pecking beaks, their wings forever flapping and beating against the sides of their cages. Peter, Simon, Paul and James, beady-eyed birds, forever watching him, forever plunging their beaks into his breast.

He could not sleep that night. His thoughts and the beating of the birds' wings woke him again and again. He heard the terrible sound of them beating their wings against the sides of their cages, hopping about, looking for a little freedom of movement. What they want is the sky, Rafael thought. He lay as still as he could, because he knew Aunt was up, listening to his soul. He slept fitfully, pursued by his nightmares. Twice he woke from his nightmare and though he was in terror he would not turn to Aunt and ask her for comfort. Once he dreamed that he was walking in a valley. The moon was out and all around him was serenity, but he knew there was something sinister in the air, though he could not tell what it was. Gentileza stood beneath the window and baaed. In his dream he heard her, just ahead of him, always just ahead of him, no matter how fast he ran. He came to a Moor's castle and something warned him not to go in, but he heard Gentileza baa and he followed the sound, as a man in the desert follows the suggestion of water. He came into a room and there was a great feast prepared for him. The lords of the world were there to serve him, popes and bishops, knights, emperors and kings. This is the world, my son, someone said, and you must choose which course you would like, but if you do not choose the proper course. The voice did not conclude. It stopped, as in a dream where one is running and never runs anywhere. Three platters were brought to him, each covered with a silver dome. Choose your course, the voice said. But remember, if you do not choose the proper course. Again, the voice did not conclude. Rafael lifted the cover from the first platter. The moon was on it. Rafael was enthralled. He lifted the second cover with eagerness. The prisoner's eyes winked at him. The cover fell from his hand, but he tried not to betray repulsion. He knew the lords of the earth were watching him. He put the cover back on the table decorously, and lifted the cover from the third platter. Gentileza lay on it. Rafael woke up.

Aunt's eyes flew open. Rafael thought if she said debes

olvidarlo, he would run away from home and never come back. But Aunt's feelings had been hurt by Sebastián's summary dismissal of her in the afternoon. She wanted Rafael to see that her feelings were hurt, although he was not to blame for this. She pulled the cover over her head and let it be known in a fussy way that her sleep had been disturbed, but she said nothing. Still Rafael knew she was listening to his heart. He heard the birds fluttering outside the window. But comfort of comforts! He heard Gentileza outside the window too. Oh! how he wanted to bury his head in her side. In all the world, it seemed to him that nothing could comfort like an animal. Human love had too much complexity. Only an animal would stand and allow itself to be loved tirelessly, panting gently, its ears flicked up, waiting for more, never in a hurry to move on, never remembering bad things to diminish the moment. His dream had been terrible. Rafael could not bear it if anything should happen to Gentileza. If he told his dream to Aunt, she would be sure to say it was a prophecy. Rafael pressed his lips together and swore he would never tell her. He did not care to be God's receptacle for such a prophecy. He felt Aunt's eyes on him, but he kept his lips locked. Hopefully, hopefully, the dawn would soon be up. He fell asleep again, and again dreamed. He was in a round room. It had no end and it had no beginning. There was a terrible sound in his dream, terrible because it was familiar. Tap, tap, tapping like the birds' beaks against the walls of their cages. Tap, tap, tapping. He looked outside through a window of the room and saw a man tied to a post. There were men all around him, in helmets, with shields, soldiers and warriors, the mighty of the earth, and they were driving nails into the man's head. He wanted to tell them that they belonged inside the room where he, Rafael, was and that he should be outside, looking in instead of inside looking out. He had not done anything wrong. He wanted to tell them that, but it did not seem to matter. The prisoner looked at him with his black eyes as if he wanted to tell him something too. That was it. Rafael knew in his dream what he had almost known in the afternoon but couldn't make out then, that the prisoner had had something to tell him. His black eyes had been filled with warning. Go away, they said. Run. The prisoner stuck his tongue out to speak, but a soldier nailed it to his chin. The light went out in his eyes. A soldier climbed to the top of the post and put a superscription above his head: All Men Die With Me. Rafael woke up. His heart was beating furiously. His palms were wet. But he held back, he held back. He made no sound and did not wake Aunt. There was some light in the sky. A rooster was crowing. If he could lay still another hour, everyone would be up. But suddenly he jumped out of bed and ran into the courtyard and within minutes, before anyone knew what was happening, he had set the birds loose. They took to the air like a pent up breath that was let out. Aunt woke up, alert with danger. She took the scene in with a glance and began to scream. She ran into the courtyard in her coarse nightrobe, her hair hanging down on her back, her arms flapping helplessly. "Maléfico, maléfico," she shrieked. She cursed Rafael and ran after the birds, trying to catch whatever she could. They fluttered to the rooftops, on the branches of the trees, on Lástima's back. They took to the air and went around in circles, crazy with this unexpected freedom.

"Come back, come back," Aunt shrieked.

Sebastián woke and looked out the window. When he saw the birds flying about, he said, "Good riddance to bad rubbish!"

"They are Aunt's friends," Belita murmured.

In the end, Aunt retrieved six and the only consolation was that Isaac was one of them. But her feelings were irreparably hurt. Not because Sebastián had insulted her, which she was accustomed to, but because Rafael, her sweet child, her consolation for spinsterhood and childlessness, had done this. His act was inexplicable, an act of inexplicable betrayal. She who loved him more than her breath! All morning she sat in a chair, dazed, with a cross between her hands and tried to make out the meaning of Rafael's act in breathless mutters.

"Why did you do this thing, child?"

"You used to love my birds. When you were a baby you used to walk with your hand in mine and I would tell you a story about each bird, David, Jonah, Peter, Joseph."

"Why did you do this thing? All I love in the world is you. Why did you drive away my birds?"

By noon she came to a decision. Rafael had been the one who had made Sebastián's cruelty to her and Belita's idiocy bearable, because of his good soul. It was for his sake that she had continued to live in their house, unwanted and insulted. Now his goodness and his magic were gone. She strung together the cages of the six birds and put her few belongings into a bag and without a word to anyone left the house. Only Belita sat under the table and watched her go.

But everyone knew where Aunt had gone. As soon as Sebastián noticed that the six birds were gone and Aunt's crucifix and her few belongings, he sent Rafael to bring her back.

"I do not think she will come back this time," Rafael said.

Sebastián considered the matter for a moment. "I do not think you should have let the birds loose. Sí, I know they are a nuisance, but they kept her company."

Rafael could not tell how he felt. He knew he had done a terrible thing, but it was good to know he would not hear them that night, beating with their wings. He was sorry Aunt had left the house, but he was glad she would not be sleeping next to him with her eyes on him, waiting for him to cry. He wanted her not to be alone or to be hurt, but he did not want her to come back either.

"She is a nuisance," Sebastián said. "Still and all, she is an old woman and we must show respect. Go, Rafael."

Rafael watched his father for a second or two, hoping for a sign of hesitation that he could exploit, but there was none. He turned slowly, hoping his father would say "wait" or "however," but he didn't. Sebastián did not have Rafael's love for Aunt and he was not troubled by her as Rafael was. He could resolve the problem with a principle.

Rafael went down the street slowly. He was in no hurry this time to find Aunt. His conscience bothered him, but he felt relieved that he might never have to share his bed with her again, or listen to her birds beating their wings at night. It seemed to him now that the only thing in the world he cared for was Gentileza.

He met up with Tomé and Alejo at the bottom of the street. They had spotted him first and were hiding in the ditch. When Rafael went by, Tomé stretched his hand out and grabbed his ankle.

Rafael jumped with terror.

"Aha!" Tomé and Alejo sprang out of the ditch. "Where are you bound for?"

"Aunt has run away again and I have to bring her back."

Tomé jabbed Alejo in his shoulder. "Aunt has run away again," he mocked. "Why does she run away so often?"

"I don't know," Alejo said, shrugging his shoulders with a broad suggestiveness. "Why does she run away so often?"

"Can it be that Aunt has a lover in the hills?" Tomé said.

"What? Aunt?" Alejo said. "A lover in the hills? What kind of lover can that be?"

"Why, only something that grows in the hills," Tomé said. "She keeps a tree stump for a lover."

Rafael felt his soul tighten, yet he could not come to Aunt's defense. He knew the suggestion was repulsive, yet he laughed with them. "I will be back soon," he said.

"Go, go," Alejo said, "we will wait for you right here." With a leap they jumped into the ditch again and disappeared.

Rafael ran at top speed. He wanted to get his errand over with and come back and play with Tomé and Alejo. He found Aunt, as usual, at the foot of a hill across the Tagus. She was sitting on a stool, facing the setting sun. She registered no expression when Rafael came into view. Her parchment-like skin slid over her cheek bones as she moved her lips in prayer.

"Come, Aunt," Rafael said, "Father insists that you return." She waited for him to say something else, something more conciliatory. But Rafael only pinched the sand between his toes. Her lips trembled and she turned away. She was puzzled and wounded. Nothing she had said to herself all day could explain his behavior to her.

"How have I hurt you?" she rasped.

"Me?" Rafael said. He shrugged his shoulders. "You have not hurt me, Aunt."

She looked up at him, standing against the setting sun.

She sensed that something irreconcilable had happened between them, but she could not find out what it was. His face had changed. His big ears did not look lovable to her anymore, but coarse like disfigurements she had seen in other children. That could not be. It was a mirage. She was allowing her hurt feelings to judge him because he had set her birds loose. In all this world, Aunt loved nothing as she loved Rafael and she struggled to swallow her bitterness over the birds. What were they compared to Rafael? Birds she could buy anywhere. How foolish she had been to chastise him for a childish act and make him feel guilty. Whose place was it to show understanding? She reached for his hand but Rafael moved perceptibly away. Aunt was astonished.

"How have I sinned?" she rasped. She leaned on her cane and stood upright. "Tell me, Rafael, how have I sinned against you?"

Rafael could not bear these questions that he did not know how to answer, but yet which struck his nerve center. "Oh, Aunt," he said, as if he were brushing away a fly. "Come, let me help you. Father says you are to come back."

His words were a dry formula and Aunt was too sensitive not to feel this.

Rafael turned to the six cages and laughed ruefully. "Well, at least you have Isaac and Peter and some of the others left." He began to gather the cages under his arm when Aunt struck him on the shoulder with her cane. Astonished, winded by the impact, Rafael wheeled on his feet. Suddenly his childishness burbled from him. Tears ran from his eyes. Aunt leaned on her cane, breathless, repentant and haggard. "Go alone, Rafael," she said weakly, "I cannot come back this time."

Rafael began to cry loudly. The conflict was too much for him. He hated her; he hated her agedness and her birds. He hated the way she made his friends laugh at her. He hated her babbling and her cackling. He hated her terrible breath at night and her red, watery eyes upon him. Only her coming back could absolve him and he did not want her to come back. He put his hands to his face and wept from so much confusion. "Oh, Aunt, you must come back. You know Father will not let you live here. And how will my mother live without you?"

"And you, Rafael?" she said. She hung on her cane, crippled and pleading. Rafael felt his soul being pounded between millstones. He could not answer her. The ground was dry beneath his feet. He twisted his toes around the prickly grass, curious that its touch could be so sharp. Aunt leaned on her cane and shook with emotions like a dry leaf. One word from this child and she would kick her heels in the air and run back with him Sebastián by himself was bitter company for an old woman, and how well she knew he only tolerated her out of pity for his wife and the guilt of his sin. But this child! Oh! this child.

"You must come back," he cried. Again he turned to the cages. "You know that Father expects you to."

"Father! Father! Father!" she screeched. She ran at him with her raised cane as if she were herself a dreadful bird about to beat him out of existence. Her old breath hit him in the face and he knew how much he loathed her. She was dreadfully ancient. Her skin looked as if it would crack on her face. Never before had she looked so ugly to him. He suddenly understood why Tomé and Alejo found her ridiculous. "Father!" she screeched at him. The word rattled in her throat. She hit his fingers and drove him away from the bird cages. Isaac and Peter hopped about in mad fright. "It was your father who drove your mother out of her wits," she screeched breathlessly. "Cry, Rafael, cry. Tell me Sebastián needs me. Sí, he needs me. It was he who made her crazy. He hit her one night on the side of her head with a milk pail because he could not stand it when she reminded him how had made her sin. Sí, Rafael, he hit her for this, and then he asked me to live with him and take care of her."

Rafael threw his hands up to cover his face. He flew here and there, away from the reach of Aunt's cane. He covered his head and his ears. "Liar!" he screamed. "Liar!" The accusation goaded Aunt beyond control. She flew at him in further rage. There was blackness throughout her head. She hardly knew what she was doing. She beat him with her cane wherever she could reach him. The birds fluttered madly, screeching and cawing. Rafael covered his head and ran down the path. He stopped midway and turned back to scream at her.

"Liar! Liar! Liar! We don't want you in our house." She lied about his father. She, his father's sister, lied about him because of jealousy and old age. "You're the crazy one," he screamed. "You are old and you smell from old age. You are crazy like my mother." Everyone laughed at the both of them. Now his aunt had hit him, a thing she had never done, his aunt who always had raisins or a cake in her pocket for him. She was a liar, a liar , and his mother was a lunatic. He turned and fled.

He did not know where he was running. He felt as if he had been beaten on every inch of his body. But worse, worse, he could not go home and tell his father that he had failed to bring Aunt back. There were dark clouds in the sky. If it should storm and Aunt did not come home, she might get sick and die. The fantasy frightened him even further. He ran up and down random streets and cried in a spasm of chaos and fears. He ran along the Moorish walls, hoping to find Alejo and Tomé who would tell him he was right to abandon aunt. She is old enough to make up her own mind. Sí. Let her sit in the hills. She was a liar. He ran back into the side streets and into the Plaza Zocodover. Every place was deserted. There was no one around to tell him what was right. Winded, confused at all the terrible things that were happening to him at once, he sat down on the steps of a building and cried. There was no end to his confusion and no end to his crying, and he had no thoughts of the future. Two priests passed him and stirred a hope that they would save him, that in their maturity, their competent, solacing adulthood, they would stop and ask him why he was crying and he would explain about Aunt's birds and how he had said dreadful things to her and now she would not come back to live with them. But the priests did not notice him. They walked on, their robes trailing the dust of the street. The world is full of crying children. Rafael buried his head in his knees. The sun went down. The sky was darkening quickly. If Aunt did not come back, she would spend the night in a stormy hill. If he did not go home soon it would make matters worse. He knew that the house without Aunt would seem dreadfully silent. There was no one else at home that he could speak to and no one else who would wake with him when he had a nightmare. Still, never would he believe what Aunt had said about his father. The look of the sky chilled him. "Aunt," he cried, "you must come home." He got up and wondered if he should go back and try again. His crying spent, he wandered, dazed down to the Tagus, knowing all the time that it was getting darker and that his crime was getting worse.

"Where are you going?" Tomé said. He and Alejo sat in a tree.

Rafael looked up and saw them. "Nowhere," he said. "You said you would wait for me in the ditch. What are you doing up there?"

"Sí," Alejo said. He spit out of the side of his mouth. "That was three hours ago. How long did you think we would wait?" They climbed out of the tree.

"Why, have you been looking for us?" Tomé asked.

Rafael had to admit that he had not been.

"What kept you so long?" Tomé asked.

"Aunt will not come home," Rafael said.

Tomé whistled through his teeth. "What will your father say?"

The sympathetic inquiry warmed Rafael, but he only shrugged his shoulders in reply. They knew what that meant. "Come with us," Alejo said. "We found the bones of a Moor."

"No!" Rafael said incredulously, but he was willing to believe it for the sake of stalling.

"Sí, sí," Alejo said. "In the ditch. After you saw us, Tomé and I were playing and you know that this dog always comes and digs in a certain spot. Well, this time we let him and he uncovered these bones."

"How do you know they belong to a Moor?"

"Oh, sí. Who cannot tell a Moor's bones?"

Rafael followed them back to the spot. They climbed into the ditch. After a full day's sun, the hole reeked with refuse and smells, but the children picked their way among the garbage, the dead rats, the rotting vegetables, as if they were treasures. "Sí," Alejo said. He uncovered the spot where the bones lay in a row. Rafael looked down at them and felt no suspense. They looked only like bones. "What?" Tomé said, "you do not believe they are a Moor's bones!"

Rafael felt empty and even baleful. Tomé and Alejo

could not whet his appetite today. "Let us play knights and warriors," Tomé said. "I will be Santiago Matamoros."
"Ach, you are always Santiago Matamoros," Alejo said. "This time I will be Santiago Matamoros."
Tomé felt caught. He decided to distribute the roles with generosity. Alejo could be Santiago Matamoros, he would be the Grand Inquisitor, and Rafael could be a heretic.
Rafael objected. He would be a conquistador. Tomé and Alejo immediately pointed out that the conquistador did not operate in the same field as the Grand Inquisitor or Santiago Matamoros. The logic was inescapable. In order for the game to be played, they needed a heretic.
Rafael knew he was being bullied again, but he agreed. Alejo and Tomé immediately tied him to the trunk of a tree that was in the bottom of the ditch and asked him if he would confess. Rafael said he would die first. Alejo wielded a broad stick in the shape of a sword and said he would cut off Rafael's head if he did not confess.
"Wait," Tomé shrieked with excitement, "I know where I can get a faggot and we can make a real fire."
Rafael's head began to ring. "Let me loose," he cried.
"We are only playing," Tomé said. "We will only place one little faggot underneath your feet. If it starts to burn, we will put it out immediately. You, Alejo, Matamoros, guard the prisoner until I come back."
Tomé left immediately. Alejo was tremendously excited. He assured Rafael they would not hurt him. It would only make the play seem more real. Alejo's voice was seductive. Rafael believed him and did not believe him. He wanted to please them, but he was afraid. He had always let them tie him up in the past, he was always the heretic, he was always the victim, always the prisoner. Many, many times he did not mind, only being glad to be able to play with them, but sometimes he did mind. He too wanted to be a conquistador por la gloria de España. It seemed very strange that Tomé and Alejo were never the heretic, and when Tomé came back with a lit faggot in a cup Rafael told him he did not want to play anymore, it was late and he had to go home.
Tomé began to whine. "You will spoil our game."

Rafael pressed his lips together. That was a terrible accusation. He did not wish to spoil their game for them and he did not know how to insist that they let him down and be able to keep their friendship at the same time.

"Two minutes, Rafael," Tomé said. "Two minutes and we will let you down." He quickly built up some dry brush beneath Rafael's feet and placed the faggot in the center. He and Alejo bent over it and blew on it rhythmically and methodically. Soon a spiral of smoke rose from the brush and the sound of dry tinder cracking could be heard.

"Confess," Tomé said at once in a commanding voice.

"I confess," Rafael said eagerly. He wanted only to be let down. He was in terror over how late it was. He could never run back to Aunt's hill now before the dark. She would have to sleep the night out there and he would have to go home without her.

Tomé was disgusted with Rafael as a heretic. "You are not supposed to confess so soon."

"Sí, I must go home," Rafael said.

The note of reality was disgusting. It robbed Tomé of all the drama of his role. He nudged Alejo in the stomach with his elbow. Alejo knew immediately what he meant. They both ran away like the wind. Rafael was incredulous. "Come back," he shouted at them.

"Sí, we will," Tomé laughed from a hiding place. "Only a few minutes, Rafael."

Rafael did believe them. He knew they would come back in time to rescue him. His liaison with the human race depended upon their word. He prayed that he would not betray his fears and call for help.

He could smell the smoke and taste it on the back of his tongue. His hands were tied behind the tree and he tugged at the cord. Its strength in keeping him where he did not wish to be humiliated him. Toledo crouched above him like a giant, here a torso, there a finger jabbing the sky. It was already so dark he knew his punishment was certain. A wind blew. It swirled the refuse from the ditch and blew up the smell of dead and decaying things. It fanned the flame. Rafael pulled at his cords again, surprised to find how expertly they had tied them, how decisive power was. He felt utterly weary with his youth and his helplessness. A flock of birds flew overhead. His heart burst with envy for them. If only he could know that they were the souls of those who had died in agony, he could find some peace for himself. One bird circled over his head. The other birds flew off. They circled over the steeple and then disappeared into the turbulent clouds. But one bird remained and hovered over the ditch. It was easy for Rafael, child, to imagine that the bird was a prescient spirit. It seemed to him that it was Isaac and that Aunt had sent it as a sign. Its presence was a consolation, albeit a dreadful one. Rafael could barely trace its flight through the dark clouds. Now and then a wing caught light in the luminosity shooting along the cloudtops. Then all locked into landscape with a title: Boy tied to a tree in a ditch. History was transformed into mood: forever apprehension. Mood is translated back into history. Civilization is memory and art is both.

Rafael, child, your terror is only a game. No matter now the name of it. Pronto, Tomé and Alejo will come back to release you.

CHILDREN OF GOD

MIRELE'S story begins in the wheatfields of Bessarabia during Easter week, 1903, when she was twelve, and she heard the ominous rumble of horses being urged to blood. She stood up and examined the horizon with squinting eyes, as someone in Kansas might do, alerted from her particular history to differences which had invaded the familiar air. She called to her sister, two years younger than her, also working in the field a few rows away,"Psst, Hinda," and jerked her chin in the direction of the horizon. Hinda got off her knees and looked in the direction her sister was looking, but the clues embedded in tiny horsemen shrouded in dust evaded her. Mirele shaded her eyes again, and watched the moving columns of figures for a few more seconds. Then she said, "Come," to Hinda, with a parental authority that irked the younger sister and, grasping her hand, began to cross the fields to go home.

She did not wish to appear out of order and tried to walk normally, not too fast for it was not clear if anything was out of order. A disturbance of air might be all. She had been accused of being melodramatic before. Ideas seized her, it was true, ideas which often betrayed her, it was true, if she tried to realize them. But it seemed best to leave the fields and speculate later on the wisdom of doing this, and Hinda was compelled to follow her, upon instruction from their parents that she was never to be left alone in the fields. Walk normally, decorously, Mirele instructed herself, but she did not.

"Hey, where are you going?" the overseer shouted.
"Hey! What's up?" a young man called.

Mirele was not detained by any of this. She jerked her chin backwards and kept walking, Hinda's hand clutched in hers. Let others explain the ball of dust in the distance. Others got up from their knees and looked at the horizon and left too, also slowly at first, not wishing to appear undone by fear; then more quickly as conviction seized them.

Heads bobbed up to see what was happening, but no one spoke. Those who were leaving merely jerked their chins too in the direction of the horizon, or rolled their eyes backward, but kept moving. More followed, quickly, then urgently. They dropped their hoes, their sickles, their scythes. Women who had lain their babies on the ground, hoisted them to their backs and began to run. Then a man gave the signal to clear the fields, and the men began to run quickly. The overseers could not stop them. Heads and shoulders bobbed and moved in unison, up and down the rows of wheat, old men with ill fitting boots on feet that hurt, heavy breasted women with babushkas and laboring breaths, not meant to run. They fled like deer from a burning forest. An instinct urged them out of the fields, and they ran toward the town, their homes, the synagogue, not sure where shelter could be found.

Mirele searched for her parents and brothers, but she could not find them. They worked in different parts of the fields. She recognized faces, but not those of her parents and brothers. Was it possible they did not see the commotion? Perhaps her mother had taken ill and could not leave the field and her father would not leave without her. Fears assailed her, but she brushed everything aside except the obsession to hold Hinda's hand and run with her. Hinda struggled against her, humiliated at being committed to Mirele's care, who fled, dragging her with her. They reached the first street of the town, already able to hear the salacious sounds of the horsemen's laughter in their ears. A few more minutes, a few more yards, a few more streets, and safety was possible. The spires from the cathedral were straight ahead. But the orderly retreat from the fields broke down. People scattered into fragments, like a shell burst apart, for the men with horses with the smell of blood on them were already in the streets of the town, blocking every path. Some had circled the fields and had come into the town from another direction. They had outwitted the Jews. They had outrun them, they had outfoxed them. The prey were caught in the claws of a crab.

In the history of suffering, among various people, there are single words, single phrases, which carry the people's history and convey the whole of what is to be dreaded by them, words like famine, slave raid, plague, or pogrom. They need no explanation. The word sounds the alarm of history. So a cry from within the belly of the crowd defined the chaos in the street. "Pogrom," someone screamed. Then the voice fell under a horse and was carried away.

Hinda began to howl. Mirele wanted to strike her, but she could not stop to do this. She held her by her wrist with a force she had never felt before, and darted in and out of the streets, but no street seemed better than another. The horsemen were everywhere, the sound of their whips over her head wherever she went, and every street was blocked with horses and human bodies. A dreamlike maturity overtook her. The word released her from confusion. Reality leaped before her and she discovered ways to outwit it. Holding Hinda's hand, she made her way down the narrowest alleyways where it was difficult for the horses to go, into streets she had never been before, into the Gentile section. She ran, and Hinda had no choice but to run too. A moan sent her in one direction, the sound of horses in another. Fleeing people were trampled to death before her eyes. Doors were flung opened, bodies were flung out, clothes, furniture, household belongings, babies.

"Shut your eyes," Mirele said, lifted into her new maturity.

"Where are we going?" Hinda cried.

Mirele had no answer. At the end of the narrow street they were now on, horsemen plunged through the opening and between the houses. "Run," she screamed, and pulled Hinda's hand so hard Hinda staggered forward without control. The two of them fell headlong, feet away from the grasp of the horsemen, who chuckled as they went after them, so little were the mice, so big the lion, it moved, sure of its prey, with feigned leisure, even as it panted to be rid of its passion. The two children fell over the cobblestones, tripping, weeping, the saliva in their mouths turned to dust, fear spilling through their bodies, their hands outstretched, clutching the air for help, their eyes shut, running blindly, running without seeing, up the church steps, falling, slipping, running, until the door met with their outstretched hands, and they banged and banged on it. "Push," Mirele screamed. They pushed with the strength of thousands, as the horsemen dismounted at the foot of the church steps and leisurely, smiling, dressed superbly as horsemen, speaking to them in the teasing voices of male desire, began to climb the steps after them.

The door suddenly opened, and the Archbishop stood there. He surveyed the scene with a swift glance and with an equally swift movement of his hand whisked Mirele and Hinda behind his robes. The horsemen stopped at the bottom of the steps. One dismounted, curiosity on his face, and came up the steps. The sun shone on his boots and on the iron cross he wore on his chest. His thumbs were hooked into the belt of his uniform. "Come, Father," he said good humoredly, "you don't mean to protect these Jews." His voice caressed the air with bonhommie and confidence.

Hinda and Mirele turned to stone. The priest did not move, except to put his hand on his cross, whether as a sign of his authority or as a request to regard his office. The horseman, at any rate, considered this an ambiguous gesture, and hesitated. Then he moved forward again, less goodhumoredly. Still the priest did not move. He blocked the doorway with his body, and the smile in the horseman's eyes vanished. He cocked his head. The thumbs he hooked into his belt whitened. His smile, which he had worn while he imagined carnally, playing a flirtatious part even under these circumstances, disappeared, and his face was cast in iron.

He was not sure whether the priest had read his carnal thoughts and disapproved of them, he was not sure what the priest disapproved of. He made a move to get around him, and swiped at the air like a bear at a fish. His comrades stood at the bottom of the steps, also confused but still expectant, still smiling, still very handsome, the sons of Belial in their leather boots, their cargo of dying bodies on the ground. The Archbishop's eyes wandered over their faces, wandered past them over the corpses at the bottom of the steps. The arm of one, half mutilated, drifted downwards through the air. The horses pawed the ground with confused instincts: the smell of blood, the absence of combatants.

One of the horsemen held up an arrogant fist to the Archbishop, to let him know his judgment meant nothing to them. Emboldened by support, their leader made another move to get past the Archbishop. Mirele and Hinda bit their tongues. The priest grasped the lintel harder. His knuckles pierced his skin. His meaning was now clear to the horsemen.

"You may not slay the children of God," he said. "You will have to slay me first."

To Mirele it did not matter what he said. All that mattered was the wizardry in his voice that made the horsemen go away. Then the priest beckoned to them to follow him and with a presumption of trust they did not question they fled after him down the corridor, down the staircase to the basement of the church where he hid them until he came, some days later, to tell them that they could now go home. The destruction was over.

Their Gentile neighbors hurried past the empty doorways, intent on getting to church or to work. They did not gossip about the affair at their dinner tables, with their families, or with their neighbors. The event made the newspapers in several European cities and in the United States. A few of the papers found their way into the town and made them feel uncomfortable, incriminated in an event which they felt had as little to do with them as a tidal wave.

The wagons started out of the Jews' quarter with the bodies of the dead, with the rabbi in front, and with Mirele and Hinda, aunts and uncles and neighbors, the mourners of other dead, behind them. The wheels moved through the spring thaw without seeming to yield movement, moved and sank, and exasperated the nerves of everyone. Neither Mirele nor Hinda grieved. They were numb and unreflective about mortality and the finality of an era. Their parents and one brother were dead. Their other brother was going to America. Some were going to

Palestine. All the young men were going away, saying they had been struck down in their souls. The disshevelment of private belongings, photographs and coins, amulets, the mayhem of memorabilia were detached from the loving hands of the dead as they clung to their souvenirs with the expectation for life, and the streets were cleansed. It was still Easterweek, and the church bells tolled.

Their Gentile neighbors hurried to service. They looked at the Archbishop as they always did as they passed into the doorway. They curtsied and kissed his hand. They came into the church, genuflected in the central aisle and found their seats. They were silent because they had resolved on silence. They were helpless to control this evil and found safety in imperturability.

Mirele and Hinda went to live with an aunt and uncle who, already having raised six children of their own, accepted them regretfully, and it was then, after several weeks of this new life, that Mirele understood the deprivation of her parents' deaths. It was not only that their bodies had been put into the ground which signified the radical passage from one state to another. It was that their passage was her passage. Death was not single. It was pervasive. They were dead, like a squirrel she had once found after the spring thaw, unfamiliar in its decomposed state, not like anything which had once resembled life. The squirrel was ghastly because one knew it once had lived, once had been familiar and instinct with life, once had made one happy to look at it. Death was irretrievable. Many things could change, but not death. Death would never change. She would change, but the death of her parents would never change.

She tried to erase from her mind the comparison between the squirrel, stiff and rigid, and her parents. Her parents were gathered to Abraham's bosom. Human death was different, more pliant. Her uncle said kaddish for her parents and her brother.

Occasionally, they received a letter from their other brother, Yousele, who had gone to America, and Mirele soon felt a desperate sweet jealousy, a feeling which grew with each letter from him and which eventually became so big that it pushed out her grief and, one spring like the sudden change in the weather, a miraculous warmth in winter, she ceased to be sorrowful. If Hinda felt such things, she did not know it, but everyone knew how Mirele felt, for she did not keep her feelings to herself, not hate nor love nor envy nor desire. Puberty made her incautious, willful, and more desperate than ever. She began to lie to her aunt and uncle. Puzzled at first to find herself lying, she tried not to lie, but it was impossible. If she told them the truth, that she walked in certain streets, spoke with certain boys when they sent her on an errand, they would not send her. They were suspicious and troubled, and questioned and pestered her. Why did it take so long for her to come home? Where had she gone? Whom had she spoken to? "Nowhere!" "Nothing!" "No one!" she shouted at them. She had twisted her ankle and had had to hobble home, and that had made her late. They were alarmed and wrote to Yousele. Hinda was not a problem, but he must take responsibility for Mirele. They were too old and could not curb her anymore. She worked when she felt like it, an impossible situation in a farming community. Chickens went hungry while she stood at the gate and stared at the road, dreaming, longing, in love with the road. The pupils of her eyes became violet and warm and sly, her skin became the color of an apricot, and her bosom grew unprecedently.

In certain communities, at such a time, there is an answer to this problem, and her aunt and uncle found it. She would be married to the miller's son. As soon as Mirele heard this, a second maturity overtook her. She became very shrewd and realized it would be useless to oppose her aunt and uncle. Instead, she wrote tearful letters to her brother in America.

"Beloved Yousele,
I am the most misfortunate creature, that my darling parents are not with me to guide my destiny. Aunt and Uncle wish to marry me to the miller's son. My mother would never have permitted this to happen, because he cannot read and is too stupid to learn. Moreover, he is short and fat and pimply, which is not to my liking. His skin is as raw as a newborn bird's and looks as if it is waiting for feathers.

KNOW THAT I WILL DO EVERYTHING
TO PREVENT MARRIAGE TO HIM"

She paused and thought what threat she could bring to bear on her brother to save her. To herself, she seemed defenceless, without a weapon to speak of, though her aunt and uncle would not have described her in this way. To herself, she seemed urgent with desire for the world and hopelessly dependent upon others who had lost their appetite for it. The summer wind outside her window filled her with burdensome languor. With tears in her eyes, she straightened the paper in front of her and wrote, "Better a Gentile." Having written this, she elaborated quickly:

"There is one here who looks at me whenever he can. His thoughts are no doubt dishonorable, but he has neither pimples nor bad breath. If I am driven to this desperate act, you will have yourself to blame.

SEND ME MONEY TO COME TO AMERICA AND SAVE
YOUR SISTER FROM DISHONOR AND APOSTASY."

She posted the letter and began to wait for a response. A letter came a few months later, but it came to her aunt and uncle who saw immediately that Yousele was not in possession of the facts. He forgot that time had moved for Mirele as well as for himself. He was going with a young lady. Her name was Eva. Here in America, men and women, boys and girls, sought each other out. They did not need intermediaries. "Freedom," he wrote handsomely, "was everything in such matters."
His aunt and uncle exchanged a silent glance, and wondered how such a system could work, and wrote back that in Bessarabia young ladies were also free, but there were no choices to be free with since so many Jewish men had left the place. Mirele was free to marry the miller's son or not, but if she did not, he should send for her so that Mirele's freedom would have more meaning in the new world where there were more choices. They concluded tersely: "We will forget the

miller's son--he has pimples--but something, nevertheless, must be done with her." The rest of the letter was shrouded in obscure warnings. Conveyed in a secret language, they wrote: her bosom is bursting. In spite of her mother and father and her brother slaughtered in the prime of their lives, her bosom is bursting. They softened their warning with an additional note: "Hinda is a lovely girl and should be given every chance to better herself. Being the younger, we are naturally anxious to see that she has a good model to follow. She has a good head and can already read very well. In America, she may become something, maybe a teacher, but here there is only the miller's son left for young Jewish girls. It is advisable that Mirele go to America so that Hinda can go with her."

Letters passed back and forth, but none came to Mirele. She watched the horizon, she watched the skies, she watched the seasons change. Bitterness struck her down with pneumonia. For three days she raged with delirium, calling to America to save her, while her aunt and uncle and even Hinda watched by her bedside, awed by the intensity of her feelings.

One day the weather cleared. The frost melted on the window. A branch with a blossom on it scratched across her window and urged her to recover. Her aunt sat on her bed, with a letter in her hand and a stamp on it from America. Mirele's eyes darted to it. Her hand shook out the contents of the envelope on to her blanket: two tickets for passage to America fell out.

Mirele rose from her sickbed with marvellous swiftness, and a few months later, in the month of June she and Hinda went to the cemetery to bid goodbye to their parents, their brother, their grandparents, and all other ancestors, known by name or legend. Sorrow overcame Mirele and struggled for her soul. She bent down and put a stone on her parents' grave, a sign of her visit for the earth to receive, and pressed her lips against the engraving on the tombstone. Hinda burst into tears. "Hush," Mirele said, recovering at the sound of Hinda's alarming misery, "even if we weren't leaving, they couldn't come back to life," and she got up off her knees.

Their belongings were put on a wagon, a small trunk of clothes, their mother's candlesticks, their father's siddur and tallis to be given to her brother, two haggadahs, one for Hinda and one for her, some coins sewn into the lining of their coats, and each other. She was given strict orders about how to conduct herself on the ship and in the new world, and not ever to let go of Hinda's hand. But she soon found that it was difficult to walk in the style she felt belonged to a woman of the new world while clutching her sister by the hand.

The rabbi blessed them and the wagon moved out of the town, past the church and the spires, past the blacksmith's shop and the baker's and the house they had been born in, down the alleyways and the streets where the Gentiles lived, past the fields and out into the countryside, down the dusty road, through the fields and out on to the sea. The churchbells rang the noon hour. Mirele and Hinda sat in the back of the wagon and watched the town disappear behind the wheatfields and below the curve of the earth, until the sky swallowed it up, and all that could be seen of the town where they had been born were the spires of the church against the sky. "Goodbye, Kishinev," Mirele waved her handkerchief, "I'm going to America, and I'll never cry again."

"Do not leave go of Hinda's hand," her aunt screeched after her, "even if the ship should sink."

Mirele obeyed, for three days. On the fourth day she told Hinda she could watch her just as well if she stood by her side without clutching her hand, and if the ship should start to sink she would grab her wrist at once. On the fifth day she told her to sit and mind their trunk, and if the ship should start to sink she would come back at once to save her, and she went forth on the deck, amazed at how many men looked at her.

One came and stood by her side. "What is your name?" he asked in Russian.

Remembering her aunt's warnings, she walked away, treading carefully over these new found ways. But he followed after her. "Come, come, don't be afraid," he said so seductively, she became alarmed and went back to Hinda.

Hinda looked up at her with a withering expression from her guarding crouch over the trunk. "I'm bored," she said meanly. Mirele consideredthe problem. "You shouldn't go off and leave me," Hinda complained. "Can't you get along without me for five minutes?" Mirele said. "What will you do in America? I can't sew you into my pocket."

Accused of immaturity, Hinda felt wounded. She looked up at Mirele who stood with her hands on her hips and a look on her face which Hinda judged as immoral. "I hope you marry a fat man with pimples," she said. "There must be such, even in America."

Mirele considered this new, harsh trait in her sister, whom she had always regarded as malleable. But Hinda gazed back at her, gaze for gaze, closing the gap between them. For the next two days, Mirele went about again, holding Hinda by the hand, feeling constrained to assert her authority, even if it was an authority she did not want and which got in the way of her new style of walking, and Hinda went about with her not because she had an interest in such things, but because she surmised that she got in the way of Mirele's new style.

In spite of Hinda, a man winked at her. Mirele was shocked and thrilled. "Did you see that?" Hinda said, only shocked.

"See what?" Mirele asked.

Hinda felt that Mirele was lying, and she did not know what to make of this.

"That man winked at you," Hinda whispered shrilly.

"So what?" Mirele warbled, "a wink can't hurt you."

But Hinda knew better, and it was no surprise to her that she found her sister in conversation the next day with the man who had winked at her, in close conversation, tête a tête, their breaths mingling in the ocean air.

"Mirele!" Hinda shrieked at her.

A wave of horror went up Mirele's spine. She attempted to make Hinda's shriek mean something other than what she knew it to mean. "My sister is not feeling well," she said in a voice overcome with responsibility. "I should go to her." She took Hinda by the hand and dragged her below deck, out of sight of everyone, and bit her cheek. After that, she strolled on the deck to her heart's content, breathing in the spray and the waves and the tobacco smoke and the gossip which mingled with the blue sky and the flight of the seagulls and the masculine glances, while Hinda sat below, nursing her cheek.

In the third week of this voyage the Statue of Liberty came into view and, like everyone else on board, Mirele was overcome at the sight of it, and the man who had conversed with her tête a tête, stood next to her at the rail with his arm around her waist. To give Mirele her due, she removed his arm, and hurried below deck to get Hinda.

"Come, Hinda," she called to her when she found her sulking by their trunk, "don't you see that everyone has gone up on the deck. There is that wonderful Statue of Liberty that has come into view. Come, hurry, or we'll be past it."

Hinda sat with her knees drawn up and crouched close to their trunk, her head buried in her lap, hiding from view the noise, the confusion and the shapelessness of a foreign life.

Mirele cried with exasperation at her. "If you do not hurry, you will miss everything."

"Go yourself."

Mirele hesitated. It did not feel right to leave Hinda at this moment, but Hinda refused to move, and the murmurs and exclamations that drifted down from the deck as the ship approached the shoreline made Mirele sick with longing. She felt like stomping on Hinda. "It's your own fault," she cried, "if something happens to you," and she turned and ran back to the deck, to be part of the noise and the crowd and the bedazzlement of this extraordinary ritual of people waiting to receive them, waving their handkerchiefs with welcome, and to shout back to them, "Hurrah, hurrah," and wave her handkerchief also, wave it wildly in the air for the triumph of arriving. She was so filled with hunger and anticipation, with sadness and fear, with looking forward and looking backwards, that she did not know whether she felt anguish or joy. She could only wave her handkerchief at those waiting for them, wave her handkerchief frantically, exhausting the act over and over, for the act was too small and she was too insignificant to signal all that it meant. She looked down at the faces crowded into the harbor and waved and waved her handkerchief at them, until her feelings burst through her throat and she lay her head on the rail and wept.

MY POOR PRISONER

THERE IS an unpleasant incident which took place in the fortress of Oranienberg in 1934, when the quixotic cabaret poet of the 1930s, Erich Mühsam, was brought there and imprisoned in the Gestapo roundup of left-wing intellectuals after the Reichstag fire.

Mühsam was known in Berlin circles as a "kaffeehaus poet," bohemian in style, outrageously satirical in his poetry, and Blakean too, as if his writing was squeezed out between bitterness and vision. He was physically unmistakeable: bushy red hair and a wild red beard crowding an emaciated face; scrawny body and wiry fingers. He was loved by his friends and hated by his enemies for the same quality: "something Christ-like," the friends said sentimentally and the enemies said snickeringly, when anecdotes were told of him, of how poverty-stricken Mühsam, who had scarcely seed to put in his mouth, gave his coat to a beggar. The comparison was subtly unflattering, and he snickered back with a manic need to bait, "Why not something Jew-like?"

Nor could he resist the visionary in him from working out a similar compulsion towards destructive acts of generosity, when some friends--for he had them not only among the bohemian writers of Berlin, but even a few randomly powerful ones--secured him a train ticket to Prague when it was known that the Gestapo was looking for him.

As luck would have it, a similar set of circumstances surrounded another young man, also wanted by the Gestapo, except that we know nothing more about him than this: as

Mühsam had his foot on the first step of the train, he saw the conductor rough-handle this man who was trying to board without a ticket. The look on the man's face tore Mühsam's caution from him. "It's all right," he said to the conductor with a disappearing smile. Anything more would have been superfluous, for when offered the ticket the young man grabbed it and ran, and Mühsam's singular generosity is recorded with the enigma embedded in his personality. He did his last act as a free man to the conductor and to a platform of strangers who indulged him with smiles.

"Quite all right," he said to them, for the young man had disappeared into the train, "please don't thank me. Think nothing of it. Well, hey! I've been in prison before. Put your consciences at rest. I can perform there as well as anywhere," and he blew them a kiss.

He was arrested the next morning. If the other young man had been imprisoned instead, if Mühsam had taken the train to Prague, if Jesus had not been crucified, the following thoughts about good and evil would not have been written for, aside from the fact that Mühsam felt an affinity between himself and Jesus, there are some events which suck the whole of an era into them. Beyond the heart-rending nature of the following episode--the torture of an animal to get at the poet (the sole aim of his jailers was to drive Mühsam to suicide) there is the fact of its parallel in the days of Nebuchadnezzar, and the difference in the two cultures: that when the lion refused to do the guards' bidding and attack Daniel, they did not revenge themselves upon the animal by torturing it, but took it as a sign from the Hebrew's God and let the Hebrew go.

Night after night, morning after morning, they tortured the chimpanzee and brought Mühsam to look at her, and whispered in his ear: "Why don't you kill yourself and save this poor animal her agony."

The chimpanzee lay shrivelled in a corner. Much of her fur had been torn from her. Keeping her conscious, they had carefully mutilated her teats. Her skin was raw with cigarette burns. She lay stunned, semi-conscious, roaming on the border of her pain.

Spared from an experiment, they had brought her to Mühsam's cell at the Commandant's suggestion that she would be goaded into attacking him (they were determined not to do their own killing), but the animal had sat down next to him, put her arms around his neck and smacked him a kiss on his cheek. Surprised and delighted, Mühsam slipped into his cabaret manner. "Well, old girl," he said, "somebody's been giving you lessons in loving. What a couple we would make on the ballroom floor, Millie and me." What her name was, or if she had a name, we do not know. Mühsam called her Millie for its comic effect, teasing her animal nature, as human names applied to animals do, as if to explore the boundary between us and them.

He wrote his wife, Zensl, about the incident: "It was the kiss of death, for they have taken the animal and torture her for this. They want to drive me insane with her cries. No," he wrote, "they don't care whether I'm sane or not, they only want me to kill myself. What can I do? What should I do?" He crossed out the last line out of sympathy for Zensl, even though he was only writing the letter in his head.

They dragged him back to his cell with truncheons under his armpits. The other prisoners watched him with the intensity of a shared destiny. His footsteps--a shuffle in untied shoes, for his fingers had been broken and he could not knot his laces-- was known--and why he was taken and where he went, for even prison life, and especially prison life, consumes itself in the social need for gossip; except for the Gypsy who kept himself apart with a wry confusion bred from the distrust of the "others," the ones who represented Europe, who "own it," as they say among themselves. The guards had left him his clothes, his baggy pants and jacket, a striped shirt and stetson hat, and the medallion he wore around his neck.

A priest--a Cardinal--he was stripped of his robes--kept his eyes on the Bible he held in his hands--a ploy--for his eyes fluttered knowledgeably as Mühsam went by. Practised in discretion he had less difficulty adjusting than Mühsam did, who succumbed to expressions of his old style buffoonery, a lifetime habit of escaping the self, or intensifying it by raising the pitch of rebuttal to folly; or Wyzanski, the young Polish communist, who still possessed vitality in spite of his beatings, and a self protective self righteousness which transformed his pain into argument. Anticlerical, he was suspicious of the Cardinal's presence in the prison. It represented a mockery to him, a tour-de-force. "The Pope will get him out," he said whenever occasion gave him the opportunity.

The Cardinal had at first been confined to a private room, on the recommendation of the Commandant, who respected his office and gave him a comfortable chamber, with a library, with a Louis Quatorze desk in it with the original inkstand on it, velvet drapes and a seventeenth century pianoforte, befitting one whose status had been created by fiat in the tenth century for members of the Roman aristocracy who otherwise would have had no place in the new Christian world. The Commandant also regarded it as a privilege of the ruling classes to creates classes, the morphology and taxonomy of history.

Here the Cardinal had spent two years, deprived of little except his liberty (which did not surprise Wyzanski). He had a good bed to sleep on, satisfying food, wine with his meals, even visitors. (Like Mühsam, he had his allies.) Still, he wrote constantly to the Pope, not only regarding his imprisonment which he took to be fundamental to the issues, but regarding the issues. ("Surely, you are mistaken in thinking the fight against Bolshevism to be our primary struggle. You cannot engage in arguments about lesser and greater evils as other governments do.") In spite of his outspokenness against the German bishops who sympathized with Hitler, his imprisonment remained a token imprisonment--he conceded--but the whole world knew of it--and as such his imprisonment had the symbolic force of the tacit acceptance of the Vatican in the face of an opposition it would not--or could not--(in the end this difference was indistinguishable) contend with.

"I should like to know," he wrote the Papal secretary, "if you have some suggestion--practical or otherwise--in which civilized people can contend with the barbarities that are now abroad. I do not speak for myself. I am treated civilly (he wanted to write, "except for the interminable conversations I am forced to hold with the Commandant who finds my company 'enlightening'--his term, not mine.") but resisted any expressions that could give rise to interpretations of personal vexation.

"Believe us," the Papal officer responded, "when we say that we have your good permanently in our hearts and that your welfare is ever present to our souls."

If nothing further was said or done, it was felt that his imprisonment should be kept in perspective: he was not in morbid danger, he was not even in much discomfort.

The Cardinal did not see the matter in this way. A growing disillusionment with silence as a strategy--the sense that it formed his essential prison--made him write constantly. He filled boxes with "reflections" and wondered if they would ever be read or, if read, would make a difference. The continual scratching of his pen, hour after hour, struck him morbidly, and he would raise his head for breath, look around at the rococo ceiling above, angels in adoration like misplaced cupids, and write more furiously. He kept up such a fury of letters--which finally found their way to the newspapers that the Papal office sent a delegate to inquire after his condition.

"My condition!" he said, vexed, waving his hands over his rooms to the Papal delegate. "Do you mean my condition or the condition of my rooms? My rooms, as you see, are in excellent condition," and he waved his hand again at the velvet draperies and gold panellings. "Perhaps you would like some wine and a canapé. I'll ring the guard to bring you some." His tone was not pleasant, but the delegate sat on a tapestried chair and said with restraint, "A cup of wine would be grand, thank you. As for the other matter, surely you see he is not at liberty to make a public statement."

The Cardinal's mood did not fit the delegate's: he exploded with anger. "He makes many public statements on other issues."

"Well, then, he cannot make them on all issues." The delegate dropped his chin and regarded his wine. "No one person can address himself to every issue. For some issues, silence, as the English say, is the better part of valor."

The Cardinal squinted his eyes, which gave him both an

inquiring and a menacing expression. "Yes, and what then of the English?"

"You know the strength of the enemy. What are we to do? England will have to fight alone which, after all, is neither here nor there with respect to us."

The Cardinal threw his hands up. "Are there no Christians in England whose lives we should fear for?"

"We must certainly hope so."

The Cardinal could not restrain his exasperation any longer--two years of letter writing--but his exasperation was also neither here nor there, an irrelevancy, as they both knew, in the historical process to which the Church itself was now tied with less choice than either cared to calculate.

"Tell the Holy Father that for some us his silences speak louder than his pronouncements."

"That may be," the delegate said, putting his cup of wine on the desk with an air of delicate conclusion, "but between the two, speech and silence, nothing is more discreet than silence," and he left. "I regret," he soon wrote the Cardinal, "that the Holy Father has no practical suggestions to make at this time, concerning those issues which you so feelingly raise and which we ourselves acknowledge with our full hearts. Be assured that the conflicts of Europe are foremost in our thoughts and that we do always plead for pity, mercy, compassion, and that the nations will be enlightened in their duties toward one another. We pray for brotherly love and faith abundant among all the nations, but of those practical suggestions of which you spoke, we are not at liberty to regard them, but be assured of our love and our faith and our continual prayers for your welfare."

The Commandant knocked on the door, and entered before the Cardinal responded. "I am sorry it is a disappointment to you," he said, referring to the letter. It did not surprise the Cardinal that he knew its contents. "A matter of time," he murmured in response, preferring loyalty under the circumstances.

"Of course, what else?" the Commandant said, eyeing the letter left open on the desk. "But I trust it brought you some comfort, at least. If it says less than you hoped for, perhaps it was never meant to fulfill expectations." He sighed, in a fully civil way, as one performing an act of condolence. "You know I used to sing in a church choir," he said, as if to extenuate his expressions of understanding, and he sat down at the pianoforte and began to play some Bach, Jesu, Joy of Man's Desiring, so well that even the Cardinal, after a while and against his better judgment ("After all," the Commandant once said to him, "you aggrandized so much of the land of Europe in your appetite for spirit, you made the rise of the secular nations a necessity in Europe's struggle against religious tyranny.")--was impressed. Noticing the effect he made, the Commandant continued, "I haven't forgotten my training," and he bent his ear to the pianoforte, appraising the notes as if they were jewels. He admired the Cardinal, and it pleased him to play for him, but when he made his mind up to it, he could resist flattery, though he was haunted by a desire for it. His chief source of gratification was in the company he kept, even in the company of his prisoners. He was addicted--he described himself this way--to good conversation, "enlightening conversation," of which he was deprived for the most part, under these circumstances, except for Mühsam, who was loquacious--but unfortunately an anarchist and a socialist and a Jew; while the Cardinal at least was none of these, least of all what the Commandant disliked more than another--an upstart. What the Cardinal's personal background was--he was the son of a bankclerk--was beside the point: he belonged to the class of Cardinals and existed within the rhythm and pattern of Europe while the cult of individualism--anarchism--socialism--bohemenianism--"modern"Jewry--Mühsam,were hurling stones against it. If only for reasons of snobbery, the Commandant's sympathies were with lineage and form.

But his respect for the Cardinal's office was alloyed with triumph: the "true" mark of respect. He closed the cover to the pianoforte precipitously, looked at his wristwatch to remind himself of an appointment, and said, "Really! Art is a whore. You know as well as I do anyone can play Bach if he has had enough training."

"What an enemy of our own making," the Cardinal thought after he left. ("Yes," he wrote, "you inquire after my condition, and how can I convey to you that what you call my condition is not anything you can see with your eyes.") He sat at his desk and looked out through the French doors into the garden and the grounds surrounding the fortress, where he often watched the Commandant do his morning exercises amid a flutter of peacocks and wild turkeys.

The land was level for several acres, covered with moss and grass and pathways trailing vines, orchids, phlox, until it fell down a slope where the villagers let their sheep run and the unsuspecting townspeople lived in a concentric circle of houses surrounding their modest church. The fortress grounds were open to them on holidays and they came in family groups not, of course, suspecting the prisons that lay beneath the solid buildings. If they saw the Cardinal standing in the French doors, why would they suspect that he was held prisoner here? The Commandant depended upon his never saying so.

It was this idea, long recognized and now ripened with apprehension, that made the Cardinal change his course of action the next morning.

The Commandant came out as usual to take his four mile jog around the grounds. His servant emerged too, carrying a towel and cologne. Watching him do his exercises, the Cardinal experienced a sequence of insights, begun the night before, which made him pace his room, made him unfit to go on staying there. The Commandant passed his view every four minutes, his body inclined so right as he rounded the trail, the turkeys and peacocks scattering to the side of him. It was the ripeness of this manner, sustained only by its form, needing only to appear upon the scene in one uniform or another, in this setting or a similar one, that was oppressive--the affinities between them-- their parallel lines traversing the greenswards of Europe--the beauty of the places--the gardens of camelias--the pools of delight--the mists of morning caught in the weeping willows-- was painful to behold--the beloved beauty of the place--the walks--the fountains streaming silver in the sunlight--so valued even by the townspeople who enjoyed it only on special occasions. Who had built this place? What cruel, seducing, lascivious architect had dreamed this prison? "Why should I blame him anymore than myself?" the Cardinal thought, pacing the floor. "What, after all, is the difference if, in the end, one belongs to a collection of things, becomes a jewel in this setting or another?"

Still, he shrank from doing anything which might seem histrionic, out of character--he hated flamboyance but, how else, under the circumstances, act? There was so little room for maneuvers. He could think of little else to do. Though it was not his nature to do it, he removed his robes and folded them on the desk, feeling cheapened by the act it took to become holy. He called the guard in and saw at once the effect his appearance had. Speechless, the guard turned on his heels and ran to tell the Commandant, even interrupting his exercises.

The Cardinal watched them though his window. The Commandant's eyes fluttered in his direction, a heavy lidded but piercing glance. He couldn't see through the glass--the sun was reflecting in it--but the Cardinal could see him--hesitate--think, with the very muscles of his face--query himself whether this was one of those times to interrupt his exercises. Apparently, yes. The Commandant put his jacket back on--but not with his customary air of having brought the morning to an agreeable finish. The Cardinal experienced a half regretful, grim pang of victory. It fortified him just enough to withstand the look of repulsion the Commandant gave him when he arrived in his room and looked at him in his underclothes, turned on his heels and said to the guards, "Take him where he wants to go."

Having inched his mind so far forward as to experience this new found level of unholiness in his doubts, of longing to go back on his own actions, against which he had to summon his resolve not to betray himself, the Cardinal shouted after him, "I'm entitled to the same prison as everyone else."

The Commandant came on occasion to visit him there, quite obviously to gauge the effects of the new surrounding on the Cardinal. "It doesn't matter," he said to the Cardinal, "even if you become a martyr or a saint, it will not change one thing. Everything is too far gone. You know that yourself."

The Cardinal proved to be as tenacious as the Commandant, and theirs became a battle of wills fought on an invisible principle. "You are probably right," the Cardinal said, "but even facts change sometimes." Months of this kind of imprisonment had made his face sallow and fleshless, like a death mask revealing the salient features. Within the confines of his new cell, he performed mass every day and the gypsy and Wyzanski joined him, making symbolic signals across their cells from which ritual movements had been stripped to the elemental communion, after which the Gypsy slid back into his hostility and suspicion of things European, and Wyzanski took up his anticlerical stand. "The Pope will get him out," he said, contemptuous of the Cardinal's prison-life, this not-believable trespass into the political domain.

Besides them, there were some others, all political prisoners of various shades: a Millenarist by the name of Vilhelm, who was equally as tenacious as the communist and the Cardinal. He belonged to a sect without church, without organization, "without hierarchy," he said, lifting his sparsely bearded chin in the direction of the Cardinal, "only with Jesus"; and with a set of tenets which apparently had sustained them for centuries, confirmed in the Second Coming, enduring a spiritual hunger for it which made everything else in life dull for them. They lived like the Gypsies, disdainful of the schools, the governments, the museums, the institutions, that had been erected on "God's land," which ought not to have anything on it but animal, plant and vegetable life and the minimum constructions for shelter. As if shot out of history, certainly out of its contemporary terms--progress, technology, realpolitick, diplomacy, negotiations, every morning he wrote on the back wall of his cell, "Jesus Saves," and placed his Bible in his lap. Every morning the guards beat him for it and erased it. Sometimes, a guard hesitated before the writing with a superstitious dread. Vilhelm, quick to note this and dreading nothing himself, pounced on the man with an onslaught of evangelism surprising in its imprisoned energy, inspiring panic in the guard that something had been found out about him, something that ought not to have been found out, like plague or disease; and he increased Vilhelm's punishment.

Wyzanski, intrigued by Vilhelm, argued on his behalf that he "represented the original intentions of communism." ("He is always looking for religious justification," Mühsam wrote Zensl) and answered Wyzanski with the touch of hilarity he always felt in the present of nonsense: "Wyzanski, you should know better. Communism is about workers and workers are about buildings and construction, history in a word, the state, etc. Remember Hegel said there is no history without the state. Vilhelm's against all that. What he wants is subsistence. Marx never wanted subsistence for the worker. In Vilhelm's state, everybody shares nothing except the spiritual kingdom. In Marx's state, everybody shares everything, and he couldn't care less about the spiritual kingdom. Do you think Jesus could come after Marx?" ("A good piece of nonsense from an intelligent person brings you back to life," he wrote Zensl. "Outside of a cabaret in Berlin, I have the best companions here. The Cardinal is a first rate fellow and not an antisemite. The communist says he's not an antisemite, but he is. He thinks because he is anticlerical he is not antisemitic, and that his religion will save him from going to hell. He thinks he has the best of both worlds. Ha! Ha! Ha! If only I had a cigarette for the proper effect of that laugh--a little smoke rising from the lips gives a man a very clever look.")

"Then what is he imprisoned for?" Wyzanski laughed with his characteristic note of contemptuous challenge.

Vilhelm did not undertake to answer for himself. He revealed nothing except the scheme of his faith, not because he was secretive, but because he had nothing else to reveal. There was no progression to his ideas and he had nothing to embroider. Many found him monotonous and taciturn, as certainly the Commandant did. Some regarded him as a "throwback"--to what they did not say. But most confronted him with disbelief and left him alone, though he said, but meant what he said, what they heard most of their lives in other contexts. Vilhelm's problem was that he never meant anything else.

Mühsam whetted Wyzanski's appetite for combat--it was the Jewish socialist in Mühsam that did it. "I'm not a communist," Mühsam said, determined to keep the differences between himself and Wyzanski clear. "What's the difference," Wyzanski laughed at him across the corridor space of their cells.

"You'll find out," Mühsam hoarsely whispered back.

"What did they arrest you for?" Wyzanski continued to

laugh challengingly. "Hey, tell me that, for being a socialist or for being a communist?" They had so much in common--even Mühsam confessed it--but rubbed each other the wrong way. "Pity," Mühsam said, "you don't know the difference. What's that got to do with anything? They can imprison me, but I still make the distinctions between good and evil. Anyway, I'm here on about twelve different charges. Think of that! Pacifism, antimilitarism, socialism, anarchism, bohemianism, Jewishism, and even for writing poetry about Jesus." He counted the charges off on his fingers with theatrical aplomb.

"I don't blame them for arresting you for that," Wyzanski said. "What does Jesus have to do with you, hey?"

Mühsam lay down on his cot and regarded Wyzanski with overt irony. "Why not?" he said, " a fellow Jew caught on the loom of history. What's Jesus to you?"

Wyzanski's answer shot out of him as if he had been waiting for someone to ask him that. "A fellow communist like me."

Mühsam whistled and laughed. ("Really, Zensl, a man could do worse than go to his execution with these, ha, ha, ha.") He did not write his laughter out--how could he?--and he erased the line altogether, on second thought (Zensl would not be prepared for it), but he wrote her about his cellmates, "his boon companions in destiny;" for her sake he composed a scenario on "his prison cabaret," for her entertainment--and wrote it out in his old style, seizing the energy of it, the electric communion between entertainer and audience that had been a magnetic field between them, so powerful an attraction they had for each other, entertainer and audience, no other audience like them, poets, intelligentsia, members of the Dada movement, bohemians in the Grün Deutschland movement, "Die Konnenden," political cranks all, "the Coming Ones," as they called themselves, bound for the future together. Even the ones who came to heckle him proved the power of his style--legs astride a chair--standing in a pool of light--cigarette in mouth--body cheapened with poverty and poor living, too many prisons, not enough food--words biting holes in the air as decisive as gems--valuable.

"Berlin! Ha! Berlin has everything but human nature."
"Now, Paris, there's a city. Paris lives, Berlin functions."
"Bismarxism! Exactly, I said, the worst of both worlds."
"They arrested me for this."
"Come," Wyzanski said, 'they arrested you for being Jewish."
"Oh, of course, that, as if that's all I was."
"Mühsam. You know my name. Mühsam. Means arduous in German."
He was always pleased by this fact. "Makes too much of it," Else Lasker-Schüler said. "He will wind up in front of a firing squad or hanging from a tree," and nicknamed him "wilde Jude,"--because of his red beard and his poetry, but mainly because of his politics. "Look out for yourself, Mühsam," she warned him, sitting in their cabaret, done up in her gaudy, freaky poverty, a feather in her hair "to symbolize hope." Good friend, she had come to his rescue before with protest letters and petitions, when he had been imprisoned with Toller and Landauer and Leviné. "Good friend and fellow poet," she warned him, "now you are free, Mühsam, stay away from politics. What has a poet to do with politics? Stay away, Mühsam. Stop writing satires and write your visions. A poet can sooner create a world than create a state."
"They're the same," he said, and wrote his essay, Die Befreiung der Gesellschaft Stat. "I never knew how to separate them--the earthly Jerusalem and the heavenly Jerusalem--the world--humanity--God--where politics left off and religion began. That's how I see Jesus."
"Whatever else Jesus and Marx have in common," the Cardinal said to Wyzanski, "one believed in God the Father and the other did not, make what you will of the difference."
Mühsam sank his head back on his pillow. "What is the difference now? Calvary is all around us--there is so much political retrogression--I think worse than at any other time. The whole world is now Golgotha. Yes, Mühsam means arduous in German. What's history without passion? I took my name for a symbol."

"German?" they asked me.
"Yes, sir, a thousand years."
"Born?"
My father should live so long.
"His occupation?"
"Pharmacist."
"Put down Jew."
"Right."
"Religion?"
"That doesn't concern you."
"Write Jewish," they said.
"Right, be a Jew at home and a German abroad."
My father should live so long.
He wrote it out satirically, the whole of it, the history of his generation--Der Konnenden--stuffed into cabarets and cells-- the anarchists, the socialists, the barefooted soldiers (the others, the practitioners of realpolitick, knew what it was all about--how to fight the enemy--how to prepare for war--how to prepare for peace--how to negotiate terms--they knew) or, if you prefer, he wrote it out in the new style of prophecy--eerily, in which he foretold how his civilization would be carried to its death in a modern invention of its own making:

Onward, onward without rest
to the north, east, south, west!
Seek, soul seek!....
See your life flash by in pain
From the window of a midnight train.
Shriek, soul shriek!

and foretold the style of his death:

An aging corpse
Hangs from a telegraph pole.
His dangling legs reached out--to--
Oh! can it catch them, for pity's sake--
The outspread branches of an oak tree

("Thank god for the innocent things of nature," he wrote Zensl.

My Poor Prisoner/122

"Will they ever vindicate us--or trust us again?") The vision scared him into wilder satire. "Yes, arduous, that is my name, also called wilde Jude by my closer friends. Don Quijote, and romantic anarchist, antimilitarist, pacifist (arrested as a conscientious objector the first time), feminist and yes, vegetarian, "a political crank" some said--you know who--those who know the world better than he did, the realpolitikniks. ("Now, I ask you, Zensl, what is the difference and how could it be otherwise?") "We bohemians," he wrote for the newspapers fond of articles about that type of life, "play with the accidents of time the better to approach eternity."
What did they understand--his audience? His performances were combats in which he struggled with forces--Europe--history--antisemitism. ("They forgive the Jewish communist and the Jewish socialist nothing," Kafka wrote incisively).
"What is your religion?" the Commandant asked.
"Humanity."
"Put down Jew, non-professing."
"Right you are."
He struggled with the New Germany--the poor--mankind. For laughter.

"...Ein Jude zog aus Nazareth
Die Armen glücklich zu machen

Applause! Applause! Applause for this man with the wild beard who lives on cigarette smoke. Yes! Thank you very much. Pass the hat around. Enough for a meal tonight. Jerusalem who stoneth her prophets! And Berlin and Paris! Now, what do you think, min herr Berliner? Who has driven out more prophets, Jerusalem or you? But for you it will not matter--you will never miss them.
("Now, Zensela, I tell you, my companion, the communist from Poland, wears a crucifix around his neck and when I said to him once, 'I'm surprised you wear that,' it touched him wrong, as if he thought I was deriding his communist faith. 'What can a Jew understand,' he answered

back at once--hoopla! flavoring his idealism with a little contempt--the parsley in the soup.
'Of course,' I whispered through the bars, 'quite right. Of course! The gulf is very deep, very deep, but not so deep here,' and I pushed some of my poetry through the bars at him. You know the ones. About the Eucharist. 'Here the gulf narrows,' I said to him. 'After all, all prisoners have something in common. I too think of Jesus as my kindred spirit.' And what do you think he did when I said this. He roared at me like a Polish communist imitating a bulldog, 'Judenschwein!'
'Look out,' I said, 'I'm glad you wear the crucifix, but be careful they don't choke you with it. From me you have nothing to fear. It concentrates my absorption into history. But be careful about the others. Do you know what is the most difficult thing in history?--who knows--maybe it's the original historical problem--to know who your enemy is--for the enemy will not identify himself--he does not come out and say, hey, I am the enemy, and takes his bow on the stage.'
'Shut up, Mühsam,' someone shouted at me. Foolishly, I thought it was one of the other prisoners and ran off at the mouth. Zensele, my love, no one put up with me as you did. But it was a guard and he came and took my pencil and paper away. Yes, he took my pencil and paper away, but I write this with my mind to you. Zensl, be well. Know that whatever you hear of me, it will not be true. For your sake, for the sake of our love, for the sake of the Jew in me, know that I will never take my own life. Do not believe it, if you hear it.")
The prisoners' eyes followed him as the guards took him from his cell. Their bodies jerked with the manic restlessness that pervades prisoners with no place to go. They whispered to him in voices of deadly irony meant for sympathy: "This is what comes of holding out, Mühsam."
"Don't worry for me," he laughed, "I'm used to prisons." He made a face at them, exaggerating the effects of his missing parts, ears, teeth, rotten gums, broken nose. "I'm no novice. Niederschonenfeld, 1924. Sonnenburg, Brandenburg, Oranienburg. Don't worry for me." His eyes were white in a face of crazy colors, swollen blue lips, swollen purple nose, red scars where his ears had been torn off, red hair

and beard dirty with lice, rotted grey gums, fingers blackened, twisted and broken.

("Don't worry for me," he wrote his wife, "you know I've been in prison before. I'm no novice. I shall always get word to you. Thank God for bribery. What would we poor prisoners do without this corruption. Or history do without prisoners who escape to tell the world. Thank God for errors and mistakes. That is what we wretches will have to cling to in the future. Blessed be the loopholes. Erich Mühsam, leader of the loophole. 'Look at him,' the Commandant said, when they first arrested me. 'Look at him. This is your famous leader of the Munich Ratrepublick, this scarecrow, this judenshwein, this target in a shooting gallery, this rooster with the red beard.'

'Yes,' I said to them when they put me against the wall to shoot me, I tore off my eyeguards and said, 'Shoot, I want to see the bastards who shoot me, Mühsam, whose name means arduous in German.'

This is what they do, Zensl. They tell me they will execute me on such and such a day, and they march me out and then they march me in. They think they will frighten me to death with make-believe. They think I will die of pretenses.")

He paused at Vilhelm's cell, his eyes blistered red. "My poor animal," he said to him, "do you know what they are doing to her."

Vilhelm did not answer. Only iron survives. Only the spirit. Only the spirit that is iron.

"Be strong," Wyzanski whispered. "Give them nothing. Nothing!"

The guards tightened their truncheons under Mühsam's armpits and pulled him away. The Commandant waited in the library for him, a sign of the respect he bore the poet--he had taken the trouble to look at his poetry--which he disliked. Still he knew that Mühsam was a journalist, a writer, one of the haute Juden intelligentsia, and a Berliner, a man who was held in esteem by many, though mostly of his own kind, bohemian rabble, people who think it clever to walk barefoot, to imitate poverty. Such people irritated his fastidious habits--a trait that was as much a part of his thinking as his dressing and which passed into his historical perspective. How could they convince a man with two dozen different dress uniforms and three personal tailors. Nudity destroys history.

Two of his tailors were Jewish, of course, for Jewish tailors were the best of the kind--there was a special competence about them. He felt this in how their tape measures drooped around their necks, handled briskly, the ends worn with years of use, the pins held precariously between their lips defying their patterns of speech, a regular barrage of humming and comments in spite of the pins which moved up and down in their moving mouths, kept there as skillfully as a laborer keeps his feet on a catwalk, and the chalkmarkers behind their ears as professional looking as an accountant's pencil. His other tailor --a Lutheran--stuck him once and exclaimed with pain on his behalf. Not Rosenbloom or Rosenberg. They moved accurately. A special knowingness in their manner. A special knowingness of things, an historic competence about goods. Which did make you wonder, as the Führer once said--one of his milder speculations as far as the Commandant was concerned, for he disliked his speeches--found them hysterical declarations proclaiming the Third Reich as "inheriting" the future. This was a false note in the logic of things; it irritated him. "Really," he said to a fellow officer, raising an eyebrow with critical distaste, "he has no sense of history."

"Don't you believe him?" the fellow officer asked surprised, very surprised, even querulous, for to disbelieve that was to disbelieve the whole enterprise.

"It's a good slogan," the Commandant said. They came down the steps of a Ministry. He looked up at the sun, as he always did when he emerged from a building, testing the lint on his glasses, "but, after all, a contradiction. One never inherits the future. One can only inherit the past. You can prepare for the future, yes--by inheriting the past. Ah, ha!" He was pleased with himself.

They stopped midway down the steps, appropriately against a noble sweep of concrete stairway. "Come," his companion said, relaxing, "do you think the Führer should have said, 'let us inherit the past?'"

The Commandant was taken aback by a confusion of thought. He wrinkled his brow. They burst out laughing together and continued down the steps. "Lucky they don't ask me to make speeches," he said cavalierly.

"Deprive them of needle and thread," he thought, eyeing himself in the three way mirror, "and they'll come undone." (He meant the Jews, for his respect and contempt for them were mixed in equal proportions.) He took first one posture, then another to see how the suit wrinkled and behaved as he moved this way and that. He had learned that the worst way to test the fit of a suit was to stand like a mannikin in front of a mirror. Therefore, he bent, he stretched, he strode, he moved about and the three tailors moved with him, pins in mouth, tape measure around their necks. He eyed himself, they eyed him, studying his form in all its postures, actually a format rather than a form. There never was such an extraordinary case of learned lineage. It was as if the maxims of a mother--walk with your head erect--keep your chest high--do not let your shoulders droop--worked as well for impressing heads of states as for a finishing school. People succumb to the proper mode oftener than to the Sermon on the Mount.

It surprised the Commandant to discover how universally this was so. The son of an insurance agent, he had no reason to know it and discovered it accidentally. He simply noticed it was so while sitting in a train one afternoon, waiting for it to start. He was gazing absentmindedly through the window of his private carriage, his head on his gloved hand, his military hat cocked over his eye, looking fortuitously moody, like a Renaissance prince by Michelangelo. An accident, but the look stuck. Every woman who went by gazed back at him. Several even gazed back as if their heads turned against their wills, as if their eyes were being moved by a magnetic field between themselves and him. He must be impressive! He could not escape the conclusion. So many people looked at him. A press photographer went by on the prowl, walked up and down the platform, waiting for a war or a suicide, and finally came to his carriage. The Commandant's career began here.

"May I?" the reporter asked, and took his picture. "I represent the---. Tell me, Commandant, in a few words--I know the train is about to start--what do you think of the situation in Poland? Do you think there will be a war? Can you comment on the economy? What's the meaning of the military maneuvers on the border? Is there anything important happening in France? Do you wish to make a statement about your recent promotion? Is it true that you had an organ placed in Oranienburg and will have Bach concerts there?"

The Commandant ruminated, among the many questions which one to address himself to. "Yes," he said, "I am a lover of Bach. His music is good for my nerves--so many irritating things these days."

"Does that mean that you are dismissing Wagner?" the reporter asked, quick to sense a possible dissension.

"Dismissing Wagner?" the Commandant said with a soft irony and an equally soft twinkle in his eye, to dispel the ludicrous interpretation that his personal tastes--anyone's personal tastes--could have anything to do with history--a sign of humility, or geniality. "How can one dismiss Wagner?"

The effect was the opposite of humility: it was grandiose. Several mysteries knocked about in the reporter's head in the form of further questions, but the train began to move. "Thank you very much, mien herr Commandant," he said. "May I take another picture?"

The Commandant fidgeted. Photographs were always such a gamble, particularly newspaper pictures, as if the subject were taken "on the run," mouth open, caught in a stammer. But his picture (he had reason to be forever grateful to the reporter) caught him like a portrait, elbow on the windowsill, head leaning on his gloved hand, thoughtful and authoritative, the angle of his hat, l'angle juste, as if he had posed for an oil to be hung alongside the oils he now had in his private gallery, robed men who never looked hasty but historical, composed within and without.

This was the Commandant's greatest asset: composure, recognized as such by those around him, so employable to history, so useful to convey legitimacy. In the archives he can still be seen to this effect, a little to the left of the Führer, a foot or two behind him with an air of readiness (like a servant to the gods?) and that air of lineage so employable to the historical moment lending to the group in the picture the claim it made, the indispensable claim, that it had come to inherit the past.

These are the only assets that matter, that can take you anywhere, at an time, in any age--as a knight or a courtier, a duke or a cardinal, one who stands in the background as a consort to rulers. Composure and calm. But they will get you nowhere as a merchant, a trader, a bricklayer or bookseller, a mechanic, an artist or a writer.

However, though satisfied with himself as he had reason to be, it was so easy to dissatisfy him. He was so perfect and so worried. A flaw--a crease--a wrinkle--and his lips tightened critically.

"What is this?" he asked, bending down to examine his cuff. "What do you sew here?" he asked Rosenbloom.

A crease of warning crossed the tailor's forehead. "Your uniform," he said carefully, "mein herr Commandant."

"And if I call you a liar!" he said, as he looked into the mirror at his offending reflection. "These Jews!" he thought. "Yes, a liar!" he said out loud, "for you know very well you are sewing something else."

Rosenbloom paused with the needle in one hand and fingered the thread in his other, like Ariadne. "To be sure, mein Commandant," he said, pulling the offending cuff into place, "I sew history. Here, I have straightened it out."

"That's better, yes. It looked foolish before, the way you had it, like a dog's ear flapping loosely," he said peevishly (a quality only his tailors knew about him), still critically eyeing himself, his trouser, as if the cuff might change back again to a demeaning flipflop. "Yes, it seems to have straightened itself out. Well, you are a genius, after all. What shall I do without you?"

Rosenbloom bowed, acknowledging the compliment. "You are too kind. The world is full of tailors. The Chinese have some remarkable ones."

"But not like you Jews."

The Lutheran pinched his eye with envy. "If you like the compliment, you may take it," Rosenbloom whispered to him, bowing out of the room. But there was nothing he could say to console the Lutheran for the slight. Struggle as the Lutheran might and have faith as he said he did, the slight was enough. The Jews always seemed to be ahead.

The Commandant waved them all away and went out to meet Mühsam in his library, a room surprisingly filled with Jewish books--stocked like a pond with carp: Bibles and Talmuds, Commentaries and Responsa, Tractates, Treatises, Medieval philosophers and poets, Mishnas, Gemaras and Kabbalahs. A staff of twenty worked daily reading them, and reported to him whatever of interest took their minds, and from their reports he made reports to the Führer. His library had other material in it too, of course, journals and periodicals of the last fifty or seventy-five years and a valuable collection of pornography. His own preferred reading was newspapers-- which he read voraciously (and for relaxation, fashion magazines, a habit he had inherited from his mother).

He chose this room for his interview with Mühsam, for its effect: he wanted him to know he respected his literary talents, even his Jewishness (though not, of course, his anarchism, socialism, bohemianism, individualism, antimilitarism, liberalism, feminism, modernism), and chose a copy of Judah Halevi to hold in his hand, a symbol of his respect, his regrets.

("Zensl, my love! remember only this. They could not make me take my life. If you hear that I am dead, they killed me. Their sole aim is to make me do their dirty work. There is a distinction they keep in mind, and so do I.")

"A co-religionist of yours," the Commandant said, laying the book conspicuously on his desk.

"A fellow poet."

The Commandant paused with his hand still over the book, caught in mid flight, not sure if Mühsam intended an impertinence. "Is he not a co-religionist?"

"I only mean to say we have many things in common."

Ah! an evasion: "Yes, but you are forever denying the main point. The Führer has nothing against the Judaic religion." (Ha, ha, ha!") "Neither do I. My grandfather----"

"Yes, your grandfather! Exactly." To Mühsam's surprise there was pique in the Commandant's voice. "That is why the Jewish people have decayed."

"Well, as for that. Surely not without company." ("Wily Jew," the Commandant thought, the thought dancing in his eyes, lightening with irritability.) "All history is decline," Mühsam said, "a regular mythology of decline." (He could not resist the look in the Commandant's eye: it compelled him to put his head on the block.) "I tell you what--I would have preferred, I mean me, personally, as a Jew" (he paused so slightly, smiled so slightly), "if you will permit me to say so, I would have preferred myself to have been a soldier in Caesar's army than a soldier at any other time."

The Commandant felt he was being baited--and by a man who had his head on the block. It did not soothe his nerves at all. "Perhaps you think Germans are not as good as Romans?" The patriotic note was sounded to suit a purpose, for the Commandant only wanted Mühsam to curtsey.

("I would like once," he wrote to Zensl, "to construct a sentence utterly at my command, from which nothing can be extracted but what I allow. To control a single sentence, to send it out into the world and nail it against its forehead.") "In many things better," he said.

"Wily Jew," the Commandant thought again, but not entirely with denigration, more with impatience and his constant irritability, for the thought was a component of the respect he felt for him, the reason, after all, why he chose his company for conversation (along with the Cardinal's) and not someone like Vilhelm. The gypsy was never considered.

Loquaciousness was Mühsam's rotten luck, an obsession with telling the world what was wrong with it. The Commandant walked about the room--the Jewish section of it-- twenty shelves or more of books, from floor to ceiling, esoteric titles that had ceased to mean anything to most--The Sayings of the Fathers, The Attributes of God, The Twelve Expressions of Mercy, and so on. "Really," he said, incredulous at the carelessness of things in his own library, and ran his finger along a rim of dust. He held it up to Mühsam and said again, "Really!" and dismissed him.

They took him back briefly to his cell and told him to get ready. They did not tell him what for, or how he should prepare himself. He knew what for. Everyone on the floor knew, and their spirits stiffened with resistance. The Gypsy inhaled a piercing breath which whistled in his ribs. He looked about with an air of searching, a random movement signifying a state of mind without an object, then he moved away towards the wall of his cell as if he had found what he was looking for--the sense, at least if only that, of moving away: an ineffectual act, for the animal's screams penetrated the walls and the prisoners were seized with a restlessness that drove them beserk, an amorphousness of physical energy as if the biological foundation of life were cut loose from social meaning and usefulness, and became a motion venemously random and nervous. They banged on their bar cells with their tin cups and shouted to drown out the animal's screams.

Wyzanski's anticlericalism bit him like a shark. He turned on the Cardinal. "You! A man of God! Why don't you do something? Why doesn't the Pope do something? Why don't you speak out?"

("I will shout with you," the Cardinal thought). He merely said, "Ssshhh," more or less to comfort.

"What can the Pope do?" Mühsam said. "It would embarrass him to speak out. That is why he keeps quiet."

As if he had skins to shed, Wyzanski came to the defense of the clergy. "You are anti Christian," he said.

"Mühsam is right," the Cardinal said.

"Yes, it would embarrass Europe," Mühsam said, laboring with the difficulty of putting on his shoes with broken fingers. "Do you think the Commandant will listen to him or to the Führer? The Pope's silence will be his strength in the future. Many books will be written about why he kept silent. Better books than embarrassment." He struggled with the second shoe. "I do not speak of the present pope. My argument is not ad hominem. I speak of the class of popes, the genre of popes, although formerly they used to speak out, now they keep quiet."

"Ha! I always knew it," Wyzanski said, "at bottom, you are against us."

"He is right," the Cardinal said again. "Perhaps we no longer have the language."

"Yes," Mühsam said, and pushed his feet the rest of the way into their shoes, "you have no new thing to say to me." He looked down at his feet, the exhaustive job of getting them into shoes with broken fingers. "I am tired of your hatred. What does it signify, here, after all?" He shuffled out of his cell and the guards brought him to the room where the chimpanzee was kept. They strapped him into a chair, around the waist and bound his hands and feet. "Even if you shut your eyes," they said to him, "you will hear her scream."

("Zensela--I have not slept since--maybe I do sleep because I seem to dream--but then I seem not to sleep, only to hear her cries--I have not slept a whole night.") Those were among his last words to her. ("There is too much darkness when I lay down. I cannot sleep. Zensela, my girl, try to be brave--it is a fact that tonight I find the darkness to be too much. I do not wish to crawl out of the cave--there is too much political retrogression everywhere--and no end in sight.")

"It will not do you any good to shut your mind away," the guard said. "You know that she is suffering. You can hear her."

("Yes, I wish to suffer with her. Can you believe this?") His chin dropped on his chest. Tears fell from his eyes, which he would have preferred to be invisible from the notice of the others, but they jerked his head up. Dimly, he heard his fellow prisoners banging on their cell bars, Wyzanski, Vilhelm, the Cardinal. They did their best to drown out the noise, but he heard her screams anyway.

She was skinned alive. Her suffering nerves and the cortical knot of her spine were exposed and she entered the history of the human race slowly, this creature of trees and vines and forest life, whose ancestors had been born in a time when there was no more mercy than at another time, but there was more justice; when logos meant law and law meant the boundary between permissible action and action which cut man off from the sight of God, for from Noah to Jesus man was sinful but redeemable, but from Jesus to now he has become abhorrent and unredeemable.

She who stopped short of being human in the evolutionary scale, never walked the halls of a museum, never listened to a lecture in science about her nature, never wrote exegesis on the Bible, never worried what divinity meant, or if the gospels and the white man had improved upon the lesser breeds, whom the Encyclopedia describes as "educable" and "capable of insight," whose instincts had been created to trust, fell out of the hand of God into the hand of man and became a mass of mutilated flesh in a corner, a tuft of fur left on her back erect with terror--the last sign of her life. The eyes she fixed upon the world were put out with a burning rod, and then she belonged forever to the night of human things.

They took Mühsam back to his cell. His feet shuffled in their untied shoes. ("Zensela, let me say it once, let me betray my instinct for life this once--let me falter once--I will pick myself up again and go on.") He stopped at Vilhelm's cell and peered through the bars at him. Vilhelm's head drooped into his shoulders. He did not look up. Mühsam's eyes drifted to the back wall of the cell. "Saves what?" he asked. Vilhelm's head sunk lower. "The world," he whispered. But then, daunted, conceded only by adding in a low voice, "They shall reap the whirlwind."

Mühsam could not hold back his tears. They fell, almost wantonly, as if liberated from a stone that had burst open. "The Jesus I know would have settled for less," he whispered back. His tears broke his resistance. Faster than his guards thought he could still move on his legs--irony and grief gave him such wings--he dropped to his knees and wept. "The hangman's bread is passed to us in this cellar, bless this blood that from the body flows from my poor animal in terror. Can you pray for her soul? Can you pray for her soul?" He banged his forehead on the floor. "Can you pray for her soul?"

We, in the outside world, when we heard of this event-- the torture of an animal to drive a prisoner to suicide--wondered why there was no argument that Mühsam--the others--the Cardinal--could have made to prevent it. Had they all passed then, truly, into a place where neither religion nor poetry availed. It is hard to imagine it--so unyielding a state of things beyond the reach of the civilization we had so carefully built and trusted.

Mühsam struggled all night to sleep. He wrapped his arms over his head to shut out the light. Not his fingers only, but all his bones felt broken. Wyzanski watched him struggle and wanted to call to him, but the Cardinal signalled to him not to. "What can we do for him that sleep cannot?"

("My heart is broken," he wrote Zensl, "at last. It is over, at least for that.") He searched in his cot for a place to put his body, and turned his face to the wall. Its clammy stone was familiar to him, the touch of his wormy blanket. ("Zensela, place a stone somewhere for her and, if you can, put her name on it. I must try to sleep--an hour or two before the next interrogation.")

"Name?"

"Mühsam--means arduous in German."

"Religion?"

"Non-professing."

"Put down Jew."

"Right you are."

"Religion? Why don't you tell us what your religion is?"

"Yes, I will tell you now. I have kept it a secret all these years. Only now that the animal is dead, I will tell you. Rahamanim bene rahamanim."

"Why don't you speak your native language, Mühsam?"

"That is my native language."

"What is your nationality, Mühsam? You speak like a foreigner."

"Yes, I am a foreigner. I and my religion and my nationality and my language. We are foreigners in your world."

But there were no more interrogations. Mühsam was found hanged from a beam on the outside wall of the fortress, near an oak tree that grew there. ("Remember, Zensl, if you hear that I have committed suicide, do not believe it. The force of life in me is greater than the force of death. I can withstand anything but them. If you hear that I am dead, know that they killed me.") He heard in his last moments, when all other explanations were silent and none were about to tell him of the future of the world, he heard the voice of God, as Job had heard it: Behold, behemoth, which I made with thee, and Leviathan, whose eyes are like the eyelids of the morning. What is man that he should destroy my creatures and contend with me. He has his day, but I have eternity, and I will give you creation forever as a consolation for this moment.

Mühsam's body was given to Zensl for burial in Berlin-Dahlem on July 16, 1934, and many of his friends--those who were not in hiding--attended the funeral. There are official records about all this (including a memo from the Commandant about Mühsam's "suicide")--but not about the chimpanzee. Wyzanski escaped and told about her. The Gypsy was castrated and then killed, or killed first and then castrated. Vilhelm's tongue was torn out by its roots by the Commandant in a fit of rage; and the Cardinal was later released--as Wyzanski knew he would be--but he became an ambiguous figure, acclaimed and then forgotten and, no longer remembered, deprived of the authority of his singular behavior, not sure if he was in the foreground or the background of the Europe he knew. But it was the chimpanzee's fate which caught my attention in reading about Mühsam's life--not the others, for their story has been told. Being a lover of Leviathan, had it not been for the fate of this animal which joined Mühsam's fate, I would not have written my story, for politically and socially, philosophically I have little in common with these prisoners, certainly not with Mühsam, nor any desire to emulate Jesus, certainly not his manner of dying. Being a citizen of the world--a townswoman --more like Zensl, needing to be comforted and prepared, I have no politics--at least, no good politics, only loyalties. As a writer, I am not fond of café literature, protest literature, of proclamations in the street. I believe in discipline and silence-- the silence of anger. Least of all do I believe in applause, or an audience, or even attention. It is dangerous--attention. Angels in the guise of writers should move invisibly and silently-- sshhh!

THE GAME

WHEN he was a child, his father used to play a game with him and his brothers. He would nail a ruler to the frame of the dining room door and measure them against it every half year, at Christmas time and at the summer solstice. The ruler was painted with Bavarian cutouts of hearts, lambs, Hansl and Gretl, and Mother Goose characters. Every Christmas morning, before they could open their packages, and every morning on June 21st., his father called them to the ruler and measured them. "Now, let us see. Who has grown and who has not?"

The numbers were very large, as in a child's toy, painted in bright green. The heart was bright red, as it should be, the lamb was wooly white, Hansl and Gretl were in blue and yellow, Mother Goose was in black, at the top of the ruler which was six feet high. She had a long hooked nose, crafty black eyes behind granny glasses, and rode a broomstick. A flock of animals and children in brown, yellow, green and blue ran after her up the ruler, trying to catch her at the top. It was his belief that the aim in life was to grow tall enough to reach her. His father always said, when he measured them, "Mother Goose is waiting for you. Let us see who has grown and who has not."

When he was very young the game was exciting. He and his brothers gathered in front of the ruler, giggling and poking each other, waiting to be complimented on the fact that they had shown progress. Growing tall was the right thing to do. Then they would rush to their presents under the Christmas tree or, on June 21st, pick up an extra piece of cake, their prize for success, and go to school.

Then, when he was ten, he didn't grow in the first six month period. His father said, "Hmmm," and "Hmmm, well, sometimes nature gets a bit sluggish. Eat more wheat cereal for breakfast and you'll see how fast you will catch up to the others."

But having lost half an inch that year, he could not make it up. He grew in the next six month period, but not enough to recover his loss. His father said, "Well, maybe it will be a tale of the tortoise and the hare." He did not know the tale of the tortoise and the hare until several years later, when the idea of it became a ruminative consolation, for he remained short and, at the same time, became intensely ambitious while, in his mind, physical stature remained an index of success. However, he never grew beyond five foot: six inches, though in other ways his body was agile and well-proportioned, women found him attractive and he was determined to succeed in his field.

The game, as it turned out, was bound to cause tension. He passed through his teenage years, more and more detesting it because he grew slowly or not at all, and the measurements arrived every six months like fate. There was nothing he could do about the yardstick.

By the time he was fifteen he didn't need a ruler to tell him that he was below average height. He could look in a mirror and see that for himself. And his brothers didn't need a ruler to show them how tall they were. They reached Mother Goose by the time they were sixteen. Next to them he felt like a dwarf. He was not a dwarf, of course, merely short like Caesar or Napoleon, but he felt like a dwarf. There were real dwarfs who came to town every summer with a travelling circus. He was in terror of being associated with them. It was not a causeless terror. His oldest brother had once called him a dwarf. It was intended as a harmless joke, but a piece of fear stuck to him which became unexpectedly acute the next time his father measured him. He stuffed his shoes with cardboard and stretched his head up until his neck hurt. All he gained was a barren eighth of an inch. "Well, all right,"his father said, but he knew he would have to cheat the next time too. Otherwise, his growth would appear retrograde.

He grew his hair high and tried other ruses to mask his insufficient growth and later detected the same ruses in the children whom he measured He had nailed a plank of wood to a tree in the yard for this purpose, a crude plank with only a notch to separate those who were of acceptable height from those who weren't. They stuffed pebbles in their socks, bunched their toes up under the balls of their feet, arched their feet up as high as possible, stretched their necks up like cranes. It was no use, of course. Cheating was not allowed and was severely punished when he caught them, and he always caught them. One could not cheat enough to compensate for a natural defect.

The dwarfs pretended to be like everybody else, but they weren't. The dwarf men dressed in suits and the dwarf ladies perfumed themselves and wore frilly clothing and jewelry. Sometimes, one or two of the women looked like a Dresden doll, good enough to play with. The men, however, always looked ridiculous to him, dressed in suits, topcoats and hats made especially for them. He wondered what they would look like in uniforms, what an army of them would look like in uniforms. The thought was ludicrous.

From time to time one heard that this or that famous dwarf pair had married. Coarse jokes would be told. His brother once told him that, when erected, a dwarf's organ was the same size as his body. He had a vivid dream about this that night. He felt his organ growing while he slept. He felt it get bigger and bigger between his thighs. Unlike his body which would not grow, his organ would not stop growing. He longed to touch it, to see if it was really as big as it felt, but he knew he shouldn't do that. He could do nothing but lay in his bed, helpless, and feel his organ grow without his wanting it to, until it burst, without his touching it. He had done nothing to encourage it to burst like that, and he wept tears of shame. In the morning he added this worry to his other worries: that his organ would grow while he was at his desk in school or sat at the table at dinner, that it might grow anywhere at any time, though he did not wish it to. It would betray him against his will, and people would point out the sign of the dwarf on him.

Whenever the circus came to town, he went compulsively to see the dwarf act. There was the famous Jewish circus, the Moskovits, who came from Romania and criss-crossed Europe every year. They came to his town in the summer and had two dwarfs who were famous throughout the world. They had gone to Hollywood and had appeared in pictures. Even a dwarf could become famous. He wondered if the dwarfs were Jewish too. It would not make a difference, however. You could not kill them twice. But he was curious and he asked for a dwarf to be brought to his laboratory and to undress. The man was amazed, as if he hadn't understood the order. "Science has an interest in your body," he told the dwarf. "This is not idle curiosity. Please undress." The dwarf cursed every wound the world had given him until he stood naked on the tile floor. His organ was the same as everybody else's. It was uncircumcised and of normal size. But what size was it when erected? It was a revolting temptation to find out, but the curiosity of the researcher is no different from anyone else's. The imagination takes lascivious journeys willy nilly, though not everyone has the inclination or opportunities to transform thought into deed. "Dress and go," he ordered the dwarf, brushing the temptation away like a nasty mosquito. But it came back and bit him one evening at the dinner table. Just as he was about to sink his knife into a souffle he saw the dwarf naked in front of him, so close he had only to reach his hand out to test the hypothesis. His restraint throttled him. He smashed his fist on the table and shouted at the dinner guests, "Who is responsible for this? That is what I want to know. Who is responsible for what I must do?" The guests looked at one another in horror. His wife jumped from her chair and ran to him. "Darling, you are so overworked." He was startled to hear her voice. It woke him from a rage that was like a pit he had fallen into. He could not believe he had lost control over himself, but he recovered immediately at the sound of her voice. "Yes," he laughed, "you don't know the half of it." The guests relaxed and commiserated. They understood immediately and sympathetically. Science was demanding.

But Irene insisted upon a change of routine. He was always running back to his laboratory, always running back to check on an experiment. He was excessively conscientious. Now she insisted he spend more time at home. It flattered him that she cared so much, that she wanted to take care of him. In fact, he loved to be pampered. Moreover, he liked nothing better than to take his children to the amusement park. At Christmas time, he put on a Kris Kringle suit and thrilled them by coming down the chimney with a sack of gifts. He romped on the floor with them and pretended to be a big bear or a dinosaur. They climbed on to his back, likewise pretending terror at his size. For them, it was always a party when he was home, and Irene was delighted at how much good it did him to be with his family. He confessed they were an oasis to him. He was a blessed man to have them. Without them! He shuddered at the thought. They were his humanity. His work was monstrous but evidently appropriate. The highest authorities praised it. No one, not a single person, said to him, "See here, I really think you are going too far." On the contrary, he received nothing but praise and congratulations for what he did, as if a genial fairy had blessed his birth. Success was like a drug, even an aphrodisiac, and he radiated a masculine intensity so that their women guests flirted with him. He saw that they could hardly control their smiles and blushes. Irene kidded him that she had to watch him, but he deplored the idea of adultery. He would never cheat on her. The flirtations were harmless wine that added a sparkle to his conversation. Is there anything more enjoyable than the knowledge of your own physical attractiveness, and that everything you say and do puts everyone around you under a spell?

Only children and dwarfs trembled at the sight of him. From the moment he appeared and cast his eye on them, a wailing would go up. The children cried whenever he played the game with them. Even the taller children who would be spared, cried. Their weeping infuriated him, because he tried to be kind by playing a game with them. It was not his fault things were as they were. He was not responsible for it. He himself was trapped by his radiation and his peers' praise. But then it matters whether your eye level hits a man's middle or you see eye to eye with him.

One day he ordered a pair of dwarfs to be brought to his laboratory. He locked the door as soon as they entered and put his riding stick on his desk where he could reach it. He studied some papers on his desk with a studious air and then, without changing his demeanor, told them to copulate. The female dwarf did not speak German and did not understand. The male dwarf hesitated to translate this for her and she remained perplexed and tearful merely to be in the room. He grasped his riding crop and explained to them: "Science has an interest in how dwarfs copulate." The male dwarf decided to translate for his partner. She had a small head of auburn curls which began to shake with comprehension and shame. She explained herself in French: "Monsieur, I do not know this man." The scientist did not understand what she said and wondered why she babbled at him. He gripped his riding stick harder and struck her. "Please," the male dwarf said, "for decency's sake."

He looked at the dwarf's creased brown face, the sweating brow, the damp hair on his forehead, the deep wrinkle across his brow like a mark of worry born in the depths of his flesh. "For decency' sake?" he repeated. "What has decency to do with science?" His rage mounted like a flame in his groin. He gripped the riding crop in his hand and said, "Copulate, I tell you. Copulate, you wretched human beings. Everyone knows the lust of dwarfs is insatiable." He struck her again on her auburn curls. She threw her hands over her head. "Stop," the male dwarf said, "she cannot, but I can. I will perform for you. Put your whip down."

The bargain was struck. The female dwarf hid her eyes. The scientist watched until the male dwarf was finished. "Enough," he said, "just like everybody else." It was an experiment without results to report, a waste of time. He was disgusted. He left the room and went out into the yard where the children waited to be measured. He took satisfaction in having remembered the game his father had devised. It was a ruse, a preposterous prevarication on fate, a mechanism which took matters out of his hands and issued decrees about life and death impartially. A ruler was a ruler, neither good nor evil.

ABISHAG FROM RAVENSBRÜCK

"...the erotic availability became a coin of incommensurate worth, in return for which the chance of biological survival could be won."

Anna Pawelczynska, *Values and Violence in Auschwitz*

In a woman's camp the smell of female blood is everywhere. There are not enough napkins, and often the guards deliberately withhold them. Women bleed helplessly. The smell of blood from the women and the smell of alcohol from the guards mingle. The guards drink all the time, from morning till night. They cannot do their work without alcohol. The SS always have extra rations in their canteens. The smell of the female blood makes their heads swim. They pant like dogs. The smell of their semen, trapped in their pants, mixes with the smell of the alcohol in their mouths. On warm days, the whole camp smells of female blood, of female interiors. It makes the guards more vicious. They stroll through the camp, truncheons clenched in their fists, their eyes bloodshot from alcohol, circling the women like sharks around a bleeding stump. When they execute political prisoners, they strip them naked. When they take the women to the gas chamber, they strip them naked. They make them stand naked in the yard through roll call while they walk up and down and examine them. The women cannot stop the searching hands of the guards, they cannot stop the teasing truncheon between their legs. The guards make them dig trenches naked, march naked, exercise naked, defecate in front of them naked, urinate, bleed, naked. They cannot get enough of looking at the women's bodies and examining them. They do this in the name of health measures and discipline. They cannot get enough of looking at the women. Their bodies excite them until they lose control, and they despise the women for this. They make the menstruating girls squat in the yard, their legs apart, so that they can watch their blood flow. They watch and pant and sweat and experience silent ecstasy. Sometimes a guard swoons on the ground and writhes. Sometimes he masturbates furiously. The other guards laugh. It is a test of will among them to see which of them will be overcome by the smell of the blood. The female odor weakens them, and they hate the women for that. The women are glad when they have lost enough body fat and their menstrual cycles disappear. Their bodies find refuge in extreme remedies. They are no longer attractive enough to be raped. Their uteruses dry up and become dessicated butterflies. They lose hair everywhere. The mound of Venus becomes prepubescent. They terrify young girls who first arrive. The vanity of the outside world still clings to the lips of the newcomers, while the other women appear shameless in their retrogression, their missing teeth, their lice-bitten skin, their breasts shrunken to pubescent pimples over pubescent rib cages, their bodies bleeding irrelevantly to their intentions. Fonya said that the only good thing about starvation was that it dried up the menses. "I have no use for all this womb apparatus." Some women agreed. "Here we have no use for it. To be a woman here is a curse. To have a baby is a curse." Others wept for children they would never have, as if they had had them and lost them. Yet they pleaded with Magda, "the Aryan," to sing romantic songs to them. She was tall, slender and blonde and had been imprisoned for miscegenation. Wild rumors attached themselves to her. The women believed she had led a glamorous life in the outside world, singing in cabarets. She denied this. "Mostly we were starving performers. No one I knew ever succeeded in anything." They ignored her pathos and preferred to believe that she had been famous on the evidence of her long legs, her amber eyes, a husky voice like Marlene Dietrich's. She had been a singer, she said, because she was unfit to be anything else. "No business skills." After the war, she made no pretense to a stage career, and became a fortune teller in an amusement park. Nevertheless, they wanted to hear her sing, they insisted upon a performance. She refused at first. She had no sense of will or purpose except not to suffer, and to sing was to suffer. Everyone knew that to remember the past was to suffer. "It is too sad to sing such songs," she said. But Magda always gave in to those who pleaded with her, and on nights when it seemed safe, she sang in the barracks in a low voice songs like "Begin the Beguine" and "Blue Moon." She was right. The women floated out onto rivers of memory and wept.

Ravensbrück was built to house ten thousand prisoners. One hundred and twenty-three thousand women passed through it. After the war, many had been accounted for, who had survived, who had died and how. But Magda, Resi, Katerina and Fonya disappeared from the records. The four women had been put on a truck one evening in February, 1943 for Dachau, and were not heard of again. Theirs was not a normal deportation. Such trucks never left the camp with only four women in them because it wasn't worth the gas. The camp was owned by Himmler and run for profit, as were the other slave camps usefully set up on uncultivated wasteland that was good for nothing except to wring dividends from the lives of the slaves. The slave camps were Himmler's property. Shares in them were sold to shareholders and revenue collected from them by him. Extermination was not the object in Ravensbrück until August, 1944 when it was no longer profitable for the camp to keep its slaves.

The real object in Ravensbrück was profit, worked out in the ratio of the cost of a slave to her labor, to keep her alive as long as possible on as little as possible, and then to liquidate her as cheaply as possible, chiefly through the principle of extermination through labor: Arbeit Macht Frei. The profit motive drove everything: what the slaves ate, what they wore, how they died. Often slaves who were going to be killed were made to stand naked in the cold, to weaken them further, so that less gas could be used to kill them. Formal executions reserved for political prisoners took place within the enclosure where the cremation oven was located, which eliminated the need to transport their bodies. Nothing was wasted, not even disease and death, which were administered with precision: how much the sick ate, who should be treated for illness, who would be given an extra blanket, the work schedules of the healthy slaves to the fifty-five factories that surrounded the camp, its four roll calls, its laundry room, its execution places, its transport system, its kitchen, its infirmary, its gas chamber, its cremation room, its morgue, its rankings of political prisoners, social outcasts, criminal prisoners, its modes of execution and identification.

The slaves were color coded. Each prisoner wore a triangle and a number sewn on the left sleeve of her striped jacket. Political prisoners like Katerina wore red triangles. Common criminals wore green triangles. Race defilers, like Magda, wore triangles with black borders around them. Jews wore two yellow triangles. Homosexuals wore pink triangles. Jehovah Witnesses wore violet triangles, gypsies brown triangles. All others wore yellow triangles. Some categories overlapped: Jewish women like Fonya who had belonged to the French Resistance wore a red triangle on a yellow triangle; or prostitutes like Resi who had spied for the German Resistance wore a red and a green triangle. The sick and the elderly were sent to the infirmary to be poisoned. Other slaves were sent to the death camps to fill quotas there. The deportation trucks always took exactly a hundred and fifty women. Administrators, professors, doctors, nurses, truck drivers, secretaries, record keepers, bill collectors, came and went on schedule. Ravensbrück was a slave thanacropolis within walking distance of a Berlin suburb. In the spring, bicycle racers circled past the walls out into the countryside; young men and women picnicked not far away. When the sun shone on them, it shone on the slaves inside the wall; when the rain spoiled their picnic the slaves shivered in the downpour during roll call. When the slaves were sent to a work detail, those who got sick or slackened along the way were killed immediately, a blow to the head with a shovel or a bullet in the neck, while the other slaves stepped over their bodies. No one registered reaction, which could slacken their own steps, and then they would be struck with a shovel.

Most often death came to the women through attrition, as they slipped from level to lower level until they broke through the biological net. You could see dead slaves standing upright, leaning against a building or on a shovel. These deaths were ascribed to natural causes. When a woman died from a beating, she may have first been raped, then starved, then denied treatment for typhus, made to stand naked in the snow or the hot sun, made to work in a factory while suffering from dysentery, perhaps made to watch her new-born infant drowned in a bucket of water. Typhus, gangrene, starvation, grief and exposure had exhausted her before the final blow from a truncheon brought her to the ground. The slaves lived in constant anticipation of death and died of dread at any provocation, a change in routine, a rumor or a glance. Sometimes they fell to the ground dead when their names were called, though no one had touched them. They collapsed and died when made to witness the strangulation of a child. They passed from weeks of grim stoicism to abject terror because of a guard's shout. The will to live disappeared if one's ration of soup was reduced.

Two symptoms revealed that a woman was coming to her end: the lice took control of her body and fantasy took control of her mind. Rumors overwhelmed her, and at Ravensbrück rumors ate the mind as greedily as the lice ate the body. Soon one believed everything and could not distinguish anything. The mind darted from rumor to rumor, from lie to lie, from truth to lie. Then a single image of a food, a special cake or candy that had been a childhood holiday treat, hooked into the slave's brain and she would monotonously describe it in loving detail, saliva running over her lips, until the other women could stand it no more and were glad when she died.

The laundry room was the place where everything was sorted out, who had died, when, where and how, for their clothing was recycled to be de-loused and re-issued to new incoming slaves. The gold fillings and hair of those taken away came back to be reprocessed, the clothes came back to be laundered and used again. When women were deported to the death camps, their clothes often came back with messages stuffed into a pocket, a piece of paper with the owner's name and place of execution so that her friends at Ravensbrück would know where she had met her end. The laundry room was the center of information. Here Magda worked and saved whatever messages came her way, hiding them ingeniously. For what reason she did not know. Neither her name, or the names of Resi, Katerina and Fonya ever came back, no message from them ever appeared, their clothes never returned. It was assumed that they had been executed in Dachau, and that their execution had been covered up for some reason.

The truck that came for them was not the usual van which took the slaves away to death camps. The typical February Berlin weather brought cold winds and sporadic hail. An abusive rain fell. The four women were ordered from their bunks in the early night. Each came from a different block and they did not know each other well. No common pattern united them except an idea in the head of SS Doktor Karl Rascher about hyperthermia and body heat, an experiment he called "Project Lazarus," a wittily deceptive term like other Nazi code language. It was the idea of resuscitation through sexual stimulation, an idea which might occur to anyone who has been impressed with the power of sexual stimulation to overwhelm other biological processes, except hunger. He had once arranged for an entertainment of mating bisons at Karin Hall at a party given by Goering. The building shook with the male animal's heat and the applause of the guests as the bison reached climax. In the Kingdom Without Limits, one could join the primordial with the scientific, myth with rationalism, the instinct for life with the technology of death. Nature withheld nothing from the men with the truncheons.

In the morning no one spoke about the four missing women. Unexplained absences were pressure points the other women dared not push, fears about the brothel or the clinic. It was known that Professor Gebhardt had a clinic nearby for experiments in bone grafting and mustard gas and that there were "rabbits" at the camp. Over a thousand women had been sterilized in the "infirmary" by Roentgen rays, had had parts of their reproductive organs removed and sent to the Research Insititute in Breslau, had had silver nitrate poured into their oviducts, had had parts of their bodies, hips, shoulder blades, their blood and portions of their muscles taken from them for organ transplants into German soldiers. The bodies of dwarfs and cripples had been immersed in calcium chloride to preserve them and had been sent to research institutes for examination. Trucks crisscrossed Germany carrying bodies, organs, human flesh, stumps, skulls, limbs and female body parts. I.G. Farben had bought eighteen hundred slaves to test drugs. Many of the women preferred to be executed than to go there.

It eventually became known, in the way of concentration camp gossip, that Katerina, Resi, Magda and Fonya had been taken to Dachau, which could mean either the brothel or the clinic, for Dachau had both, and the better looking women were taken from Ravensbrück to service the brothel there: a term of six months and two thousand men. Resi joked that she preferred the brothel to the clinic on grounds of experience. She said she had worked in Kitty's in Berlin, but that was temporary. The prostitutes there were never arrested, for the German generals went there, and Resi had the manners of the streetwalker, beaten and tough. There was nothing tempered about her. She could not survive without brashness, a brashness topped by the tufts of red hair that remained after her head had been shaven. She had a hard time keeping her mouth shut until she was whipped twenty-five lashes for it, which left her crippled and subdued for three months.

Fonya's head was shaven too and covered with a black fuzz. She had joined the Communist Party, but left Russia when Stalin and Hitler signed their pact. Then she went to France and became a messenger for the group known as "Noah's Ark" in the French Resistance. For twenty years she had been on the move to find a political sphere for her restless body, for her unappeasable loathing of corruption, tyranny and cheating men. She had made a haphazard living writing articles, but they were too intemperate for most journals to find her work acceptable. Eventually everything disgusted her. She was a utopianist and could belong to no group for more than a few years, for as long as it took to reveal its hypocrisies and rivalries. Betrayal was ontological in her world. The other communists at Ravensbrück shunned her as an apostate. She didn't care. Contempt for human beings gave her an odd liberty. She maintained a resolute discipline in the camp: that she would do nothing that would help the enemy.

Katerina wore a crown of braids when she first arrived. She had come of the Russian aristocracy that had fled the revolution. She was her parents' only child, rooted in their exilic world, her nature shaped by their history, her intelligence formed by Russian tutors who were indifferent to altering circumstances of poverty and relocation. She spoke six languages and translated Tolstoy into German and Goethe into Russian and helped her father publish a newspaper for other Russian aristocrats living in exile. Some of the women called her "the snow princess," and endowed her with vestigial powers to "survive anything." They disliked her and respected her. She was not unkind, but she was armored, having decided that human evil was always incipient and its provoking moment was irrelevant. What mattered was a code of life that transcended human proclivities. Her family lived in a Russian world of Russian friends, Russian restaurants, Russian books and Russian music, confident that they would return to Russia when Europe returned to its senses. Her father had acquired a scar of honor in a duel with a German socialist, from his left earlobe to the top of his neck. When he protested Hitler's pact with Russia, he was arrested and their paper was ordered shut, but Katerina continued to publish it underground until she was also arrested. After the war she went back to publishing the paper and waiting to return to Russia.

The night they were put on the truck for Dachau was cold, wet and sleety. An icy precipitation that was neither rain nor snow fell. Each drop of wet struck the ground like a missile. The four women were put into the back of a covered army truck which had been made comfortable for them and therefore aroused their suspicion: their status had been elevated to that of privileged prisoners. There were mattresses on the floor, thermoses of hot coffee, warm blankets and cigarettes. Resi clicked her teeth, "All the comforts of the barracks. Well, what do you think, ladies? When men get generous, what do you think they want?" The others shrivelled under her words, but Resi stretched out on a mattress and said, "What the hell. I've been paid in worse coin."

Katerina retreated into a corner of the truck, clearing a decontaminated space around herself, and said in a voice futile in its authority, "They cannot mean to rape us here." "Why?" Resi snickered, "are you particular about where the enemy fucks you?" Magda said, "Let's not talk about what we do not know." "Bullshit," Resi, said, "we know." Her clarity rebuked them and they stopped talking. The icy rain hit the canvas covering over the truck and drew attention to the cold outside. The truck lurched forward into gear and was soon travelling at high speed. They paid attention to everything the truck did, when it stopped, when it seemed to turn, when it slowed down, when it picked up speed again, though their knowledge would not make any difference. They did not know they were going to Dachau. They did not know where they were going or why and preferred not think about it. They preferred, at first, to sit suspended without thought or speech until their silence began to suffocate them more than their fears. They were powerless to stop the truck. They could only suffer thoughts until they would know why they had been removed from Ravensbrück and then suffer reality. One could die of their thoughts.

The trip took ten hours and time moved slowly. Every so often someone stirred, lit a cigarette, stretched a leg. The muffled movement made the silence more apparent and encased them in isolation from each other. From time to time the truck slowed down, perhaps waited for a light. They heard the noise of the huge windshield wipers. Then the truck started again to their relief. Anything was better than arriving. There was a hair's width of space between the canvas covering and the truck. An occasional beam of light from an opposite car on the road swung past the opening like a knife's blade, its occupants strangers to their destiny, the sound of its motor sadly delicious until it disappeared into the rain, and they sat again in silence, suspended inside the machine.

"It's better to talk," Resi said resolutely, and lit a cigarette.

Magda agreed. "But not about now."

"What then?" Resi asked. She passed cigarettes and matches around. Fonya and Magda accepted. Magda shivered, though they had been given coats to wear over their striped shirts. Resi pushed a blanket at her. "Might as well have it," she said. "They will never be this generous again."

"I will take some coffee," Fonya said, and reached for a thermos.

Katerina took some too and said, to dispel the poisonous silence and make a pointed comment such as visitors or tourists make, "What an awful climate Berlin has in the winter. In Russia at least cold weather is beautiful."

"You miss Russia?" Magda said with aimless sympathy. Katerina did not respond, but Fonya said to her, "Why should you? You've been here more than twenty years. I don't miss Russia. I don't miss anything or any place."

"Neither do I," Resi said. "The past is a bummer. Besides, how can you remember what the weather was like in Russia if you were three years old when you left? My parents died when I was three, both in the same week of the flu. I can hardly remember them. I'll bet you don't remember Russia at all. You only think you do."

Katerina did not care to discuss how memories persist and Resi said, "I had a picture of my parents that I kept for years, but when I left my uncle's house he took it from me, and now I can't remember what they looked like."

"I remember everything," Fonya said, "but I didn't leave Russia until I was twenty-two. If you stay in a place until you are grown it's easier to remember it."

"But you don't miss Russia?" Magda asked.

"No. I don't miss anywhere," Fonya said again.

"Did you grow up in Berlin?" Magda asked Resi, determined to keep the talk going.

"No, in Lübeck. That's where I came from. I ran away to Berlin to become an actress. Every prostitute thinks she's going to be an actress."

"Why did you become a prostitute?"

"No special reason. After my parents died, I was sent to live with an uncle. I hated him and he hated me. He never let me do anything. He hated the music I listened to, he hated

American jazz, he hated the way I dressed, he hated everything I did, he hated the way I talked and walked. So I ran away to Berlin. Six months later I was starving and a pimp set me up. He said I would never go hungry again if I stuck with him, and he was right about that. There's permanent occupation in sex until you grow old. Frankly, I don't care where they fuck me, as long as I get fed. I've been fucked so often, I know how to shut my eyes and disappear. I've been a prostitute since I was fifteen and now I'm thirty. I averaged two men a night, seven nights a week, for fifteen years. The number comes to 10, 080."

"Good for you," Fonya said."

"Oh, God," Katerina said.

Resi acknowledged both tributes. "The number surprised me too when I added it up. But I think my experience has saved me so far. I'm sure the Gestapo would have killed me by now if they didn't think they could fuck me some more."

"I was an actress," Magda said. "You can also starve as an actress."

"Tell us," Resi said. "I like to hear about any life that was more successful than mine."

"You'll have to get someone else to give that story. I was a very bad actress. Actually I never got on to a real stage. Mostly I did song and dance routines in cabarets. My boyfriend wrote the songs and I sang them. We starved together." She laughed uncomfortably, aware of disturbing their illusions. "He was very talented, but I was an ordinary singer. His songs needed someone with dramatic flair, like Lotte Lenya. Mostly it was my fault that we starved, but he wouldn't leave me."

"Well, obviously, I was not a successful actress either," Resi said, "but I was a successful whore. After fourteen years on the street I managed to get myself a job at Kitty's. One of their girls succumbed to a disease just when they were giving a big party for German generals. They were desperate and picked me up, cleaned me up and dressed me up. I realized one can actually have a good life as a whore."

"Well, then you were successful once," Magda said. " I worked for the worst nightclubs in Berlin. Maybe our patrons were not so different."

"Yes, they were different," Resi said. "The patrons who

came to Kitty's were very high class, diplomats and generals."
"Why were you arrested then?" Katerina asked.
Resi declined to tell her that the underground railroad of information and rescue went through brothels and convents, from streetwalkers to partisans. She said instead, "I guess I just didn't like big pricks and the Gestapo found out. I've seen too many men naked in bed to take a uniform seriously. I'd been arrested before, many times. So what the hell, I thought, another night in jail and I'll be out. Why would I think anything else? What about you?" she asked Magda, "why were you arrested? You're so pure Aryan looking. You'd think they'd keep you as a prize."
"Yes, of course, but that's why they considered me a traitor. My lover was Jewish. Either I betrayed him or I betrayed them."
Katerina said, "At least you had a choice."
Fonya exploded. "You call that a choice! I'm from Russia too, the other Russia, the one that never had a choice. Besides, after Stalin came to power, what was the choice between him and the other one, between one evil or the other?"
Magda intervened. "It's always a choice between evils, don't you think? Werner and I had been childhood sweethearts, I can't remember for how long. He seems always to have been part of my life. He was very talented, wrote songs like Brecht, when he was only sixteen, he played three instruments in the jazz bands, piano, trumpet and drum. I loved his life more than my own. My father was a school teacher, my brothers joined the Sparticists. We quarrelled constantly. My father wanted me to break off with Werner, so I ran away and joined his band. It was fun for a while, but we were always out of money. We were so poor that we were often hungry. Then they began to arrest our friends. Werner pleaded with me to leave him, but I wouldn't, and I pleaded with him to leave the country, but he would not go without me. My father had died and I could not leave my mother. Then my mother died a year later. Poor woman. It was terrible to think that we had waited for her to die so that we could leave the country. But as soon as I closed her eyes, I called Werner and said, 'We're free. Nothing holds me here anymore.' But it was too late. They had found out about

us. We also thought it was ridiculous, that it would not last. We gave peroxide parties. Everyone bleached his hair. The whole band, even the Negroes from America. We gave out bottles of peroxide to our audience. People bleached their hair then and there in the cabarets. We had wonderful parties, which is strange to think about now, because we were always hungry and frightened. We played all the American songs and danced until dawn. Werner and I loved to do the tango and the two-step. Slow dancing, any kind of slow dancing. He was a wonderful dancer."

"I would rather dance than fuck," Resi said.

"Me too," Fonya said, "especially if it's slow dancing. Once I had a boyfriend in Paris who danced very well. He was impotent, but what a dancer."

"I should have such luck," Resi said.

"No," Magda said, "You should not. The truth is we danced until total exhaustion so that we wouldn't have to face our empty cupboards. We thought it was fun because we were all together, everyone gripping someone around the waist, sleeping on our feet, moving around and around until dawn, the whole cabaret swaying."

"It sounds like fun to me," Resi said. Magda did not respond to this, and Resi amended her judgment: "I guess it wasn't."

"Not, it wasn't," Magda said, "it was desperation, but we called it fun."

"Where is Werner now?"

Magda stirred in the dark, a hardly discernible movement, like her talk, barely audible in the historical record.

"He is gone. Everyone is gone. Little by little everyone's hair turned back to its original color, and more and more cabarets were shut down, more and more of our friends were arrested. I became depressed, and when you are depressed your thoughts are very strange. I don't know why I thought suicide was better than our parting, but so it seemed at the time. Many of our friends were committing suicide. We threw suicide parties. Perhaps if I had had more to eat, I would have had the strength to think of something better to do. I decided I would also throw a suicide party. Many of our friends were doing that. I bought bottles of champagne and wonderful cheeses and set a table in my apartment, with balloons and ribbons. I spent all the money I had. Then I called my friends to come to the party, I swallowed a bottle of pills, lay down on my sofa and pinned a note to my chest: 'Please do not revive me. And please make sure I am dead before you bury me. I do not wish to wake up in my coffin, underneath the earth, alone. I will wait for you, Werner, but do not hasten to join me. Let me hear the band play my favorite songs and I will dance away into the night. My eternal love, Magda.'

Well, when you are young, you sometimes do things like that," she laughed. "Yes, I wanted my friends to celebrate my death. I was tired of being cold and hungry. I was always shaking with fright, even before Mühsam's arrest, and Werner was always consoling me. 'It will not last.' I do not know where all my fear came from, and I was tired of it. I seemed to have been born frightened. But Werner revived me. He lay down on top of me and wept. I smelled his hair, his breath, his grief, and I returned. Everyone thought it was a good joke. We had a wonderful party. Then one night when Werner walked me home from the cabaret, he told me I must go, I must leave Germany. He did not think he would be able to get out anymore. I must go myself, he said. I tore at him, 'Then why didn't you let me die. You know I can't bear to be lonely. I don't know how to live by myself.' It was bitterly cold. I had barely a decent coat on me. We spent maybe five minutes together and quarrelled. It was so dangerous for us to be on the street together. 'Listen, Magda,' he said, 'I will not have you staying on my account. Go away, you must go away while you still can. This won't last and eventually I will find you.' I shook with fear, maybe from the cold, I don't know. I could barely talk. 'I'm not the one in danger,' I said.

'Yes, you are,' he said, 'you are in danger because of me. We must stop seeing each other.' I could not bear to hear him say it. I began to scream and two SS appeared immediately on the street. Werner ran off, he melted away into the dark. The guards asked me what was the matter. I said I had been seized with a stomach cramp. They called a taxi for me and it drove me home. From a shadow on the street, I saw Werner running away. That was the last I saw of him, darting between the buildings. I was afraid to roll down my window and call to him. All night I imagined that the guards had shot him in the street while he was running. When my phone rang six o'clock in the morning it was his roommate. I thought he was calling to tell me that Werner had not come home last night. I knew he was gone. I knew it in every part of my body. 'Come quick,' Gunther said. 'Where is Werner?' I asked. He paused for a second. 'He is here.' He's lying, I thought, as I ran down the steps. But why would he lie? What would be the use of it? Werner must be there, after all. I arrived fifteen minutes later. Gunther opened the door. He was pale and dissheveled. He took my hand. 'Be brave,' he said. 'You lied,' I screamed. 'You said Werner was here.'

'He is here,' he said and pushed open the door to the bedroom. Werner lay on the floor, his head swimming in blood, a gun in one hand, a note in the other. It said, 'Magda, my love, go.'"

Her voice changed. It affected a silly irony. "My suicide note was more interesting, don't you think? And anyway I had nowhere to go. I am as content to be here as anywhere else."

Katerina said, "That is defeatist. One must not think that way."

"Yes," Magda said.

"Yekaterina," Fonya said warily, "You want to know why I became a communist? To save me from people like you. I ran away from home too, I ran away to become a communist, a free woman, so that people like you could not step on people like me."

Katerina considered this statement. "And did you succeed?" she asked.

"At least I tried to put my destiny into my own hands, not into my father's."

"You women are so fucked up," Resi said. "I wish I had had a father who cared about my destiny."

"No, you wouldn't," Fonya said, "if you had had a father like mine who cared more about your virginity than about you."

"Why shouldn't he care about that?" Katerina asked. Resi shrugged her shoulders and only said, "It's tough to be fifteen."

Fonya agreed: "It's too bad we have bodies before we have wisdom."

"That's why we have fathers," Katerina said.

Magda asked Fonya, "Were you raped?"

Fonya thought about this for a moment. "Yes," she said, "in a manner of speaking."

"No one is raped in a manner of speaking," Resi said.

"It was worse than rape," Fonya said, "I was raped in my soul. My father didn't like anything I liked anymore than your uncle did. We lived in a small town. My father was the baker there. Everyone bought bread from him, even the Gentiles. He was the only baker in the town, and I used to help him. There was a boy, a Gentile, who used to come every Thursday to buy bread from us. His mother was bedridden and he did the shopping for her. He was so handsome, with blonde hair and blue eyes, a real shaygitz, my father called him. Everytime he came into the store my body turned to water. I was about fourteen and he was probably sixteen. When he came into the store and looked at me with his blue eyes I felt flames shoot through my thighs. I could hardly stand on my feet or touch his hand when I gave him the bread and took the money. Week after week he came every Thursday morning. I was a nervous wreck waiting for him. If he touched my fingers, they shot into flames, if he touched my arm it burned the whole afternoon."

Fonya was astonished at how vivid the memory still was, though she would have like to cut it out with pincers. Still, she succumbed to the memory: "All week I could think of nothing but seeing him on Thursday. I lived for the few minutes he came into the store and if a week went by and he did not come that Thursday, I got sick. I couldn't eat. I ran a fever. What an incurable disease! When he came into the store, sometimes I thought his eyes rested on my face longer than necessary, and I felt my cheeks burn. Sometimes I thought his eyes looked directly into mine and tried to send me a message. I imagined all kinds of things. I imagined he was lonely and longed for me. I imagined he stood by his window as I stood by mine and watched the street to see when I passed, as I watched the street for him. I imagined I was being unkind to him because I never smiled at him when I saw him in the store. I was too frightened because of my father. I imagined that he knew it would be dangerous for me to smile at him and that he was thinking of a safe way to contact me. One day I went to visit a friend in the next town and was coming home through the meadow. It was spring. My breasts were so heavy. They ached. The sky was filled with birds and the earth smelled of clover and buds. My body was filled with longing, even before I saw him. He was crossing the meadow too, almost directly in my path. My legs turned to stone. I could not move them. I could not move from the spot. I saw that he changed his direction so that his path would cross mine. Immediately I thought that this must be the plan he had thought of to see me, that he walked here every afternoon hoping to meet me here. Where else could we meet? Why else would he be here now? I felt terrible that I had not thought of this before, that I had kept him waiting. I felt remorse that I had been stupid, that I had caused him pain." She laughed ruefully, "Can you believe that? Innocence is terrible. As he approached me I thought I saw in his eyes desire and acknowledgement. He smiled at me with such a wonderful smile. I could not stand on my legs anymore now that he was so close to me, his eyes against mine, his legs against mine. We fell to the ground together. The grass covered us. Flocks of birds flew across the sky like a banner. 'Do you love me?' I whispered. 'What?' he said. I sank into the earth. When he was done, he buttoned up his pants and continued on his way. I lay there for hours. My father and my brothers came looking for me and when they found me they asked me if I had been raped. I said I had become dizzy and had lain down to rest. I should have lied and said I had been raped. It would have been better for me. I had been raped, I had been raped in my soul. My father was suspicious, but said nothing. But now he watched me all the time. Every day became a burden. He would not let me out of the house, I could not even help in the store anymore, which was just as well. He said I was a woman with naked eyes and that he would find me a husband to cover them up. When I missed my period for two months I became terrified and ran away to Moscow and found some Jewish girls there who helped me deliver my baby."

The truck stopped momentarily. Everyone became alert. The rain fell, each drop hard as a stone on the canvas. They expected any moment to see the searchlights swing into their faces and to hear the guards shout at them, "Mach schnell, mach schnell." But the truck started again, and they were relieved.

"I have nothing more to be afraid of," Resi said.

"Me too," Magda said. "It is odd that I am no longer afraid."

"What became of your baby?" Resi asked.

Fonya's voice lowered to a confessional tone. " She was a girl with blonde hair. I gave her away for adoption to a Gentile couple." Then her voice hit its customary stride. "It has always seemed strange to me that a woman can bear the child of a man she has scarcely known. Nature cares nothing about us. Nature is our enemy. It was all for nothing."

Resi laughed. "I wouldn't say that. At least you had a five minute illusion. I never even had that much."

"Five minutes!" Fonya spit. "One can also say at least you never had any illusions, which is better. I was raped in my soul, and I should have told my father that I had been raped, because that was the truth."

"You never had other lovers?" Magda asked.

Fonya replied derisively, "Yes, of course. I had other lovers, I had other lovers all the time, if you wish to call them lovers. I could never get rid of the need for sex, but love, please!" She clicked her teeth with disgust. "Listen, Resi, a woman can live without love, but some women like me cannot live without sex. Nature is our worst enemy. I have no use for men but I cannot change myself."

"You've never had a lover?" Resi asked Katerina boldly.

Katerina answered equally boldly, "My parents have selected a husband for me and I do not allow my mind to wander."

"And you've never seen him?" Magda asked.

"Pictures," Katerina said.

Resi digested this for a while. Then she asked, "How do you know you will like him?"

"How many of the 10, 080 men you've slept with have you liked?"

"None."

"Sex is over-rated," Fonya said, "but apparently inescapable, like an avalanche. So why am I required to equate it with my eternal soul?"

"People write songs about love," Magda said. "They don't write songs about avalanches, unless you lose your lover in one."

"It's ridiculous," Fonya said. "Either he has egg on his beard, or his breath smells of vodka and cigarette smoke. Half the time I get a headache."

"Or he doesn't have an orgasm and wants his money back," Resi said. "Dancing is better."

"True," Magda said, "especially the tango. Especially the wonderful tango, When Orchids Bloom in the Moonlight," and she began to sing it. "It's true," Resi said. Fonya said, "It's all a dream. It's either a dream or a nightmare."

The truck stopped again and Magda stopped singing. Then the truck started again, but slowly. They surmised they were no longer on the highway, most likely on a side road. They surmised they were arriving. Yes, they were arriving. The truck rolled to a stop at a gate, questions were asked, identification papers were passed. A soldier unpinned the canvas to the truck and ordered them out. "Mach schnell, mach schnell." They climbed out of the truck. The gates of Dachau rose out of the morning fog: Dachau, the first camp built by Himmler in 1933 when he turned a swampy wasteland into a profitable slave camp. The sight was familiar, the slogan over the gateway was familiar, the architecture was familiar, utilitarian, dismal, barren. The fog shrouded the slaves in the camp in their thin striped pajamas. Their gaunt forms rose like shadows from the mists as they pulled tractors and trucks and shovelled snow. A prevailing western wind carried the smell of burning flesh. The four women rushed into the administration building, registered, paid for, and taken to the hospital. Their nerves unravelled utterly at the sight of its white functional concrete walls. They were pushed into a shower to be deloused with shouts again of "Mach schnell, mach schnell," and taken to a room with beds, a table and chairs. Clothes and food were brought to them. Nothing was clarified. No one explained anything to them. The sight of the food made them weepy, but Katerina reminded them that the Nazis would not waste clean clothes on them if they intended to poison them. They ate the food meticulously, then waited for their destiny to unfold.

No one came to explain it for several hours, and the silence became omnivorous again, eating into their brains. Resi tried to joke: "I hope it's a brothel." No one responded. They could not make the effort at conversation again. The room was warm and they perspired. Their bodies melted in the silence. Outside, slaves went by in the fog carrying bricks in a wheelbarrow. In the distance other slaves marched to a factory. A patch of cold sun emerged and lit up the heads of two slaves who had been hanging from poles for several days. They were probably not yet dead. Only the circling birds would know when.

At last, the door opened and Dr. Rascher in pressed military uniform and another doctor in a laboratory coat entered. They looked as if they were in opposition to each other, the military man and the medical man, rather than accomplices as they were. Dr. Rascher surveyed the four women for a few seconds. They had an impulse to move together, to cover their bodies, but dared not move. For his part, he was pleased at the combination of women he had acquired for his experiment. He had hoped to carry out his hyperthermia experiments at Auschwitz on a grand scale, but had had to settle for the acres of cold foggy fields and a few tanks of icy water at Dachau. Nevertheless, he had adequate means. Dachau was situated within sight of the Alps. Winters were severe here. Snow often fell from the end of November through April. If the natural climate could not freeze a naked man by prolonged exposure, his temperature could be lowered by submersion in icy water. They knew nothing of his ambitions and when he finally spoke, his speech nonplussed them. He told them that, as a Nazi officer, he had great reverence for women; he explained the scientific usefulness of his experiments which were being conducted on behalf of the German Air Force; that everything was being done to assure the scientific quality of the work, measurements of the test person's body heat were taken every ten minutes; that the gain for humankind might be immeasurable; that they, as women, were being honored in their role to contribute to this undertaking.

The sweat crawled through their bodies like lice. They failed to grasp what was expected of them and registered confusion with every word he spoke. He hated to be unromantically explicit. Prudery and vulgarity combined in him in a new manner out of different limits. He decided they were being deliberately obtuse. There was an unsavory aspect to this part of the experiment which he had not clarified in advance: could he trust their compliance, their meaningful compliance? When you came down to it if you couldn't trust their compliance, this part of the experiment was useless. There were many instances when men could dispense with women, except as a germinative thought. The German resurrection, after all, was a male event. Last night he woke in the flush of a spontaneous erection and his wife was asleep like a stone. But who was master of whose fate? He had grasped his organ in his hand and moved it slowly, and then faster. But this was not one of those events. Compliance was required here. It should not be difficult for them to understand what was expected of them even though it was difficult for him to tell them exactly what he expected them to do. The doctor by his side did not attempt to help him, for he too was prudish, and preferred not to put into speech, beyond the endearing statements of 'embrace them and bring them back to life,' what they did not hesitate to put into action. But in the Kingdom Without Limits, citizens can go from charm to hatred, from good manners to rage in the twinkling of an eye. It was Dr. Rascher's prudery that had confused them. As soon as he screamed at Resi, "You! Don't pretend ignorance!" they understood.

Still as enlightenment crept across their faces he thought he detected craftiness in them and his rage increased. He raged at Fonya, whose recollection of the passage was hazy, "You Jews thought you could save your king this way. Why should you be embarrassed?" He chuckled as he grasped his precedent; in fact, he grasped several: "There is nothing new under the sun," he said with brutal emphasis in case anyone should blame him for this innovation, and turned and left. His assistant followed with relief. The door closed and the women sank onto their cots, relieved not to be in the presence of the two doctors any longer. They lay like corpses, like stones, incredulous, while the sweat dried on their bodies.

Resi said after a while, "Jesus Christ, this must be the limit. I'm not going to screw a stiff. Who's Abishag anyway?"

Fonya told, as much as she remembered of the story. "So, it is true," Resi said, "we really do have incredible powers."

"That seems to be our misfortune," Fonya said maliciously.

"But not enough to warm a stiff," Resi said.

"Don't use that language," Katerina said with disgust. "Anyway, they're not dead."

"They'll be close to dead," Magda said. They tried to understand this.

"How close?" Fonya asked. No one knew, or cared to say. Something imponderable was in the circumstances, something beyond the imagination of sex, romantic or obscene, something without a history to it.

Katerina covered her eyes with an arm. "I won't do it," she said, "I won't do it." Fate had outwitted her: a first embrace in an arctic region on a hospital floor under the gaze of instruments and doctors.

Fonya said wearily, "I can't kill someone if I think I can save him."

Katerina jumped up from her cot, the blood drained from her face. "That is a stupid idea, to put life above everything else, above dignity and honor. Is that part of your Jewish communist training?"

Fonya screamed at her, "You're a fascist like the rest of them. The fact is you're a frozen virgin fascist and you're afraid even to give your precious virginity to save a dying man."

Magda cried, "What is the use of our fighting with each other? The fact is that if we succeed it would also help the

Germans. Let's not forget that."

"My God," Resi said, aspiring to brazen reality, "if we succeed, they'll round up every prostitute for this work."

They were silent again. This time the silence was a concrete wall they could not scale. It would not go away with talking. It would always be there, the final end beyond which their thoughts could not go. Fonya hissed under her breath, "Under no circumstances will I help the enemy. That's the last piece of honor I have left." Resi agreed: It was one thing to fuck for money, to save your life, to save a king; it was another thing to fuck to help the enemy to victory. "But they will kill us if they suspect us," she sneered, "of withholding our meaningful compliance."

"They'll probably kill us anyway," Fonya said, as if that was a consolation. "Let's not be tempted by an illusion, and let it not go into the record that they succeeded in this experiment because of us."

No one argued further after this. Now their silence spoke for them. They were prepared, all except Katerina, to buy life with their bodies, but not to help the enemy. It was the one thing they all agreed upon.

But they were not killed then. Death came to them in other ways. By a chicanery of circumstances they were deported from Dachau, each to other camps, finally liberated with "certificates of disappearance," and went their separate ways. When the information about the hyperthermia experiments at Dachau came to light at the Nuremberg trials it was known that women had been brought to the men, that they had embraced frozen lovers, but as no useful data emerged from this aspect of the experiment little mention was made of it in subsequent references to these experiments, or of the women who had been brought there. After the war, Fonya went to the United States, where she moved from job to job and place to place, still restless, belonging nowhere, waitressing in San Francisco, doing housework in New York. Once she lived with a young man for a few weeks, until she woke one morning and saw an eye on her full of cold agony, and flesh that felt like fish in a barrel of ice, its gills barely palpitating. Perhaps her lover had died. She could not tell. In very cold temperatures, the boundary between life and death is unclear. Signs of life become puzzling to interpret and it is difficult to know when one is choosing life. One could embrace a dead man and not know it. The blessing had turned into a curse, but Fonya did not care. Ice is good. Disease cannot spread in ice. Her own body was finally dead. She was glad about this and took no more lovers. Katerina went back to her small apartment to nurse her aging mother, and put the photograph of her intended husband away. She did not plan to marry. Resi went back to the streets, and pretended she was Abishag being brought to King David to heal him, but she knew that the men she picked up had the anonymity of frozen flesh.

Magda had a one room apartment on the third floor of a walkup in a poor neighborhood and took refuge in small comforts: fresh flowers when she could afford them, an old velvet sofa which she used as a bed, a phonograph bought from a junk shop, old records saved from destruction: the Dorsey band, Harry James, Brecht, Benny Goodman. She still preferred the music from this era. The cabarets were opening again in Berlin, but the music was different, the entertainment was different. In the poorer neighborhoods on her route from the amusement park to her apartment, she passed caverns that showed underground movies with strange titles and live sex shows. Flesh was everywhere, promising everything, dissolution, violence and orgasm, an end to the dilemmas of the body. Last week a dead prostitute had been found, her head here, her torso there. Organs and limbs and body parts had surfaced for days. Memories returned to her of women sitting in their menstrual blood, their bodies dissolving on the ground, and there was no antidote for this, no future to prevent the past from returning in memories or otherwise. All eyes looked dead to her, all flesh numb, all faces frozen in their expressions, unbearable to touch. Her old love, preserved like an ideal from youth against such betrayal, a flower pressed between granite, became more powerful than life itself, and she acquiesced in this. Only death could save her love from the betrayal she saw around her. One night, she put a tango on her phonograph, turned on the gas in her stove and laid down on her couch. This time she did not leave a note.

Father Woytzski Leads A Jewish Youth Group To The Holocaust Memorial In Oswiecim, Poland

He began this work eighteen years after the war had ended and he had been liberated from Auschwitz. Nothing in his previous life, not even his internment in the camp, had prepared him for this kind of work; but then nothing in his life, or anyone else's that he knew of, had prepared him for the camp, for his flight, not prompted by political motives, from his native country, a rural village in the Malapolska hills between Lodz and Cracow; nor for his subsequent life in a lower middleclass neighborhood in Brooklyn, a neighborhood without hills and few trees, with many schoolyards and playgrounds which he passed daily on his walk from St. Stephen's Parish to the multitudinous meetings that fill the time of a clergyman.

From meeting to meeting, he passed through these Jewish neighborhoods, the schoolyards crowded with children swinging bats and books, the girls on bicycles, already flirting, already recovering: the children of the next generation, the generation of the sons of Noah, born after the flood. Though he had been in Auschwitz with their parents, he never tarried here. His life of recovery had its own pattern. The war had caused disruptions in many lives, but it had shattered him differently. A more than ordinary sense of discontinuity haunted him so that he seemed not to have spiritual autonomy any longer.

Since his internment at Auschwitz he suffered from this lack of "spiritual familiarity," and was prone to dreams and experiences that were inexplicable to him which, as he described them, seized him "with an outside force," explicable perhaps in someone else's life but not in his; for he was temperamentally a moderate man, of middle height, well read in Plotinus and Patristic literature, and not given to a Gothic sensibility. Nevertheless, these experiences arrived in due course. And for all their regularity, occurring every three or four months, weakened him for days. They were like "an attack," or a "fit" of illness, something one had to recover from. Which he always did, though they left a residue of anxiety, layer upon layer after each attack. The last experience had occurred in his own church while he was performing Mass: the feeling that Christ had descended from the crucifix behind him, not to embrace, but to assault him.

He recognized the aberration as one of the many he had had over the years, and forced himself to continue with the Mass. He refused to allow "private" experiences to expel him from his traditions, from his framework of reality. He was unprepared for a radical departure, for his own saintliness.

The first experience had occurred eighteen years ago, upon his release from Auschwtiz. Before his internment he had been a village priest in a farming district, when he had been seized and taken prisoner: he was not sympathetic to Jews. In fact, there in the Malapolska Hills where he had been born, the problem was remote, a theological problem one read about in the Gospels, or a political problem one read about in the newspapers. If they were the People of the Book they were also the people in the Book. Like everyone else in the farming district he lived in, he had seen Jews on the few occasions he had gone to Lodz or Cracow where they were for him disembodied figures in the modern structure.

Then one night a Jewish woman materialized out of nowhere at the door of his house in the village somewhere between Lodz and Cracow, materialized out of the night and the impact of history, banging loudly on his door. His terrified housekeeper refused to answer the knock. He went himself, prepared to confront police, German soldiers, people with helmets, guns! For what? He had done nothing, was guilty of nothing. This innocence gave him the assurance that whoever was knocking on his door had come to the wrong place, and he opened the door. A woman, about his own age, unkempt and bleeding for some reason, a frantic, brawling child in her arms, collapsed into his room. Immediately he put up his hands, forewarned and asked her not to reveal her identity, and said to his housekeeper, "It's only a woman with a hungry child. Make something to eat."

The child--about two, he surmised, and rather a good size to carry a distance--was so frantic, it could not swallow. His hunger had made him self destructive. They had to hold his arms down and force the food into him. The woman sat at the table and ate, and called his name (Pietzka) between mouthfuls, and begged him to be good and eat, "for you see," she wept,"these people are kind."

Little by little the child's screaming stopped. When he was finally at peace, the housekeeper, watching from the doorway, relaxed from her tension. For at all times and everywhere it is unbearable to listen to a hungry child. They hurriedly dressed the woman's wounds, conversed minimally, gave her bread to take with her, and she departed, her child strapped to her back.

They stood in the dining room, he and his housekeeper, and looked at each other. She spoke first. "Well, that's that."

Two days later he was accused of giving refuge to a Jew and his church was ordered closed. He explained that he had no idea who the woman was, but that he would comply with their orders. From week to week, from Sunday to Sunday, from Mass to Mass, he intended to comply. Until they came one morning on motorcycles, helmeted. His arms, raised with the host, remained in midair, paralyzed with terror (they described it as "intractable rebelliousness"). They tore the Crucifix from its place, dismantled the altar with an ax, and marched him into a car, into a prison, into an office where he was interrogated, into another prison where he was tortured, and into Auschwitz where he was interned.

He emerged two years later, very old, and went back to his village, to his church, out of habit: every familiar stone, every bit of color from the windows anticipated with hunger.

Someone had replaced the Crucifix. To his surprise, he

noted this with resentment. He had come to replace it himself. Someone had disturbed the sequence of events, his place in the restoration of order. A rebelliousness broke out in his mind: "We can no longer say that Your death was quintessential in its suffering. Calvary is everywhere." The thought--so unprepared he was to have it--seemed to demand that he leave the priesthood. One for whom distant events were no further away than yesterday, Calvary as omnipresent as Auschwitz, this meditation seemed inexcusable.

It was the nature of his temperament that he rose from his bench in the church, prepared to follow the dictates of this argument and leave the priesthood. He slept that night in the village inn and there began those dreams of the Crucifix that were to follow him the rest of his life. The figure spoke to him with presumptuous candor, a message he was doomed to hear. This dream, as most dreams with a message, was imperative, but he could not understand it. Upon waking, he was acutely uncomfortable to realize that in his dream he had prayed that he never would understand it. There began that feeling of hiatus, of a split in his personality, of being borne whither he would not go, of being seized by a spiritual current whose direction he distrusted, of being the unwilling carrier of a message he prayed not to hear.

Within the next few days he made up his mind to leave Europe, to cut loose from this past which had become disorganized in his mind so that he was rapidly losing the historical sense of it, without which he could have no theology.

In the aftermath of the war, such feelings came too rapidly and violently for him to digest. In the face of so much disintegration he could hope only to save himself and not his priesthood, and so came to the United States with the thousands of other refugees in that time. He remained a priest, for practical reasons only. It placed him quickly, occupationally, and severed bureaucratic knots. Officials were assured he was not a "displaced person." These gratuitous assumptions fed his sense of shame. He sat huddled in a deck chair on the boat, remorseful that he was granted a "saving faith."

Many Jews were on the boat with him. He recognized a few as having been in his camp, but he felt no desire to talk with them. Almost everyone stood at the rail and watched the ocean beneath them or the horizon ahead of them. Subject to perverse moods, he thought: "These are the generations of Isaac---why do they always suffer such ludicrous fates?" unmindful of the fact that he shared this one with them. He felt no grudge against the woman whose life he had saved and bestowed upon the incident no further sentiment. "They had been caught offguard." "They had acted instinctively, out of mere human charity." "Even animals do as much." Statements he had made in defense of himself, but when asked to denounce his "regrettable error," silence had afflicted him.

Neither did the rolling ocean or the blue sky or the first seagull, when it was sighted and faces lifted towards it and eyes fluttered at it, neither did these call him out to life. He sensed no future for himself.

A Jew stopped in front of his chair, his shirtsleeves rolled up, his number apparent on his hairy arm. "So," he said, "so now we know. Before Hitler God was helpless, Christ was helpless. Even the Pope was helpless. Now, what?"

Father Woytzski shielded his eyes from the amazing sun. He was surprised, again, by his emotions. A pugilistic reflex to defend himself made him say, "You resent Christianity? Christ?"

The Jew clasped his hands behind his back: a philosophical pose. What had he been before the war? A professor, a lawyer, a tailor? Impossible to know in the nondescript refugee clothes he wore. "He's not Christ," he said. Father Woytzski dropped his arm. The man shimmered in the sunlight. "He's not Meshiach. When Meshiach comes, he won't fail."

Father Woytzski was greedy for the sun. This man cast a shadow on his face. "You'll never change," he said to him.

"What's to change?" the man said, "me or the world?"

"They'll burn you again."

The obscenity bounced off him. "Me they didn't get, and even if they did still wouldn't make 1+ 1=3. Akiba was wrong and so was Jesus. We saw right away he was wrong. And that other one, Sabbatai Zevi. We saw he was wrong too."

Father Woytzski put his arm over his eyes. In spite of

the man's shadow they were tearing from the light. "Why do you deny Christ?"
The man snorted. "Who has a better right? I'm the opposition. But you? What's your reason?"
A sibilant sound went up from the boat, sigh or moan: land was sighted. He took his arm away from his eyes. All the faces at the rail were indistinguishable, all eyes were in one direction. No one stood in front of him.

Father Woytzski did not leave the priesthood. He suffered it. He undertook it as the cross he no longer believed in, "the burden of his atheism," and paid the price of self reproach and the world as shadow. He committed no transgressions, for nothing tempted him. He suffered sleeplessness and loss of appetite in everything, even for intellectual activity. Messages of his coming crisis reached him from within: the troubled dreams, the "aberrations," the inexplicable sensations that someone waited for him behind closed doors, that someone had a message for him; and always waking at dawn, someone coughing surreptitiously, coughing behind his hand, getting up the sputum with an effort. Father Woytzski hated the sound of it, with its memories of sickbeds, urinals and latrines, the smells of bodily decay eating away at his faith in immortality: history and theology reduced to the problem of fecal matter. "Go away," he groaned. The man obliged. He rolled off the edge of the bed and rocked on his heels, broken with hunger and spite.
The fool would rock forever if someone didn't stop him! Someone stopped him. The next night it was quiet and Father Woytzski slept through. Five, six, seven nights until the coughing woke him again. Eventually, it always did. And he always had the same response. Enough! "Damn you, go away!"

This nocturnal argument continued for years. His nights acquired a shadow history, a dialogue without language, so old that gestures sufficed. This argument between himself and his "opposition" was immemorial (he could not remember when it had begun), and irremediable (would not yield to the intellect). They wrestled, he and his "opposition," this specter of resistance clinging to life, coughing up sputum, wiping the saliva from its lips. Extraordinary for European history to have taken this pathetic form. Only he seemed aware of this, "visited" with this chilling information. In the daytime, he ignored it. In the daytime he followed the same course from meeting to meeting, Sunday to Sunday, Mass to Mass. Though he wrote many articles for religious newspapers and journals, he never discussed this problem in them. He believed that his personal fears had no place in the daytime world of dialogue.

But at night it was otherwise. He was transformed into a morbid consciousness, a register of antinomians. The idea that "nothing makes sense," neither Jesus' divinity nor the Jews' rejection of him, could be understood philosophically. He required a reconciliation which would allow him his faith. The Father, the Son, and the Holy Ghost co-eternal, and in contradiction of the first commandment: a jealous God debased by the coming of the Son whom Father Woytzski's faith glorified: debased and glorified *their* God, *their* Father the devil who so loved the world He gave His only begotten son. To what conclusion had the centuries brought him: to the conclusion that none of it made sense: easy enough to say if you're not looking for God; difficult to shake the terror of it if you are.

"Enough!" he called out. "Eighteen years. Enough!" But to whom did he address these words. At the end of his bed was nothing but the cluttered gatherings of his blanket where his feet had pushed it. The figure continued to cough and to wipe the prayer in his mouth with his shawl, the blanket on his bed. History and personal memory conspired. God knows the number of Jews he might have seen like this in his own camp. But now he could not remember if he had ever seen a Jew in such a posture, or was constructing his memory from photographs he had seen. He both remembered and didn't remember. History and memory lost their boundaries, became each other, the past and his present. The boundaries of his psyche became fluid. At night, more and more often, he could not remember what century he belonged to, and wondered if it made a difference. Fear told him it did. Fear told him to cling to the mortality he knew was his own, to stay in his own flesh and to die in it, above all, above all, to stay in his own flesh, to cling to the century he was born to and vindicate it. The figure at the end of his bed rose, as he remembered it doing a few minutes ago, rose and rocked on its feet in prayer, as he knew it would, for whatever reason he knew this. A conspiracy of shadows attacked him, a merging of dream intentions, an everlasting Protean wickedess of nightstuff: The Lord shall smite thee with madness and with astonishment of heart!

No one can account for the deepest springs in another, for what is called simply "a change of heart," or melodramatically "a conversion." Here comes one who halts one day in front of the schoolyard of a yeshiva. An action arrested Father Woytzski's attention. A boy of eleven, yarmulka on head, cracked a bat, hit a two base run and took off. Cap on head hit the wind and flew off. The retrieval was instinctive, and the batter was knocked out by the infielder. His disappointment, always plain on the faces of the young, arrested Father Woytzski's attention. He had a generous impulse to tell the boy that it was not his fault--if he hadn't bent to retrieve his cap--that you mustn't be distracted from the game. He walked away, amazed by his thoughts. A perilous irony hung over them.

That night he dreamed that he was back in his village, in his church, in his own church in the Malapolska Hills, and he had come to restore the Crucifix to its rightful place, for no one had. He had been mistaken in that. He woke and prepared himself, as a Jew, to read the Bible, and discovered, that he could not. Incoherence rose from the familiar pages.

Throughout the years, Father Woytzski dreamed of many things that bore resemblance to the dreams of others: of being pursued, being buried in pits, in holes, in wells, all suspect of Freudian meanings; being buried in impossible situations, "implacably totalitarian," as Poe intended in "The Pit and the Pendulum" where man searches for means of escape from the conditions of world and history by means of the rational self. But upon waking, he always knew that he had dreamed of Auschwitz, for prior to his imprisonment when he was a village priest and a young man, he dreamed very different dreams: he dreamed he was being pursued, buried in pits and in caves, in holes and in wells, but he was always rescued, mysteriously and sweetly rescued, justifying faith in God and the world.

Now, waking in the middle of the night, he would turn on his light and reach for his Gospel. Then he would remember the shadow in his dream that was empty of content, that had no salvation, no rescue, no marvellous deus ex machina, the saving hand of dreamers.

In the morning on the way to a hospital or a visit to someone's home, he passed the yeshiva schoolyard crowded with schoolbuses and children. Quaint! Quaint! All this restoration! These pushing, shoving children waiting for doors to open, their voices already hoarse with morning prayers and jibes at each other, mothers waving their goodbyes, as if none of it had happened. Babies in their arms, babies by the hand. Quaint! He shared a nightlife with them, a nocturnal dialogue, but in the daytime their alliance was rhetorical. Quaint! He dreamed about them every night. The quaintness of it struck him again. A cold calamity sprang from the ground. There, on the brink of spring, the trees stiff with buds, the air hovering with green, in the shouting of their optimistic voices, cold calamity sprang from the ground. Everything hung in the balance: air and sun and bird pinned against the sky, and his soul wrestling for recovery.

He dreamed that night, again, of his church in the Malapolska Hills. He entered and found the Crucifix where it had fallen eighteen years ago, and bent to pick it up, but was prevented by his weeping. He could not pick it up. He could do nothing but weep at where it had fallen. When he woke, he did not feel guilty that he had failed. But neither could he remember whether he had gone back to his church after leaving Auschwitz. He had only the impression of having done so, not even a memory anymore. But, surely he had gone back! Why else had he left Poland? Because he had gone back--and had seen what? What had he seen that would have caused him to leave? Memory, so dependent upon the personal self, wavered. The boundary between events became more obscure; his crisis deepened.

He sought avenues of "religious rehabilitation": ecumenical councils, neighborhood interfaith discussions. He encouraged his parishioners to attend a seder on Passover night. He initiated interfaith prayers on Thanksgiving evening. But these did not give him the peace he sought. His dreamlife continued until it began to usurp his waking life and to exhaust it. The liaisons he assiduously promoted felt too fragile, too contemporary, perhaps too American, to withstand the pressure of the past. Everything hung in the balance.

Beset with fears about his "true feelings" on this matter, nevertheless, one year he accepted Rabbi Zellenberg's proposal to accompany him and a dozen children to Dachau. His work in the community and his feelings on these matters were respected. He, himself, had been in Auschwitz. He had the credentials of Lazarus. The invitation stirred his uneasiness about the world's gratuitous assumption about his "saving faith."

That first trip--he was to take half a dozen with Rabbi Zellenberg--was fraught with his self consciousness as the "expert," the "survivor" among these children who sat on the plane, intensely sober and frozen lipped. Rabbi Zellenberg was nervous and kept setting the yarmulkas straight on the boys' heads. Weary, he finally fell asleep next to Chaim, his "star pupil," the one who would vindicate him as a teacher. As they sighted the coastline of Europe, three children began to sing Hatikvah in thin voices. Then they landed, and filed off the airplane behind Rabbi Zellenberg, prepared to meet their nightmare with a few rituals and prayers.

Still, Father Woytzski went the next year and the year after that. Rabbi Zellenberg became "the expert," and Father Woytzski left the discipline of the children and the singing to him. Each year brought changes. The trauma acquired specificity; the boundary between black and not-so-black determined the discriminating details so necessary for the register of reality and survival. The forces of good and evil became clarified, lifted from the anarchy of mystery and nightmare; and their singing became stronger, their repertoire of songs fuller.

Each year brought its own embarrassments, differences, limits, constraints, revelations. Each year he felt himself travelling in altogether different directions, further back, further apart from the others, for the children changed from year to year. An appetite for knowing colored the sobriety of the first trip. Afterwards, they were inevitably more sophisticated, mastering the wave, putting distance between themselves and this past, taking their measure of life against this shadow; except for himself who seemed to be travelling elsewhere, into a knowledge which he wished not to master.

Then Rabbi Zellenberg took ill and died. It was the year they planned to go to Auschwitz. Father Woytzski's position as a native of Poland, as a former inmate of Auschwitz, one who was not Jewish, one who was a priest, helped persuade the Polish officials. But other than Peter Zelkin, age twenty, member of the Youth Council of the temple, no other adult accompanied him. The new rabbi, Rabbi Scheller's wife was expecting their first baby. Father Woytzski went himself, with the twelve children. He it was who had to address the Brotherhood on financial matters, he it was who received calls from anxious parents, advice as to allergies, food problems, homesickness, letter writing. He it was who went to visit them to discuss that which fell into the category of "special problems." He preached a sermon the Sunday before he left on "the True Sepulchre of Christ, for Auschwitz," he said, "and "not Calvary had been omnipresent these forty years."

The weeks prior to his leaving were filled with the flurry of activity that used to fall to the responsibility of Rabbi Zellenberg. It was Father Woytzski who arrived at Mrs. Rosenbloom's house, cluttered with the treasured photographs of weddings and babies, trays of candlesticks, silver and brass and glass, and wallhangings of Sfad, the Galilee and Jerusalem the Golden. Her mother-in-law, a stubborn babushka on her head, followed after them with scruffy footsteps, after her grandchildren, Danny, aged twelve, and Sharon, aged fifteen, "the special problem."

They sat in the living room and discussed Sharon, budding in a T shirt which girls now wore, some with alarming messages written on them. Disingenuously, hers read, "I'm Heaven Sent and Earthward Bound."

"Sharon needs watching," Mrs. Rosenbloom said.

The old lady sat at the window and "watched the outside." She grunted her disagreement.

Mrs. Rosenbloom did not say anything more. She wished only to hint and to find herself at the conclusion of the conversation, without using words to get there. She wished Father Woytzski to understand without her having to explain anything. She got little further than "things would have been easier if Rabbi Zellenberg had not died." He had known Sharon since she was born. However, they had promised her this trip this year and they could not go back on their word. She pushed tea and cake at him. He accepted and pondered her message. The old lady continued to sit at the window, seemingly excluded from tea and cake and comment. Danny added, "I've read Shirer."

"In school?" Father Woytzski asked.

"Are you kidding?" he sneeered, "they don't teachya anything in school."

Danny arrived at the airport a month later, Shirer in hand, Sharon in a blue T shirt that read, "I Get Better on Acquaintance." Twenty-four parents, eight grandmothers, three grandfathers, and twelve children assembled. Rabbi Scheller conducted a prayer service in the waiting room for the safe return of the travellers. A thousand "Be good's," "Be careful's," and they were boarding. But not before the old lady pushed her way through the crowd on shuffling feet to Father Woytzski, babushka on head, yellow teeth hising in his native Polish, the very dialect of his hills, "Go with God, I'll pray for you. My prayers are special. Go."

They boarded: to fly to Warsaw, to visit Lodz, to take the bus to his village in the Malapolska Hills, to take the train to

Cracow, to take the bus from there to Oswiecim. Through the whole of the trip Sharon's wardrobe consisted of two pairs of Levis, one dress (for shul) and T-shirts in assorted colors and assorted messages for the Polish world: "To Know Me Is To Love Me."

In Warsaw she sat on the bus and two boys, flaxen-haired and blue-eyed, made out the message and sat down in front of her. Danny jabbed her in her ribs with his elbow, and went back to his reading. Her shirts caused stares and comments wherever she went: On Monday, "Try Me." On Tuesday, "To Know Me Is To Want Me,' on Wednesday, "Too Hot to Handle." On Thursday--Father Woytzski averted his eyes.

He wondered that her parents allowed her to pack such shirts. But then, all the girls in America now wore them with a curious innocence. Even the girls in the schoolyard of St. Stephen's school. No one else in the group noticed, not even Peter Zelkin. Peter himself wore a shirt which froze Father Woytzski's blood. Black on grey, it read, "I Explode On Contact." Sharon seemed not to notice the attention she caused, or did not wish for the others to know that she noticed. She stared out the window of the bus at the streets of Warsaw, the disarming bearer of a message to the flaxen-haired and the blue-eyed. She was, no more and no less, a child of her generation, the children of the sons of Noah who had floated on the waters of destruction.

They spent three days in Warsaw, one day at the site of the ghetto, walking around it, walking through it, huddled in its museum. In their dungarees and T shirts, in the freedom of this fashion, they seemed fragile and unprotected.

On the fourth day, they took a bus to Lodz. It was crowded with other passengers, other young boys in Levis and leather jackets who themselves seemed transformed into American figures: brisk movements, good spirits, curiosity about these Americans, self conscious, defensive, arrogant, good humored. Father Woytzski's clerical garb and Polish past was a bridge. They asked questions. He explained "the pilgrimage." They knew something about it. They asked him about America, many questions about America. They asked him what was written on the shirts. Father Woytzski forebore. "Sayings," he said. One winked and said he could read a little English. He read the message on Sharon's shirt. They laughed. They were intrigued. American girls were always so interesting. They pushed to sit down in front of her. Sharon kept her face out the window. Danny jabbed her again in her ribs and said, "Now see what you've done!" Sharon jabbed back. "I haven't done anything." Danny knew this was so, but that was not enough to appease him. He jabbed her back. "Yes, you have," he whispered. Sharon suffered the ugliness of being accused unjustly. Her blue eyes leaped to the fight. The two boys in front of her had no idea what caused the flare-up in her eyes, but they were intrigued. "What is your name?" one asked in Polish.

She did not understand. He tried the sentence in English. "Your name? What is?"

"Sharon."

"Sharon? What means Sharon?"

It was time to intervene. They were not far from Lodz. Father Woytzski directed their attention to the view outside, though he himself regarded it with armored distance, testing his thirty-five years of residence in the United States against it. They--the American group--and the four Polish boys--parted in Lodz. They--the American group spent two days in Lodz, circling the ghetto there, that unique European creation, a "neighborhood" with names like Judenstrasse and Judenplatz, which had breathed its affects into so many aspects of European life, its restrictions a curiosity for children who at age ten know how to cut a hole in a hurricane fence with a pair of pliers and enter any playground at will. Nevertheless, this is their past. Though they do not remember the flood, they know that it happened and move through its neighborhood accordingly.

Then they boarded the bus again, this time for Father Woytzski's village in the Malapolska Hills, prepared as they had agreed to do, to go all the way back with him, to see the village where he had been born, the school where he had been educated, the house he had lived in, for whatever he had become to them in their Jewish neighborhood in Brooklyn, here is where he began. And they were prepared to do him this honor.

They boarded the bus and struck for the hills, not only for the cities with its defined circumferences and its life labelled with street signs where you can find your way around with civic accommodations--but for the open country where change is slow and freedom is only apparent, where old religions, as the Christians discovered among the rural pagans of Gaul, take a long time die. It was here, in one of these small villages, that six Jews had returned from Auschwitz to collect their belongings, and were murdered by the villagers. "Lynched," as they say in the United States.

What did Father Woytzski have to fear for his American charges? He suddenly felt nervous, confronted by memories which brought him into judgment upon his own people. But the consequences of this trip took another turn, though given the quixotic nature of a tradition, even the religious tradition, it could just as well have taken the earlier fate. Traditions are like Greek masks and can slip from one expression to the other with a sleight of hand. In this case it wore the expression of geniality.

Two of the boys--the ones with the flaxen hair and the blue eyes--in Levis and leather jackets, boarded the bus at Lodz. They too were going all the way through to Cracow. They too were stopping off in the Malapolska Hills. They had a grandmother who lived there, an uncle in Lodz, a sister in Cracow. This was their holiday. They were visiting everyone. They were travelling through Poland. Some day they hoped to come to the United States. They were very interested in this American group, also touring Poland, yarmulkas discounted. In America, things were different. If they could come to America, they were prepared to be different too. They slipped into the seat behind Sharon and Danny and engaged them in conversation. They wished to engage Sharon, but Danny was the informed one. He happened to have an almanac in his pocket. They listened politely, learned very little, and kept their eyes on Sharon. Soon they were in heat and it made them silly. They giggled a lot and became very friendly. They flashed their stunning hair in her eyes. They became ardent supporters of anything she might want. They could show her a lot in the village.

The American group practised indifference. Flirting they understood (except for Danny) but history warned them against it here. But Sharon was not indifferent. She was embarrassed but excited. Father Woytzski intervened again. His tactic was to distract with loftier conversation. Of course it didn't work. They answered him perfunctorily, and went back to paying attention to Sharon. Danny's method was more direct. He jabbed Sharon in her ribs again. She turned her pent-up emotions on him and began to pummel him. At once, this made her more appealing. Nothing now could prevail against their ardor.

Seeing that levity didn't work, they too became serious. They discussed Poland's offenses against the Jews which they attributed to economic malaise, the innumerable invasions by Germany and Russia, medieval superstitions, and an impoverished peasantry. But now with economic reform, all was different. They were different. They swung their hair.

Sharon gave way. She said she had nothing against the Polish people. (They were very glad to hear this.) In America all ethnic groups were equal. Polish people had the same rights as everyone else, Jews and Germans and Blacks.

They listened with respect: America was a wonderful country.

The bus arrived in the late afternoon on this agreeable note. The depot was the parking lot behind the village hotel. They got off, shaking hands with everyone; with Father Woytzski, whom they now treated with more respect, with Peter Zelkin, whose T shirt and yarmulkah seemed unstably mixed, with Danny who quoted Orwell's famous aphorism to them, and with Sharon, whose hand they held longer than the others. Could they come and visit her this evening? Their grandmother's house was only a block away. They would love for their grandmother to meet her, to meet them.

Father Woytzski thought not, and felt the peculiarity of his reservations. What grounds did he have for objecting? They wanted to know. In America, everyone was equal. Was this not so? They were puzzled. They wished to place the hospitality of their village, their country, at his disposal. Their grandmother baked wonderful breads, always ready in the oven.

Peter told Father Woytzski to accept the offer but he looked about at the village, its two or three dozen houses, the dusty road, the hills in the retreating background, straightened his yarmulkah on his head, folded his arms on his chest, and kicked the tire of the bus.

Sharon felt required to attack his churlishness. The terms of her American upbringing seemed to her to require this. "They're only being polite," she said. She went further. After washing up, they came down to the dining room, where she also said that she was humiliated by the way they behaved. Peter's kicking the tire of the bus was like kicking them in the face--for what?--"for inviting us to meet their grandmother?" Peter denied nothing and added nothing.

Father Woytzski saw himself as the cause of Peter's constraint, the motive for Sharon's defense, though what he had wished for most ardently was not to be the pertinent factor in their behavior.

The two brothers came at dusk in high spirits, still in Levis and leather jackets in spite of the twilight warmth. Their grandmother was expecting them, they said, particularly Father Woytzski. She was beside herself with surprise and joy when she heard that he had returned. The brothers beamed their message. They looked at Father Woytzski with more vigorous respect. Would he remember his old housekeeper? He was startled. "She must be over a hundred." "Yes," the brothers said, "but wonderfully strong."

The group walked down the dusty street behind Father Woytzski and Peter, his arms folded on his chest, the two boys with the flaxen hair on either side of Sharon, outdoing each other in garrulity. "Their grandmother's bread was wonderful." "How wonderful that she should be Father Woytzski's old housekeeper." "What a wonderful homecoming for him." "American girls were wonderful." "Could they maybe write to her." "Maybe someday they could come to America and see her." "Could they have her address?"

Their grandmother was already in the doorway, watching for them. She could not believe that Father Woytzski had returned. He had disappeared after the war. Everyone thought he had died in Auschwitz. A miracle had happened. She gathered him up as if his true place had been restored to him. Her joy, so genuine, embraced only him. He introduced the children to her but her eyes, filled with the miracle of his return, swept over them casually. What had America made of him? He thought that his appearance there with this group explained it. Her grandsons explained to her in Polish, the object of their trip. She brushed their explanation aside as if they had said something naughty and it wasn't worth her while to discipline them for it. What mattered was that Father Woytzski had returned. He had not forgotten his birthplace. All these years she had been praying for his soul in heaven, and he had been in America.

After the visit, the group returned to the inn, not really a group any longer. In Warsaw, in Lodz, they recognized their history. Here, in this village, among the eternal hills, it was different. They had come with a different set of rules about ethnic parity and "not excluding people." The old woman had ignored their rules. She ignored America. Here everything was the same.

"Well, you can see why," Sharon said. "After all, she was his housekeeper. Naturally, she wanted to spend all her time talking with him." The others were not persuaded. Their spirits sagged. They looked forward to leaving the village.

To his surprise, Father Woytzski was dismayed by Sharon's defense. He was pleased to see his old housekeeper, but the feeling was guarded by the sense that the bridge between them had collapsed. She only imagined that he was back, and it had embarrassed him, again, to be the recipient of religious goodwill. On the other hand, he had an impulse to shake Sharon from her American armor, but the sense that he had no rights over her stopped the words that came to his lips. He only said, mildly enough, ""Oh, child, really!" But that was wound enough to her, and she went upstairs to her room, conspicuously insulted.

Father Woytzski retired with unpleasant reflections. He wanted above all not to dissipate the spirit of the group, not to be the instrument of its loss of momentum. Not recompense, but recovery, was possible, was on the wing, and he wanted to be part of it and not dissipate its energy. It had not been pleasant for him to realize that in his old housekeeper's mind, nothing had changed, not even him. She was a difficult yardstick, that old lady. She was his old human attachments, his womb of memory.

He planned to visit his old church in the morning, but he was beset with hesitation, with a feeling that he had not earned the right to go back, because the return, so longed for humanly, now seemed to bargain on the sanctity of the children in his charge. The feeling of hiatus occurred in him again. It was not as sharp as it used to be. He did not have the sensation that he was being literally torn apart. His energies were not consumed in protecting himself, and now he remembered when he had first felt it. It was when that woman had knocked on his door and he had responded instinctively, like an animal leaping to the defense of its own: life calling to life through the chaos of history.

A dusky moon hung in the sky, his sky, the moon of warm summer nights in rural places that brought such richness to a country night. He could not forget it nor account for how he had squandered it. Had he not convinced himself, here, many years ago, of the beneficence of life. It had been his own youth which had convinced him of it. Yet a chill struck him. The very moon and its richness was pregnant with premonition. He put on his bathrobe and slippers and went down the stairs to the small lobby. There were whispers in the doorway. Two blonde heads bobbed in the moonlight. Father Woytzski felt a wrath invade his bones. "Sharon," he called sharply. There was a muted exclamation, and she fled. "Go away," he said to the blonde heads. "We came only to say goodbye," they said affably. "Go away," he said again. They did, but not without mumbling about his sourness. Sharon waited for him at the top of the steps, still in her dungarees and T shirt. "How could you!" she said in a shrill voice, wounded in the marrow of her womanhood.

He went back to his room and lay down, a prey to introspection. He took himself to task for over-reacting. He went over it a dozen times, but each time became more convinced that she was wrong and he was right. He was right to have been indignant, even if she was a child. How else should one react to a foolish child? Oh! child, child. How many hearts have burst for you? He could not sleep anymore. He must walk off his thoughts. Again, he put on his bathrobe and his slippers and went down the steps. He should have gone first to the church and not delayed to see if the Crucifix had been restored. That should have been the first thing he should have done. He hurried there now. In the moonlight of these streets, all the skeins of this history shone twisted and braided. Child! Child! he mumbled as he ran, overwhelmed with the everlastingness of her fallible humanity: Even the generations of the sons of Noah, the ones who came after the flood.

The door was open, waiting for him. The pews and the benches were in order. The Crucifix was in its place, over his old altar. The moonlight came in through the open door and the windows, washing over the ivory body, lighting the carved face. The eyes gleamed at him. The message stared from them. How hard it was to accept it. Oh, fallible humanity! How awesome was this fallible humanity! Whose heart could stand it? Whose heart could die for it? "Take me instead," Moses had said. "If Thou must blot out this people, take me instead." Oh, treasure of caring which had never ceased. "I have come to save the House of Israel." Oh, heart! Oh, terrible failure! Oh, terrible heartbreak of history.

His knees bent under the weight of this revelation into the wounded heart of his Savior, the pathos of this history. It was his own heart that broke, his own tears that fell.

GUIDO, MY GUIDE

*More vividly than in their
extant works, the Middle Ages
present themselves in the absence of works that to one's
mind had been so vividly there.*
Eleanor Clark, Rome and A Villa

*Anywhere at any time, with
anyone, one may be seized by
the suspicion of being an alien.*
Elizabeth Bowen, A Time In Rome

To Someone who has never suffered from claustrophobia, the first experience is shocking. The attack came upon Michael precipitously like a black hood dropped over his head, suffocating him in darkness. He suddenly could not hear or see or feel or think and called out to his guide in the catacombs. Guido's response echoed from a short distance, but to Michael not reassuringly. He ran to catch up with the voice, terrified that he would lose his way and be buried alive with the curiously sterile dead who lay there.

His guide walked through the chambers as rapidly as was compatible with the reverential pace he thought the place deserved, but rarely stopped to explain anything to Michael.

Nor were there any of the customary explanations in place for the casual visitor which would be expected in a tourist area. The catacombs had not yet been put into condition for receiving tourists after the war. The lighting was poor, the air bad. They were still left largely to the archeologists to explore. Guido was sure that this would change and that the catacombs would soon be as popular as the Forum, the Vatican, the Coliseum, and the Via Veneto. They were, after all, unique. Other countries had gardens and palaces and castles and museums, "but only Rome has catacombs," he told Michael.

They had come to explore its potential for this event, and had to find their way through the mazes with makeshift arrows that often separated at a fork and went in different directions. To Michael, the caverns seemed to unwind endlessly. The dead lay in berths along white chalky walls, piles of naked bones. Nothing distinguished them. Their flesh of identity was gone. Their sex was gone, their history was gone, their language dead. Nevertheless, they had been preserved for a makeshift posterity as if their bones would one day talk. The place was eerily sterile. The earthen floor was compact and clean. No dust. No rats or mice, no insects or bats. Nothing except caverns which forked in different directions, and the dead who lay chastely inside their walls.

Michael hated to call out to Guido for help, but he lost his sense of direction, he lost all sense of himself except for the clammy sweat dripping from his armpits. Finally his terror stripped him of every thought except to keep up with Guido, and to escape from this underground maze as soon as posible.

When they finally emerged above ground, he felt nauseous and looked about for a water fountain. There was none. The area was deserted. The August torpor was relieved only slightly by the cypress trees whose tops swayed in currents too high to cool the air below.

The hot sun shone off Guido's black hair, worn slicked back in the style of the day, though he sweated in a suit too tight for his build and envied Michael's chinos and polo shirt, his camera slung over his shoulder, his American cigarettes which he accepted freely, with pleasure and envy, when they were offered. Americans amazed him. He preferred them to all other kinds of tourists. They were generous and naive, something like what angels should be like. He was glad they had won the war.

Michael did not tell Guido about his terror in the catacombs, and Guido's lecture on the Christian martyrs was dissonant with his effort to recover from it, and with his ambition to write a travel book that would be more than a guide to budget hotels and historical declamations: Here lies Flavia Domitilla, noblewoman, deaconess, Domitilla Sancta, Domitilla martyr, her bones lying in a scheme of dust more naked than naked flesh, exposed willessly in a crypt protected by a glass wall lit with an indecent pink light, her elemental decay unnervingly public, her skull and bones innocent of identity other than the tag on her crypt, her empty eyesockets staring at viewers like himself as if they might suck him in.

Michael worked for Touristrotters, Inc. in the United States, which hired college students to search out travel bargains in Europe for other students. Their logo was a sneakered youth with a globe in his hand balanced like a basketball. Jet propelled planes were making their first transatlantic flights, and Michael had boarded one to Italy twelve days ago, congratulating himself on his opportunity. His assignment embraced a singular moment of American cultural appetite, penniless wanderlust and the entreprenuerial tourist industry. The war was over and Americans could return to Europe in seven hours to retrace the steps of ancestors who had fled from there. Michael was nine when the war had ended and had taken its place in time for him as remote as the Peloponnesian War. Rome basked in the aftermath of having been declared an open city. Everyone respected its history. Even the Nazis had tempered their fire. The only rubble to be seen were historic ruins, Mussolini's reconstructed Roman past as a monument to his ambitions. It was said that a map of classical Rome had hung in his office in the Palazza Venezia, which had inspired his politics and his city planning. The Jubilee Year in 1950, announced by the Pope, had officially opened Rome tourism and three million tourists arrived in that year. Jewish peddlars who had had their licenses revoked in 1943 were given them back in response to the problem. Tourist card vendors were on every street corner and Guido, Touristrotter's agent in Rome, knew them all. They all worked for him. Fourteen years after the war, Europe functioned for the future and waited for the Americans to return.

Graffiti were on every building: "Yankee go home," and "Welcome, American tourist." Guido wiped away unfriendly messages. The future of the world belonged to the travel industry: transportation, airlines, highspeed trains, lightweight luggage, wrinkle-free clothes. He stopped to check a pushcart in the Roman Forum, putting the photographs of his favorite monuments in prominent places. His eyes canvassed the area, stones and cats, oleanders and vendors, like an artist judging proportion and effect in the arrangement of material.

"Shalom, my friend," a vendor smiled at Michael. The friendly greeting struck him as a dart from a blowgun, not lethal but unexpected and out of place as many of his experiences were proving to be. The experiences he had expected to have in a calendar of cultural events had become secondary to the experiences he had not expected to have: panic, lassitude, loneliness, his lust for adventure dissipated with satiety and homesickness. Venice had undulated for three days and Florence had blended Renaissance architecture with postwar bourgeoisie respectability. Michael adored Venice and searched futilely for an erotic liaison. He respected Florence and bought reproductions. Rome and the hips of the Roman female exhilarated him for three days. Then he was suddenly exhausted, victim to lassitude and a schizophrenic apprehension of too many realities: common reactions to tourism glut. In six days he had travelled through the three ages of Rome, from il Teatro di Marcello and the Arch of Titus, to the Vatican and Mussolini's residence at the Villa Torlonia. The Middle Ages were missing. Mussolini had demolished them to excavate the Forum, where the vendor stood his ground against a marble column with characteristic Roman cynicism concerning fate. He was slight and skinny, with baggy pants held up with a hemp belt, a wraith with street smarts, slyly unpretentious.

Michael snapped a picture of him for a photograph of local color in the Forum. Guido kicked urchins and cats to a side, and despaired over pigeon droppings and graffiti.

History required housekeeping, and he battled against surly messages. If nothing else, the history of Rome was not trivial, and he was possessive about it. Anyone could see that it was on a grand scale. Guido appreciated that as a businessman. Americans came in waves, and they were always grateful, sincere, a little bashful, even when they came as soldiers, brash but embarrassed to be there. He had come to know them as one of their prisoners and had opened an office in Rome for Touristrotters to greet them on their return as civilians.

They exited the Forum by way of the Arch of Titus. Guido clicked his teeth with disgust at the graffiti on its base, "Am Israel Chai."

"Vitale," he grunted and wiped the chalk marks away.

He was genial to Michael's questions about the war, but matter-of-fact and brief. "The war? It was terrible! Terrible!" Michael felt Guido's pronouncement like a judgment against his innocence. They sat at a sidewalk table on the Via Veneto. Guido drank wine. Michael drank warm coca cola. Stylish women, smelling of magnificent perfume, thronged the street and paced the swing of their hips and their walk to accommodate the fashionable sack dress, film directors, and other gazing eyes. Shops glittered with the objects of greedy vanity. Sidewalk tables did brisk business in aperitifs and, off the avenue, the first fast food hamburger restaurant had opened. Though ice was still unavailable, the Via Veneto was Italy's competitor to the Champs Élysées as the most glamorous street in Europe, bright locale of la dolce vita. Within a decade it would be overtaken by fame and sink into carnival sordidness.

Michael was solicitous for Guido's unkind memories, but where had the war gone to? "What happened to you?" he asked.

Guido was surprised by the question. "To me? Personally? I was captured."

The answer felt punitive to Michael, who conjured scenes of grotesque prison camps. "By whom?"

"By whom?" Guido said, undismayed, "by everybody." Surmising that one question led to another while tempus fugit, Guido snapped his wristwatch out from his shirtsleeves and declared that they should go at once to the catacombs so that they could return for siesta. "When in Rome," he flashed a meaningful smile, knowing that the afternoon rest was a difficult concept for Americans which the tourist industry would have to deal with, "do as the Romans do," he concluded also meaningfully, declaring again Rome's special status.

After their visit to the catacombs, he whisked Michael back to his pension, speeding down the Via Appia in the automobile provided by Touristrotters with its name and logo in green on the white car. They drove past yesterday's forays into the Coliseum, the Vatican and the Forum. Guido mastered Roman traffic with Roman style, blowing his horn and cursing loudly. "It's amazing Rome wasn't bombed," Michael said, struck again by the sensation that the war was a rumor. Though the good fortune was due to the Pope's request, Guido's eyes flew heavenward, grateful to all other deities as he drove victoriously through Roman traffic. He felt entitled to the spoils of war, having been wise enough to invest in the future of history. "A miracle," he blew out between curses, mindful that it would have been the ruin of his business otherwise, and delivered Michael to his pension across the street from the Fontana di Trevi, "the best place in Rome to stay." Again he consulted his watch and told Michael that he would pick him up at "five o'clock exactly to see Rome by twilight," and kissed his fingertips enthusiastically to byegone gods: "The lights from the city, not even the stars in the sky can compare with."

Michael climbed the three flights of stairs to his small and exceedingly warm room, $2.00 per night, with toilet down the hallway. Its location alone was a bargain, across the street from the world's most famous fountain. On the first night, he was intoxicated with the combustible scene of Romans and tourists that filled up the plaza before his eyes. By the third night he felt smothered in history and was lonely. He discovered that he did not like to mingle in an anonymous crowd, his tourist identity as obvious as a pebble in a glass of white wine. He was not, he realized, anonymous, but conspicuous and felt suspended in a peculiar exile. Romans avoided him, except for those who wanted to sell him something. His window was open and, without a screen, insects dove in and out of his room. In the street below buses disgorged tourists sixteen hours a day: tired American businessmen, dumbfounded and pious; elderly women from the American midwest, in seersucker suits, sunhats and swollen feet, warm, breathless and uncomfortable in the Europe of their dreams; secretaries in brief skirts and sandals, who had saved from their salaries since the war had ended; and a few German and Japanese tourists tentatively among them in the aftermath of the war. All were as foreign to Michael as the ancient Romans were. Still he was conscientious and hopeful of capturing the essence of place and people. It is the ambition of every tourist to discover the hidden trails and realia beneath the official history which tourism endorses, but Michael was heedful of his editor's advice: Remember your audience is other college students like yourself. You're writing for them. "Writing for them," he felt should include advice on how to cope with exhaustion from history and car fumes, inability to read road sign, menus, and historical markers, and what to do in case of sexual loneliness and panic attack.

He had almost vomited in the catacombs, but knew it would be fatal to include this fact. Truth was he had felt like a voyeur there. The woman's nakedness had struck a wayward prurient response in him. Her powerless bones seemed arrayed with intent to compel one to gaze at the parts of her which had once been private. Her mouth was open as if she were about to speak to him. Her empty eyesockets stared at him more intently than living eyes he knew. They were cavernous with beseeching, and even hours later fastened themselves to his brain like suckers.

The Roman caesura did nothing for him. The memory of his experience in the catacombs prevailed and retrospection neither diminished it nor yielded an explanation for it. The terror held no revelation, except that he now knew what terror felt like, but the knowledge was indigestible. He would expect as a writer, at least, to take advantage of the experience, and was humiliated by incoherence. It was useless to stay in his room, a victim to heat, loneliness and writer's block. He consulted a map and a guide book and found the subway connection to Ostia Antica, a spur off the mainline originally laid by Mussolini to take visitors to see his model city of classical

Rome, EUR, which was now a pleasant suburb one stop before Ostia Antica. Building the subway had been traumatic for Romans. Digging had uncovered more catacombs and an underground bordello with Christian symbols where livelier bodies than dead bones had lain in the private cells. The subway route was changed accordingly, and Rome adjusted to its newer underground world with inevitable graffiti on the subway walls. Reading about the controversy, Michael speculated fancifully on his disorderly reaction to Domitilla's stare. Maybe the dead woman had been a prostitute.

The train was crowded with commuters, businessmen trying to go home for the siesta, peasants with vegetables and dead chickens trying to get to a market, women nursing babies. He made a friendly memo in his notebook that Americans might prefer to leave Rome in mid-afternoon to solitary confinement in their rooms. American habits should be given their due, he thought, as he stepped out of the train station at Ostia Antica.

Ruins stuck up out of the sand like giant toy blocks the Romans had left behind in their war games. Bits of the old marble wharf and remains of warehouses, shops, baths, temples, a theater and private houses bled through the sand. Much excavation was in progress. An ancient synagogue was emerging from a field of corn, unearthed during the construction of a new highway to the airport. A statue of Minerva stood idly in a temple to Mithradaites. Nature and Roman history clutched each other here as it did all along the Mediterranean littoral to Caesarea. The fertile antiquity was exhausting and the temperature was 97 degrees. The afternoon sun tortured Michael's eyes. He had forgotten to take a canteen and eyed a nearby water fountain with the stranger's fear that he might catch a rare disease which was prevalent in places like Rome, but which American had no historical immunity against. He felt marooned in his national habits. A vendor smiled familiarly at him, but he distrusted the smile as soaked in a longing to sell him something. The vendor greeted: "Yesterday, in the Forum, you took my picture, remember?" Michael did not remember. "You work for Guido," the vendor said.

Michael was mildly vexed. "How do you know that?"

The vendor smiled gnomically and shrugged his

shoulders, the characteristic response of Romans to replace the inconvenience of explanations.

"Doesn't Guido know anybody else but tourists and travel writers," Michael asked, pained that his position was obvious.

The vendor smiled authoritatively. "I know Guido. We all know Guido. Everyone in the tourist industry works for Guido. Guido works all the time, except on Sunday. Guido works very hard." He waved his hand around the place. "Sooner or later everyone works for Guido, even the builders and the diggers, because Guido really knows his job, but he never works on Sunday."

"Why is that?" Michael asked. "Sunday is a good day for tourists."

"True," the vendor said, apparently willing to discuss the problems of his trade, but the Church does not permit him. Sunday is the day for the Church and the family, and the tourists are very unhappy on Sunday. But they should be grateful. Because of the Church, Rome wasn't bombed."

Once again Michael was impressed by the fortunes of war. "True," he said also. "One would never know there had been a war here."

"True," the vendor said. "We should all be grateful that Rome was spared. Are you interested in pictures about the war?"

"Not especially. Only curious because everything seems so normal."

"Everything is normal. Even the war was normal. I have pictures of Il Duce. Would you like to see one?" He rummaged in a cigar box on his cart and took out a snapshot of Mussolini in a bathing suit, with his arm around his mistress. "My brother took this picture. He had a concession at Vecchia Pineta where Mussolini swam. It's worth a fortune to have a picture like this. And this one," he took out the photograph of Mussolini hanging upside down by his heels. "My Uncle Dante took this one. He went to America in 1938 and came back with the American army. These are very special pictures."

They had no value for Michael's guidebook. His editor

would veto them, but they were interesting souvenirs. "How much?" he asked.

"One dollar for the both."

"One dollar! That's a fortune, half the price of my room."

"Two dollars for a room!" The vendor spit. "I can find you a cheaper place."

"Not necessary," Michael said quickly, "I'm on an expense account and can afford the extra dollar."

"Then you can afford a dollar for these pictures."

But Michael did not make an offer and the vendor slipped them back into his cigar box, disdainful of Michael's inability to grasp an opportunity. "It's o.k., my friend. You work for Guido. I know Guido. He's my friend. He's not a bad guide."

Against his better judgment, Michael leaped to Guido's defense. "What do you mean not a bad guide?"

The vendor scratched his unshaven cheek. "He's a good guide," he said with pompous generosity. "Believe me, my friend, stay with Guido, in the Forum, in the Vatican, the Via Veneto, he's the best. But not in the catacombs. You want to see the Catacombs?"

"I've seen them," Michael said tersely.

"Ah, I see," the vendor said, "you saw them with Guido. With Guido no one can truly see the catacombs, because Guido is not from Rome. I am from Rome. Guido is from Trieste. Guido can't read the stones. He can't read Latin or Greek. He does not know what the signs mean," he said with disgust. "If you want to see the catacombs you should go with my uncle Caius. He's an archeologist in the museum in Naples. You know the famous museum in Naples? My uncle graduated from a university in America. He can read the stones. He can read Latin and Greek and Hebrew, and knows what the signs mean. He will be here on Sunday. He has permission from the pope and he can take you to the catacombs and read the stones for you. He will be happy to do this. I know my uncle."

"Don't bother," Michael said.

"No bother," the vendor said.

"I'll be busy on Sunday."

"Why, do you go to church on Sunday?"

"I don't go to church, but it doesn't matter. I'm flying back on Monday and I need the day to finish my notes."

The vendor dismissed this contemptuously. "How can you finish your notes until my uncle shows you Rome? My uncle Caius is very smart. He has lived here all his life. Believe me, he knows Rome better than Guido, he knows Rome better than anyone, better than the pope, but don't tell Guido that."

The tourist temptation of an unscheduled experience attracted Michael, but caution seemed advisable: the vendor was a stranger. "Thank you," Michael repeated and began his retreat. "Thank you for the offer, but I really need to pack on Sunday." He was seized by sudden alarm and turned and ran to catch the train back to Rome.

Luckily, he returned to his pension just as Guido's car drove up in front of it. "Ah, Americans," Guido said, catching sight of him like a naughty boy with his fingers in the jar of peanut butter. Michael confessed that he had not taken a siesta, but had gone to Ostia Antica instead. "Met one of your vendors there," he said, to establish a professional reason for his escapade, but Guido snapped at this as if he had caught a fly in his mouth. "Vitale! You met Vitale. Vitale's a liar! What did he tell you, what? I bet he told you his uncle is an archeologist in the museum in Naples. That's a lie. Caius is a stonecutter for the cemeteries. I know what Vitale was doing in Ostia Antica. This is the thanks I get for giving him work. He tries to steal my business."

He put the car in gear and they lurched forward. They climbed the Janicular, wrapped in Guido' surly silence and reached the top, luckily, just as the sun was setting in a conspiracy of light and stone. Rome was spread out beneath the ray of the heavens portentously. The view was inspirational and Guido recovered his spirits. Buses and carloads of tourists wound up the hill with them. Dozens of people watched the lights of the city go on in sync with the stars in the sky.

The next day they spent seeing Rome's environs, Villa d'Este and Hadrian's Villa. Michael would have to fend for himself on Sunday. The loneliness of it crept in already by

Saturday evening as he sat in the plaza around the Fontana di Trevi and watched the buses of tourists arrive until midnight. They came like pilgrims to the famous landmark, gratefully threw their money into the fountain, boarded their buses and went back to their hotels. He climbed the steps to his room. Some time during the night the buses ceased. Roman boys with their pants rolled up above their knees waded into the fountain to retrieve the money thrown into it, amazed at the largess of Americans. Some time during the night, the last boy whispered, "Ciao," and the last pair of high heels walked down the street. Some time in the morning, at the first sign of dawn, Michael heard the marvellous murmur of water in his sleep, waves on a foreign beach, Brighton in Brooklyn, warm sands covering multitudes of tracks. A beam of sunlight penetrated his left eye like a pointer pressing into the layers of his brain, stirring memory of friends and family. He woke, struggling to remember where he was, what day it was, dreading the day, feeling the dispossession of the traveller, space without relevance.

Sabbaths are difficult for tourists. Cities gather themselves into family unions, families vacate cities, go on picnics, to the beaches, or retreat into backyards behind fences and walls. In Jerusalem everyone has a house to go to for the noonday meal, or goes to Tel Aviv; in Rome everybody climbs aboard a Vespa and leaves. Houses and stores are shut. Only the tourist places stay open, museums, the Vatican, the Forum.

Michael tried the Vatican again, but alone, its crowds and huge spaces, built for the imperial sensibility, swallowed him up. The Forum, on the other hand, was empty and hot. Cats eyed him from behind marble pillars as if he was a stranger in their domain. He walked along the Tiber, envying tourists who walked in pairs. He crossed the Ponte Fabricio and wandered into the flea market in Porta Portese. But once in, he could not get out, and again felt swallowed up, as if he had fallen into a funnel of narrow streets packed with shoppers. Women covered with dirty white aprons exhorted him in Italian to buy a birdcage, a footstool, a box of ribbons. The debris of centuries was stacked on tables and hung from makeshift lines: cloths, damasks and tapestries; old books in cartons: Cicero,

Suetonius, the Medici, Michelangelo, Savonarola, Guide to the Catacombs, Guide to The Vatican, Guide to the Villas, books on The Age of the Emperors, the Age of the Popes. Crucifixes and busts of emperors jostled each other on stands, replicas of ancient coins, little marble pantheons, the relics of history in bronze, our splendid idolatries. He did not understand Italian beyond emergency expressions and smiled vacantly at the barkers' urgings. Some whispered messages to him in broken English, "Change money, cigarettes, cameos." Jars of olives and tubs of cheese whetted his appetite, but a variety of worries suppressed it: inability to communicate and fear of being cheated. His distress was diverted by a familiar face that bobbed up from behind a table piled with cloths. "My friend," Vitale called to him with succulent pleasure, "I told you I would see you today. Everybody comes to Porta Portese on Sunday."

"I thought you worked for Guido," Michael said irritably.

"I do, I do, but not on Sunday. I told you. On Sunday there is no work with Guido, so I work here." He held his hands out providentially. "So how fortunate that you are here now too. Now I can take you to meet my family and you will see for yourself true Romans. Guido is not a true Roman."

Being a tourist is a schizophrenic experience. Michael was happy to be rescued, but suspicious of his rescuer. Vitale, however, was not to be dissuaded. Michael's being there was a sign of fate to him. His motorbike, he informed him as if this was an omen, was on hand, parked by the side of his table. He unlocked it and told his partner to mind the business for the day.

Michael was not sure whether he had agreed to the invitation or not, but he ran after Vitale through the aisles of pushcarts, tables, vendors, boxes of ribbons, pens and pins and books, down through tunnels of streets packed with people, worried that he would lose sight of him and be sucked into a side tunnel. But when Vitale revved up the motorbike in a plaza, Michael's doubts took firmer shape: riding on the back of Vitale's motorbike was definitely a dubious thing to do. He mumbled expressions about not intruding. "No problem," Vitale said with persuasive optimism, "get on." Distrustful, nevertheless Michael mounted the bike and grabbed Vitale around his waist. They sped out of the Trastevere, across the Ponte Fabricio towards the Teatro di Marcello settling its old stones in a field of wild anemones, into a neighborhood of Corinthian columns lying about in medieval courtyards, and medieval houses brought up-to-date with new windows, into the Via della Reginella, "the only street of the ghetto that has survived," Vitale told him. Balconies, potted plants and fluttering laundry decorated the architecture. Old women sitting outside on stools mended impressive piles of clothes. Rows of shops, shoemakers, repair shops of everything, cafés, and multitudinous strollers defined the neighborhood. They entered the Via del Portico di Ottavia at the Via di S. Maria del Pianto, "the very spot where Titus and Vespasian met after the fall of Jerusalem. Guido did not tell you this?" Vitale asked, and parked his motorbike in front of his house ornamented with balcony and a dozen potted ferns growing in this historical humus. He swung open the door to the family gathered for their afternoon meal, two aunts, two uncles, a cousin, an elderly grandfather, a fat grandmother with a large grey bun perpetually slipping from its moorings of two pins; Vitale's parents, three brothers and a sister with raven black hair, Gypsy black eyes and blood red lips. Her name, Domitilla, alarmed Michael. Chairs were found. A steaming plate of pasta and spicy broccoli was placed in front of him; fried artichokes, spinach, bread and olives were pushed toward him, wine was poured.

Vitale made the introductions: one Aunt Cara Regina, sister to Vitale's grandmother, shorter and fatter with portentous breasts in black dress, a widow and a chain smoker; one Aunt Giulia, sister to Vitale's father, also short but not fat and her grey hair was doubtfully bobbed. Her husband, an uncle, was a slight man, exactly the same size as she was. A photograph of him on the sideboard showed that this had not always been so. In white uniform decorated with medals from the First World War he had been a head taller than her. Their wedding picture revealed that he had been taller than her even then. Other pictures on the sideboard revealed Aunt Cara Regina to have had normal sized breasts at one time. Her eyes gleamed with revolutionary malice into the sunlight of a Palestinian desert where she had gone as a pioneer.

Vitale and his sister were photographed at every event in their lives, Vitale in barmitzvah suit, Domitilla in a graduation dress. At every stage her eyes were the same and looked into the camera with precocious disdain. The three brothers, Umberto, Cesare and Amato, unlike Vitale, were burly and leaned against a fallen marble column where they worked as dockhands, three heads covered with dark curly hair, their faces bronzed as old coins. An aunt in a lace dress and garden hat, perhaps Giulia, was self-consciously delicate. A picture of Uncle Dante at Brighton Beach in Brooklyn, a bachelor of long standing who had tried America, hung next to his picture of himself in an American soldier's uniform. Uncle Giuseppe with a plumed helmet shook hands with the Emperor Vittorio Emanuele. A framed letter from Garibaldi, autographed to an ancestor, had pride of place above the menorah. Everyone spoke little English, except for Uncle Dante who had tried America, and Domitilla who worked for the government as a translator.

"Michael is a writer from America," Vitale said.

Everyone was impressed, except Uncle Dante who took this information with unsettling amusement.

"He writes travel books about places in Europe for a big company in America."

"Ah," they exclaimed, impressed again.

"He is writing a book about Rome for Guido."

"For Guido?" Vitale's father said. They fastened their gaze on Michael and suspended further impressions.

"Guido is Touristrotter's agent in Rome," Vitale explained to them.

"An agent from America?" his father asked. A wave of dismay went about the room.

Vitale's sister spoke. Her incredible lips parted. "No, Papa, not for America. For a tourist business in America." She translated this into Italian for their benefit. They registered approval again.

"America is interested in Rome?" Uncle Giuseppe asked.

"Well, of course," Michael said, "everyone is interested in Rome."

"Ah," they exclaimed. Actually they were not surprised by this, but gratified to hear it corroborated by an American. Except for Aunt Cara Regina and Uncle Dante, no one had ever been anywhere or cared to go anywhere. Aunt Giulia's husband had drifted in from Milan to marry her forty years ago. It was not a surprise that she would not leave and that he had stayed. Aunt Cara Regina had come back to take care of her sick mother. Once back, she married and stuck. Her husband would not leave. That was not a surprise either. The outside world might as well have been the moon. Uncle Dante returned after the war, "now that Mussolini was dead." They always knew he would. Except for Aunt Cara, who was a puzzle to them, ambition to be anywhere else was unknown to them. Suggestions to travel "and see the world" brought the comment, "Rome is the world. Everybody comes here." They were Rome's most loyal citizens. Now that the war was over, it did not surprise them that Americans came here. Where would rich Americans want to go? As for themselves, all their relatives and friends, their neighbors and shopkeepers, cousins and aunts and uncles had always known each other forever and ever. They all remembered the same things, the same events, the same sorrows, the same enigmas, the same deaths. They were Rome's oldest citizens. They had been shaped with the shaping of time like its stones and its landscape.

"True," Vitale's grandfather said. "There are many tourists here now. Wherever I walk there are foreigners. There are no more Romans." They laughed politely, except for Aunt Cara Regina, who said, "We are the only Romans left."

Uncle Dante said, "But we are no longer free to urinate in the streets as we used to. Americans are offended by this."

This was a sobering thought. "Where do Americans urinate?" Vitale's grandfather asked, "when they are in the streets?"

"Are there toilets in the streets?" Vitale's mother asked, prepared to believe that anything was possible in America.

Vitale's grandmother straightened her bun. She rarely spoke and rumor in the family had it that she could not hear, but she refused to wear a hearing aid. What was there to hear?

His father said, "In America I have heard that there are

still Indians. Are they the oldest citizens in America?"

"Not exactly," Michael said. "They're not thought of that way."

"That is not the government's policy," Aunt Cara Regina said pointedly. Everyone ignored her remark in order not to give offense to their American visitor, but Aunt Cara Regina went on, "We are the oldest citizens here." Everyone ignored this remark too, and silence followed. Vitale's grandfather finally said, to give Aunt Cara her due because he knew one had to, "True." He was indifferent to this issue, but said as a matter of record and to give Aunt Cara her due, "We were here before Caesar." They waited for Michael to say something to this, but the statement puzzled him. Instead, he said, "The Indians really would prefer something else." Aunt Cara Regina grunted.

Vitale's mother said, "Caesar was good to us. We named our first son after him, Giuliano. He was handsome, a good swimmer, he worked in Ponte Vecchio where Mussolini used to swim. Do you know Ponte Vecchio? The Nazis took him away. I have his picture here." She took out the locket from around her neck.

Vitale's grandmother rocked on her chair and straightened her bun.

"True," Aunt Cara said, "we did not always live here. We lived first in Trastevere. From the time of Caesar until the time of the Pope Paul lV. You have been in Trastevere? Trastevere is very beautiful. We used to live in Trastevere before the pope locked us into the ghetto."

"That was the old pope from long ago," Vitale's grandfather explained. His grandmother straightened her bun again and hummed to herself.

"The Pope, Paul lV," an uncle said.

"He was bad to the Jews," Vitale's mother said.

"Not all the popes were bad," Vitale's grandfather said, to set the record straight. "Pope Leo Xll enlarged the ghetto. He was good to the Jews."

"But he shut the liquor stores," Umberto said.

"True. He was good to the Jews, but bad to the Christians," Aunt Cara laughed ostentatiously. They all laughed too, to be agreeable, for they had heard her say this a hundred times.

Vitale's sister wet her lips devilishly. Michael was startled by the glisten. A drop of saliva sparkled like a diamond in the petal red. "You should not bore our guest with these old stories," she said. "You should talk about today."

"About today?" Vitale's father asked speculatively. He would like to know how Americans felt about the war, but remembered that Italy and America had been enemies. Perhaps he should not remind Michael of that either. It was kind of America to send a writer to Italy.

Aunt Cara Regina ignored him. She had other subjects she wished to discuss with this American visitor. "We are the only Romans left in Rome. You should write about us in your book."

Michael was embarrassed. "I don't choose the subjects," he said. They were amazed by this. They had heard that in America everyone wrote and said whatever they wished to. Michael sensed that his response was not impressive, perhaps not believed. Domitilla eyed him satirically. "In a guidebook," he said, laboring to choose words that would be understood, "one writes about subjects that have pictures to go with them."

"Pictures!" Vitale's grandfather said.

"Pictures!" his mother repeated. "We have many pictures," and she ran to get their photo albums.

"He doesn't mean pictures like that," Domitilla yelled after her. "He means historical pictures, pictures of monuments and famous buildings."

They thought about this for a moment. "No problem," Vitale said. "You know il Teatro di Marcello. It is the oldest building in Europe. We hid there when the Germans were here, everyone in the ghetto, hundreds of us, because we know all the secret rooms."

"Yes," Uncle Giuseppe confirmed. "No problem. We will go there and take a picture."

"He doesn't mean pictures like that either," Domitilla yelled. Vitale's grandfather ssshhhed her for her brazen tone, but Aunt Cara did not care. Three amulets, a chai sign, a mogen David, and the Hand of God competed for space in the cleavage between her breasts.

"What then?" Vitale's grandfather asked.

His brothers did not care. They finished eating and left to join the passeggiata, the evening stroll where there would be girls to look at. Aunt Giulia also excused herself and took her husband home because she predicted he would have a bad stomach within the hour. "Too much food," she said in Italian, by way of stating that the meal had been wonderful.

Vitale's father said, "You should take him to see Caius. He will know what to show him." Vitale's grandmother nodded her head so that her bun slipped out from its moorings.

"True," Vitale said. "You remember I told you my uncle was an archeologist."

Uncle Dante snorted, "A gravedigger."

Vitale's grandmother muttered in Italian that he had a foul mouth.

"Come," Vitale said, "I will take you to see my uncle."

Michael was happy to leave because the conversation had not gone well, but he wished also to stay for Domitilla's sake. Her anger was so interesting. Her lips were so wet with fury. His eyes were torn from their sockets as he said goodbye and his glance fell on her. He said silently through the air that he would return, but she knew he wouldn't. Outside, he said it was getting late and he should get back to his room to pack. Vitale countered that it would be a shame for him not to meet his uncle. Michael protested, but Vitale revved up the motorbike and they sped away down the Corso to the Piazza del Popolo, to the Via Nomentana where the palace took up the entire block. Twilight was settling on the place like grey velvet. Old trees grew there. The ground beneath them was soft with the moss that accumulates in undisturbed places of shade. Vitale parked his motorbike beneath a tree and found an opening in the ground nearby and called to his uncle. "Caius works down there in the catacombs," he explained. Michael shivered with memory. Vitale's uncle soon emerged like a giant gnome, the biggest man Michael had ever seen, with the biggest beard, stained yellow with nicotine. His fingers were yellow, his lips were yellow, his saliva rolled yellow in his mouth. Decay and humus clung to his face and hands. "This is my uncle," Vitale said. "He knows everything about Rome. Michael is a writer from America. He works for Guido."

"Ah," his uncle said. "You should have come earlier. It is too late now." He looked up at the sky and shook his head doubtfully.

"Perhaps you can take him down to the catacombs," Vitale said. "There is light down there which my uncle has put in himself," he told Michael proudly, but Michael shivered at the suggestion. "I have seen the catacombs," he said desperately.

"Yes, but with Guido, no doubt," Caius said.

"What's the difference?" Michael said irritably, "bones are bones."

"Not our bones," Caius retorted. "Our ancestors are buried here."

"These are the best catacombs in Rome," Vitale explained. "They are right underneath Mussolini's palace, and no one knew they were here until a few years ago."

Terror gave Michael courage, and worry that he was being bamboozled as a tourist discouraged his interest. He looked at his watch and said, "It's getting late. I have to get back to pack." Caius squinted at him in the darkening air. He stood by the opening to the passage like a sentinel piqued by Michael's resistance to his treasures. Michael was sorry he disappointed him, he disappointed himself, but the force that shaped his terror was stronger than good manners. He shook Caius' hand, but resisted his invitation and begged Vitale to drive him back to his pension.

He returned to his room, relieved and unsettled with longings: Domitilla's lips called to him. Impulses seized and drained him. But decisions about his going and his coming were not his to make. Flight plans dictated them, and he packed without enthusiasm. It was too late, he had found her too late, the arrow of his destiny was pointed homeward. But when he heard his name called from the street below an hour later, hope flamed in his heart. It was not, however, Domitilla. It was Vitale, waving to him to come down. "Come down, come down, I have something to give you." Hope flamed again: perhaps it was a message from Domitilla. It was not. It was a gift from Vitale, the photographs of Mussolini. "Take them,"

Vitale said, "Here is something to remember us by. Maybe someday you will return to Italy and my uncle will show you around. But come directly to see me, don't tell Guido." Already the future too was problematic, not only the past. "Why not?" Michael asked, suspicion about Vitale aroused by Guido's warnings.

The difficulty for Vitale was a matter of fate, la forza del destino, to be taken philosophically and cautiously. He shrugged his shoulders: "Guido's the boss."

Michael thanked him for the pictures, regretting they were not of Domitilla instead, and went back to his room. Guido came for him in the predawn morning and drove him to the airport in the company car. "Arrivederci," Guido said companionably, shaking his hand. "Ciao, bon voyage, safe journey, regards to America and tell everybody to come to Rome."

Michael boarded the airplane. Ineptness supplemented fatigue as he settled into his seat. The dawn was grey. The light seemed to have been sucked out of the air. He made out the figure of Guido on the ground, waving affably against the rising sun, kissing the tips of his fingers goodbye, or greeting the sun.

THE ETERNAL ROMAN

Unpleasant dreams can burden one the whole day, though some go away upon waking. With a blink of the eyes, the psyche crosses the boundary between the night world and the day world, and the subconscious repository of multiple pasts makes an adjustment to the salvic standards of the workaday world. But some dreams will not go away. They persist in invading the common day. Like a weed, like a growth from the winter underground that has no place in the established terrain, they push their way up. Persistently, night after night, year after year, they ferment beneath the ground and come spring, come any random spring, they are there between the bricks again. Ask any gardener about this! The persistence of growths from the underground is astonishing.

That's how Paolo Christiano felt about the bad dreams he began having a year or so ago--perhaps it's been two years-- who can recall the onset of change? Who can say when a habit begins--a disease--a thought--since his son married, or just before--since his arthritis began, or soon after? Who can say when arthritis begins? Twinges and aches--he had had them for years. But now he could not hold his pruning shears in his hands without pain--his fingers that were so important to him-- more than a means of livelihood--he saw with his fingers--knew when a fruit was ripe by the touch. Such pain was a new experience for him. Blessed, he had never known bad health. And how recast a soul of seventy? He was a sober man, sometimes withdrawn when moods of abrupt bitterness erupted in him, a forlorn jealousy that he had been cheated in life. His wife thought him surly, but otherwise a domestic man of predictable habits, home, gardening, and work.

These fingers that had given him such pleasure--he had talked to the earth with them--now a petal was too much to hold. Their pain was terrible. It reminded him of the dreams he was plagued with. Terrible pain in these dreams. His wife said it was because he rolled onto his hands while he slept, but it was not so. When he woke up, he was always on his back. The pain in his dreams belonged to someone else. This he was sure of, and he told his wife he was being transported in the night. "Some evil thing carries me away," he said. "A devil is taking me away every night."

At first she did not believe him, not because she did not share such beliefs, but because his miserable condition was a surprise and an annoyance to her. He woke her every dawn to tell her about it and to have her help him on with his work shoes. She lay on her heavy arm, her grey bun unrolled and looked as she always looked to him, bloated with contentment. He had married her out of pity and conscience. He had expected her to suffer, but it turned out she would be happy in hell. "Teresa!" he hissed. "Teresa, you want I should die of pain and hunger?"

"I want you should go to hell," she murmured, and rolled her heavy hips into place.

Her movement made his mood ominous. She had made her quietus with every dark thing, and had a joke about it. In view of the bad dreams he was having, which she knew about-- he confessed more to her than to his priest--it was bad for her to say that. Now that he was growing old--faster than she--there were more differences than ever between them. Sometimes he thought she took an opposite position only to vex him. When their son married out of the faith, at first he forbade him in the house, but she shrugged her shoulders and said it was no worse than his nieces. "None of them is Italian here."

For his part, he did not mind the girl, if she had married someone else. He did not like her--there did not seem to be anything to like or dislike--but he did not mind her. She was too skinny, but so were his nieces. No hips. He tried not to think about this. She couldn't cook either, but neither could his nieces. He couldn't visit her home because there was nothing to eat there. He could not understand this. He had understood that Jews like to eat, like Italians, but he saw how she sat at the table and ate half of everything they served her.

"It's very good, absolutely delicious, very good, but I'd have to run five miles to work it off tomorrow," she said cheerfully.

"Run?" He did not understand her language. "Where do you run?"

"Jog. Around the track."

"You're so skinny," he said compassionately.

"Me!" she squealed with delight. "I'm at least four pounds over."

"Four pounds! Thas' nat so bad," he said with peculiar ferocity. The glitter from the gold star around her neck caught his attention. "Four pounds!" he clicked his teeth menacingly, "an' you wear that star around your neck."

"What's that got to do with it?" his son asked, but not seriously. He knew his father made strange connections. His path of ratiocination seemed never to go where it should--where Carl thought it should go--but ended up in out-of-the-way places. He asked the question to let his wife know he was a different man from his father.

"What you marry her for?" Paolo asked. A darkness flooded his mind. "What you marry her for? For being Jewish or for being skinny?"

His son's answer did not enlighten him. His answers never did. "Neither," Carl said, "I married her for herself."

"Whas' that?" Paolo asked. He studied his son's wife and tried to find out what that was. Skinny, blonde, corrected teeth, she looked like his nieces. When they visited all together on a holiday, they all talked about the same things, diet and exercise and jogging.

Paolo shifted to his other problem. "How come she don' eat?"

"Pop," Carl said, "I told you she eats."

"I never see her eat," Paolo said vehemently.

"It's not good to eat too much," Carl said.

This was a puzzling answer to him, and he thought about it for a while. He did not wish to appear ignorant about something new in the world. "Maybe," he said, "but it must be worse to eat nothing."

Americans did not understand food. On this subject, at least, there was unity between him and Teresa. "Get up," he hissed with a final sharpness and flung the alarm clock across the room. "It's half past five."

She sensed the crisis and got into her slippers and bathrobe. "You have a bad conscience," she said to even the score, "that's why you have bad dreams."

He crumbled at this remark, and grasped his head between his hands. She sensed power, but goodnaturedly retreated. He was truly in pain. His shoes were still untied, his fingers stiffly trying to make a knot. She felt a stab of pity and contempt, remembering the power he once had.

After his breakfast, he walked to work along the shore, a ritual walk every morning. The waves pierced him with homesickness, even after forty years. He used to take Carl fishing here at night or to fly a kite in the morning, and he would say to him when the sky was clear, "Look! There! Thas' Italy," imagining he could see the outline of land.

He kept his Mediterranean habits, working from dawn to noon, with an afternoon break, walking to work in the mornings, the birds rising in the warming air at the sound of his footsteps, past the cottages with gardens along the wetlands, tarred roofs, clotheslines. His home was one of them. Roses grew best in the salt air, Mediterranean or Atlantic. The sand blew through the dry beach bushes. The waves rolled towards him. As always, he heard in them the waves of other oceans and the voices from his past, his family, friends, girls he had lusted for. The foam curled over his boots. The tide was rising and brought in debris. He moved away from the water to keep his shoes dry, but walked close to the edge and watched the bits of wood float in--always bits of wood--was there a wreckage some place?--apple cores, wet matches, a prophylactic. Always that too, wreckage and seed thrown into the ocean, apples and pieces of wood from a ship that's gone down somewhere.

Such thoughts came and went in him and made him restless. He followed a footpath that meandered over the dunes with a human intention but whose purpose was lost, for the path ran out in the sand. When he arrived at work, the truck was there, Carini and Bros. He was an extra hand, moonlighting in the spring when the work was heavy, doing the small jobs, flowerbeds of pansies and anemones. He put on his gardening gloves as much to hide his swollen fingers as to work with them. By the end of the day his shoulders were tense with the expectation of pain, and his mood was grim with the knowledge that nothing would make the pain go away, that there was no position he could shift to, to make it better. It would not ease, no matter how courageous and enduring he was.

He woke every morning with the sweat of this nightmare, that the pain would triumph, even though in his dream there was no pain in his hands. It was transferred to someone else. During the night, it was miraculously transferred to someone else. He told Teresa about this. She believed him, but she did not want to hear about it. It confused her, and she advised him to go to the priest. He fell back on his pillow and dozed and listened for sounds in his head that would tell him what was going on. Clues in the noises he was familiar with. The sound of hammering. He had been Longinus in a school play when he was a child and had hammered the cross together. No pain in his hands then. What does an eight year old know about what will become of him when he is seventy? He had carried a spear and a shield and a hammer, a real spear and a real shield, and they were not too heavy for him. He was very strong for his age. He had carried the sword like a true Roman, the priest had said, and he did not envy the boy who played Jesus. He died later, just before Paolo left for America. He was thrown from his motorcycle, sixteen feet into the air. The priest said at the funeral that his was the greatest glory, for he had portrayed Jesus. Paolo stood at his graveside and searched through the other faces. There was Teresa. She was Mary one year and Magdalen the next, the year they became engaged. Primavera she was that year, with a garland of flowers in her hair. Primavera, like the joke says. Spring and autumn. She was fifteen. He was already thirty. In his sleep he was crying. "Teresa," he said, "it is time to get up." She played possum and pretended not to hear him. Primavera. She got up grudgingly, tossed the ragged tail of her grey hair over a shoulder, and bent own to tie his shoes. She was not unsympathetic, but it was difficult to believe that such a big man could not tie his laces. He walked five miles a day, carried a trowel and a shovel. He had always been a strong man. "Hot blooded," he laughed, proudly lascivious. In time he became domesticated, but not so that she forgot how he had been. It seemed unreasonable that he should wake her for this, but he could not tell her that each of his moments were now planned, that he was jealous of what was left of his strength and hoarded it for the things he could not do without.

He moved inland, across the dunes. The sand lifted in the air and whistled through the dry grass on top of them. Behind a dune, sticking out like rag dolls, he caught sight of the lovers' legs, hers skinny, his hairy, naked and writhing. Not for the first time he saw them. Lover's lane. Every strip of beach in the night. The dune covered the rest of them. Except for their little pile of clothes which flamed against his eyeballs.

It took him the whole morning to recover. He worked intensely, fighting the pain in his hands, the images that rose in his mind, the bitterness that he could not hold a flower without pain.

In the evening Carl and his wife came to dinner. Barbara was her name. She was studying to be a psychologist. She had already graduated from one college, and went to another. She studied all week, and played tennis on Saturday and Sunday. Sometimes they came by on their way to the tennis courts, the little star gleaming on her white clothes, but she never spoke about anything but dieting and jogging and playing tennis. He was curious about this, but did not know what to ask her. She never spoke about her past, except to say once that her mother's family had died in Bergen-Belsen--that's why she had so few relatives at the wedding. What did she have to do with those faces he saw staring from dark, threatening photographs, this thin, unspotted girl. Primavera. She defeated his ideas.

In his dream the hillside was swollen with summer heat. All winter the hillside had been as barren as a planet. Now it was tense with expectation. He, Longinus, had been the guardian of this landscape for thirty winters. He counted the skulls at the end of each season, from the time of Pilate to the time of Florus. No one obstructed him in this work, though the plotters and the revolutionaries did not dissemble their enmity. The priests had embarrassed, degraded eyes. The old women looked away when he passed by. The faces of the young girls became vacant when he approached them. Their eyes became stones when they glided past him. The curse of empire, that it fell to him to put them to death. Primavera. To death.

Every summer the hills were covered with poppies, with roses and anemones, with bodies swaying on the crosses. The hill was heavy with the odor of flowers and the smell of decaying women, the musk of their organs. His loins were weak, his sword heavy, his loins so weak every morning when he took down their bodies, some with their children crawling on the grass near them, like lambs surrounding the stricken she-goat. Biological facts governed even on the cross; dying, their breasts filled with milk at the sound of this hunger.

It is a special burden to crucify a woman, and Paolo woke in a confusion of dread and desire, awakened by a shuddering in his loins. The woman beckoned to him from the cross. Her mutilations were healed. Her body was whole. Her husband carried her down the hill while he, Paolo, was left, a lonely soldier with the passions of lonely soldiers in alien lands. His knees weakened. His loins were heavy. He wanted to fall. To fall among the poppies. The sword in his hand was too heavy. He wanted to fall. "Teresa," he called out, "I cannot bear these dreams anymore."

She did not argue with him this morning. She even felt sorry for him, there was such fear in his voice. "I tell you the devil is taking me away," he cried. "It is an omen of my death." He said it, finally, the thing he had feared to say.

Compassion moved her to ask, "Where does he take you?" though she was afraid to speak about the subject.

He took command of himself. He twirled his hand in the air, shrugged his shoulders mockingly, and said, "Would you believe to Golgotha?" The answer impressed her.

He nodded gravely, but a smile on his lips and an old obscene expression in his eyes made them both laugh. "Why not?" he asked. "You think I am too much of a sinner?"

She put his breakfast on the table and laughed too, but did not ask him any more questions and he too, walking to work later, was enveloped in a different mood. He was bitter that she had not asked him anything more. Like that, with a snap of their fingers they went from laughing together to recriminations. She said later, "You should tell the priest all this. He will know what it means," and he knew that she did not want to hear anything more. She washed her hands of him.

He did not have to rouse her the next morning. She roused herself and made his breakfast, and though he had held it against her for years that she got out of bed in the morning begrudgingly, this morning her alacrity made him feel mean. When she bent down to help him, the look in her eyes slandered him.

"Awright, awright, I will tell the priest," he said. It was a retaliatory move. He wanted her to feel he was doing it because of her. She understood and resented this. His whole life he never took responsibility for his wicked deeds. Not even for his own dreams. She snorted to herself. For her Paolo was not a likely candidate for a vision.

Father Melita was also cautious. "Whom do you see on the cross?" But Paolo, who should have been eager to disburden himself, looked around the room with a disagreeable expression. The furniture was not in the right place. At first he thought the crucifix was missing, then he spotted it on the wall between the draped windows. The new priest had re-arranged everything. He told Father Melita: the figure on the cross is veiled, but beckons to him.

"Beckons?" the priest asked.

Paolo crooked his finger coyly "Like this," he said. Father Melita asked him analytically, "Where are you when she beckons?"

He tried to concentrate on the answer. "Me? I am standing beneath the cross. I am looking up." The young priest's appearance disconcerted him. He was as young as his son. "Why do you ask me so many questions! Enough!" He had been tortured for a year with these dreams--maybe two years--he could not say--ever since his hands had become cursed--once he had been strong--he had carried a sword and a shield and the hammer--it was Easter--everyone came--his parents--his brothers and sisters--everyone in the village--he had been chosen because of his strength--he was tall for his age --there were flowers everywhere on the stage--lillies and gardenias--the audience in the dark applauded him--his brothers and sisters--his father called out, "Paolo. Longinus! My son!" He plunged the sword into the side of his friend and there was a burst of noise, a shower of lillies, the applause roared in his head. His father shouted over the crowd, "My son! Longinus! My eternal Roman!"

Ah! Father Melita thought he understood. He said eagerly--"You were a child--chosen for the part--you mustn't feel guilty--it was only a play--all these years--you've harbored guilt feelings about the part you played." The expression in Paolo's eyes was not encouraging. His eyeballs slithered beneath his lids. He did not wish to contradict this priest, but he found himself saying, "No, Father, it was not like that-- everyone applauded--even later when I was a grown man-- everyone remembered--Teresa--her mother said when she heard we were getting married--oh, him, Longinus! Everyone liked me. Everyone applauded." Father Melita persisted. "Surely--" he groped for the proper word, "surely your performance was excellent, but you felt," he hesitated, "forlorn at the part you were made to play."

"In the play I was the Roman," Paolo said indignantly. It was useless to talk to this priest. He felt, again, alone inside his head, a swelling silence in there, with muffled voices. Outside the ticking of the clock on the mantle. He lived alone in a different world from the others. No one could find the path to it, no matter how much he tried to show them where it was. It was useless, and he got up to leave. The priest told him to come again. He told him to write his dreams down, to keep a journal of them. "Try to see who is on the cross," he said. "Try to see."

"I am tired, Father," Paolo said dejectedly. "I do not wish to see anything. I do not want to dream anymore." He had expected the priest to know how to stop his dreams, but the priest wanted him to keep a record of his dreams. Teresa helped him on with his jacket and buttoned it for him. Perhaps it would be better to go back to his dreams and stay there. There was no pain in his hands then. He was emperor of the world, a powerful Roman who carried a sword and a shield. His hands could hold a woman, bouquets of them, their skulls like flowers broken from their stems. "That is who I see on the cross," he told the priest a few days later. "I see her, the one who spied for her husband."

"Come," he beckoned to him that night, "come, I will show you who is on the cross." He took Father Melita up the hill in the dawn when he did his work. By noon, the odor was too bad to stay there. Even the families of the dying could not approach their kin, the hill was so overpowered with stench. He worked in the early dawn, followed by the other soldiers who came for whatever clothing and sandals they could scavenge from the unclaimed bodies. He went through the rows of the crucified to see who was dead and who was still living, who could be bribed for reasons of mercy or for their belief in the resurrection.

"Come," he said to the priest, and crooked his finger. This was his kingdom. Skulls and crosses on the hills surrounding the city, jackals prowling in the distance, the half eaten heads of children next to their mothers. The wretched sounds of pain from those who were still alive. "Come, I will show you. You want to know who is on the cross. I will show you. Follow me. She is on the top of the hill. I know her very well. She used her motherhood to play the spy--carried messages in her shawl--I have been watching her for more than a year, deciphering the messages she carries--listening to their secret plots. There are others like her. They think they go undetected, but we have more spies than they do. I have let them pass through our lines for months, but soon I will catch this little fish from the Galilee."

He woke, trembling, no different from other mornings. Teresa was already up, her bun unravelled, watching him with her old eyes. He had been trembling in his sleep. His face was twitching. He would not let her help him on with his shoes, and he left for work with his laces undone, his clothes unbuttoned. She saw that the situation was grave, and she called her son as soon as Paolo was gone. It was six o'clock in the morning, but her anxiety would not let her wait another hour. She rasped into the telephone, "He is losing his mind."

Carl came at once--but to what? Teresa was evasive. She knew what she must not talk about--visions--devils--dreams--but what was left to talk about if not these? "Better you should let the priest explain," she said adroitly.

He went reluctantly. In the little he heard over the telephone from his mother, he heard nothing to alarm him. A bad dream! He went to appease her. "I'm already up," he said to Barbara, "might as well go."

"People have bad dreams," he told Father Melita. "So what? I have them myself."

"He has them all the time," Father Melita said. "Every night."

"He's getting old. He has severe arthritis. His hands hurt him when he sleeps. I know my father. He's a proud man. It humiliates him that someone has to help him on with his shoes. He was a very strong man. Don't make something else out of this."

Father Melita understood the accusation. He made the case as plain as he could in Carl's terms. "Your father was here this morning. Agitated. Laces untied. Clothes unbuttoned. Said he must confess that he was guilty. I tried to make him see that such feelings were nonsense. But it's not Jesus he sees on the cross."

"Who does he see?" Carl asked, flagrantly sarcastic.

One cannot talk across a gulf of time. The ticking of the clock on the mantle made its own statement. "I don't encourage him, believe me," Father Melita said. "He dreams he is crucifying a woman."

Carl felt a sour disgust. His brain filled up as if someone had blown gas into it. Why does sickness have to take the form of obscenity?---why don't old people go mad in pleasant ways? He wanted to badger---"So he isn't a visionary--just a sick old man who can't take the pain anymore." But he didn't. He thanked the priest for his help, and turned at the door and said, "What he needs is a doctor, I mean a psychologist, something like that."

"Of course," Father Melita said. "I advised him to see someone. But I also advised him to come here as often as possible. That's what I'm here for."

The concessionary tone deflated Carl's combativeness. He grasped, finally, the seriousness of the problem, unidentifiable as it was. He did not wish to tell Barbara. "Nothing much," he said in response to her questions, "just seems to be having a lot of bad dreams. He's getting old. His hands hurt him when he sleeps."

Teresa called three times the next week, then four times. "What does he dream about?" Barbara asked. "What difference does it make," Carl said. She was piqued. "Maybe I can help. After all, it is my field."

"It's just his hands," he said.

Soon Teresa called every morning to give a report. "Like an alarm clock," Carl said.

"I'll drop by tomorrow to say hello on my way back from the tennis courts," Barbara said.

"Don't talk to him," Carl said.

"What!"

"You know my father. It would embarrass him to talk with a woman about such a thing."

"Oh, my God!"

In the evening, she reported stiffly, "We didn't discuss a thing. Happy? He gave me a bouquet from his garden." She paused, flint-eyed. "But your mother watches him all the time and it makes him nervous, and he watches her and that makes her nervous."

Is this what declining years means? Carl thought.

Neither did the doctor suggest anything else. "He's overwrought, nothing more. His hands keep him awake at night and fatigue is making him nervous."

Paolo claimed he slept. "I sleep," he said. "A devil takes me away while I sleep."

The doctors said that insomniacs often don't know whether they sleep or not. Often they doze off, but don't remember dozing off, or when they're awake they're only partly awake. "They live in a kind of twilight zone when they get that fatigued." He prescribed sleeping pills and a painkiller for Paolo to take before he went to sleep. But Paolo would not take the pills. He insisted that his hands did not hurt him while he slept. "My hands are powerful in my dreams." He claimed the sleeping pills kept him awake and then he was in pain all night. It was bettter to sleep. He needed to go back to his dreams, and he threw the pills away. Instead he came every morning to see Father Melita, and shared every detail with him, and the details became more and more elaborate, what the crucified were wearing, who their families were, what plots were being hatched, what revolutionary groups and sub groups and counter revolutionary groups there were, even scraps of intimate talk between a husband and a wife.

Father Melita told Paolo to go on a vacation. "Back to Italy for a while." Paolo felt that he was being asked to desert his duty. This was his post, here, at the base of the hill. How could Father Melita ask him to desert it? The voices were familiar now, he understood their language. For the first time he knew what they were saying to one another, husband to wife, father to son. Father Melita--like Teresa--did not wish to know anymore. They wished him to go away, on a vacation, they called it. Again, he was alone, inside his head, alone among the crosses, the families waiting at the bottom of the hill to claim their kin, the knots of mourners, the soldiers on the hillside with him, searching for clothes and sandals. Was it true, then, that he had killed Jesus? No one, not even Father Melita wanted to know. Not even Teresa, when she knew what his hands were like. Could kill a bear. He had waited at the crossroads for her when he came home from the play, and walked beside her in the forest, among the swellings covered with moss, with wet leaves and debris, with the smell of gardenias from her hair and decay along the footpaths. Every spring it was this way. The old earth turned and uncovered herself.

"Come, Teresa," he said afterwards, "wasa' difference, I will marry you." She stopped trembling, but lay unpleasantly still. "It will be all right," he said, "I will marry you." He tried to joke with her. "Hey, comon."

Primavera. He did not want her to get up to help him. He did not need her anymore. "Hey, you think I am an old man." He rolled himself out of bed, laughing. The light was parting in the sky over the ocean. A flock of birds fanned out into it. The odor of flowers and salt air surged in him. His longing was terrible. He went outside to breathe the air. His garden was on the verge of blooming. Ha! Everything was beginning again, pink cyclamen, anemones, hawthorne, the desert tulip, old desires. Everything flourished in his garden, even in the sand. From beneath the silent ground even the dead branches bloomed.

Teresa came to the window and beckoned to him, punishing him with her old eyes, but afterwards, as he walked along the beach, the morning light hardened and cleansed him. The waves came into shore with their collection of things trapped in seaweed--a leather boot--a sandal--a piece of skirt--a half torn book with blurred words--such flotsam--a pile of clothing laying by the side of a dune--a crab crawling towards it --their legs so still--were they dead, or exhausted?

The sky was filled with degenerate birds. The families gathered at the bottom of the hill, desperate with cravings. The decades of crucifixions had made them wild, had turned them into crabs that creep between the rocks, salamanders licking stones for food, worms dried by the wind, left as husks, their souls gone, others like bloated frogs inflated with all manner of spiritual debris. Necromancers had invaded the countryside promising relief and like madmen whose bodies had been set on fire, the people ran in circles. Some said that the age would end, and that after the end there would be a new beginning. Others said there would only be the end. Some prayed for the end. In a house on fire only consummation made sense. But others could not imagine the end to everything and constructed provisional ends, ends that would be preludes to other ends, or to beginnings or to the beginnings of ends. But the night did not end and the house continued to burn.

Finally, after all these years, just as his term of soldiering was coming to an end, he understood every secret thing they said among themselves, but he did not tell Father Melita anymore. He kept to himself the secrets he unravelled, especially of that one who came and went with a silent smile.

"When does the daylight begin?" her husband asked her, but Yael did not answer him because she had no tongue. It had been cut out by the Roman who had crucified her father. But she heard everything very well and knew by now that a tongue was not necessary. To everything there is nothing to say. Everything was like the middle of the sea in a storm. Which way to go for safety? The answer was anywhere else. But anywhere was not Judea. It was everything and it came from everywhere, from Rome and from Parthia, from Damascus and from Egypt. Everything was an animal devouring them. Its mouth was larger than the country. In the whole land, the only safe place was in a tree.

"What do you wish, Yael?" Bar Shem teased her. Her eyes travelled out towards a cypress.

"My poor Yael," he laughed mordantly, "what would you do with that tree? You have not even the tongue of a bird to sing with, and you could not fly away. Tell me, Yael," he bit her ear with lust and greed for her stillness.

She smiled slyly. He could not tell whether it was because of him, because he bit her ear with his naked heart under the naked sun, or because she kept secrets to herself. If she could talk, she would tell him that if she had a tree it would be enough. A nest in a tree was better than the stones they lived under. On top the hill was pink and fuchsia, the color of wine, but inside it was stone. A tree was better than stone, a nest was better than a funeral chamber. Praise the birds that inhabit the air. They inhabited the bowels of the earth, her husband and his mordant followers.

"The Heavenly One will arise from His throne and wipe our tears and take His eternal children to His home. Blessed be His kingdom for ever and ever."

She neither believed or disbelieved. It was enough for her that Bar Shem loved her. She heard everything and let it be. Some had turned to worshipping the sun, others to worshipping water, the moon, the rising stars, and none knew what a Jew was anymore. She had stood with her father on the shores of the lake and listened to Rab Zakkai prophecy that the Galileans would make common cause with the Romans. Her brother had gone to the Waterbathers and preached the Kingdom to Come, and he was crucified. Her father pleaded with the people not to make war and he was crucified. Her mother sat at the bottom of the hill and turned to stone. Like her, she was silent, though she had a tongue. Her uncle contended with the priests, and the Galileans had laid hold of him and set him aflame. Bar Shem had run away to live in the desert among the holy men who would not bear arms, and all had come back with weapons to defend Jerusalem. His brother was an athlete in the gymnasium and a servant in the palace of Agrippa, the king who lay with his sister.

How was it possible for one house to contain them all?

Just as well she had no tongue to answer these questions. It was enough that she heard everything and that it sank to the bottom of her soul where it gathered layers and became an old city.

"Your silence has made your eyes deep," Bar Shem said, "and very hard. Do you see far or deep, Yael?"

Provocatively, she slid her eyes past his face and settled them on a cypress. Her silence teased and suffocated him. It evoked emotions of joy and pathos for the strange manner she had acquired in her longing to speak.

He told her his fears. The land was filled with strange shapes. Families lived in caves and tunnels. No man knew his friend except by a sign, and no more than six were loyal to each other. Those who had sworn not to bear arms had turned into warriors. Assassins had fled into the desert and turned into wailing stones. Nothing and no one remained the same throughout a day. By night all the parties had changed and become the opposite of what they were in the morning. He himself would have to kill his brother if he met him on the way. How was it possible one mother had borne them both? And he told her of his brilliant hope.

A shrewd grief suspended her judgment, but she gave herself to him as a wife and a spy, as an instrument of his plans, because her silence was his camouflage. She received instructions, heard everything, went everywhere, said nothing.

Trust no more than three
Consult with no one who appears suspicious
Do not speak with a coward about the war
With a merciless man about kindness
Do not barter with a merchant unless you know him by name

Trust your soul and the Holy One. For us there is no one else, neither watchman nor priest.

In this way she passed through the Roman lines. She carried two nails from her father's cross as charms against evil, and walked with a shawl and her son, Bar Adir, who always accompanied her. His presence stopped tongues about a woman travelling alone and kept the licentious at bay. He was her tongue and her accessory. What she could not say to the guards and the merchants, he said for her, but he rarely spoke to her because the shadow of the things she could not say crept into her eyes.

She carried a shopping basket, went to the market and knew whom to barter with. They hailed her from their tents and their stalls. "Bat El." It was a secret name, like everything else about her. Their cause was secret, their hope arcane, their methods hopeless.

Beware of the priests. They are more Roman than the Romans

Beware of the Templekeepers and those who guard the doors to the Kingdom of God

Beware of the priests who wear long robes, intone through their noses and burn incense, for they eat the fat of the flocks.

She brought her fruits back from the desert and from Jerusalem and spread them on the stony floor. Their brotherhood lived in caves and beneath the hills, in Sepphoris, in the Galilee, in Megiddo, in Ashkelon. They sent her from cave to cave with a piece of sheepskin with a message on it, "Holy Liberty," and they made plans, Simon from the tribe of Levi, John of Galilee, Eleazar from Sepphoris, Bar Shem, and his father who opposed all their plans.

"Do not do this," Rab Hanna exploded. "I know what is in your hearts. I beseech you, do not give into this council. Bear with Florus another day. He is mortal. He will die."
"Another will come in his place," Eleazar said. "Rome has many to send."
"Would that she sent us Caesar," Simon said. "Our quarrel is not with Rome but with whom Rome sends to do her work. Send us Augusta, not Pilate."
"Still, I beseech you," Rab Hanna said. "It is Florus who is here. It is Florus you must contend with. Give him what he wants. It is nothing. It is a pittance, a sullen Roman's memento of honor. Salute his cohorts on the road. Do not send Yael with a message to do otherwise. I know what is in your hearts. I know what you plan. Florus himself is nothing. Even Rome holds him in scorn, but Rome will back him. Even the queen has gone down on her hands and knees to him."
But this last only aroused them more. "Let her grovel," John said, "let her beseech, let her beg, let her whimper. What is it to us? Her lovers drink wine in Alexandria and Rome."
"Pity a people whose leaders have sunk into corruption," Rab Hanna said. "Still, she has shaved her head and has gone into mourning for the massacred. She is many things, true, an Egyptian, a Roman, but also a Hebrew, like your brother."
"In Tiberias they cannot count the dead," Simon said crossly. "Only the number of merchants who come from Parthia and dangle bells in their stalls. In Tiberias the king sleeps with his slaves and even the Hebrew has his eunuch."
"I have never been there," Eleazar laughed, drunk with sardonic anger. "They say that the donkeys of the rich are carried on the shoulders of the slaves and that the queen who mourns our dead wears a girdle worth the price of our kingdom given her by her Roman conquerors."
"Which they unwind every night," Simon roared out.
Rab Hanna covered his head with his shawl.
"My holy father," Bar Shem said, "you wish Israel well, as I do. How can our counsels be so different?"
"Where there is a clear path," Rab Hanna said, "we all

know how to go," and he stretched his trembling body out on the ground.

Bar Shem became morose again. Yael put a finger on his lips. "Here is one who hears all," he said tersely. "Her empty mouth makes her ears sharp."

"Do not send her," Rab Hanna groaned from beneath his cover.

Yael's mother stirred the ashes. Like Yael, she heard everything but said nothing, even when Yael paused behind her back. Grimly she bent towards the ashes, and would not acknowledge her going nor move nor eat until they returned. She knew how to be a stone.

Outside the night air was cold. Bar Shem wrapped Yael in her shawl. "My speechless one," he said to her, "do you have your ear to the mountain?" She nodded her head playfully. "What do you hear?" he asked, but his mood was different from hers. "I hear rumbling," he said, "but my father does not hear what I hear. The mountain is going to erupt. Tell me, Yael, can we prevail where Athens, Macedonia, Gaul and Egypt have failed?" She put a finger on his lips. "Wise Yael," he said, "wise was the Roman who cut out your tongue. But you can listen. Come back to me, Yael. Do not linger anywhere. Bar Adir will stay with you, and may the Holy One Whose Name will not part from my lips bring you both back to me," and he kissed her fingers and her lips, her hair and her eyelids and whispered into her neck, "Come back to me, Yael, come back to me."

Then she was gone. She and Bar Adir travelled along the coastal road towards Caesarea, then towards Lydda. The country was deserted and the trip tedious. Yael had no stories to tell Bar Adir, nothing to entertain him with. Sometimes he exclaimed at something in the distance, a crow sitting on a branch or a column of soldiers, and she shielded her eyes to look where he pointed.

They found a place to stay for the night in Lydda, with friends who warned them to travel fast. "The Romans march from Caesarea. They are already on the road, and the priests march from Jerusalem to greet them. Harpists and choristers go with them and they carry their holy vessels. You can already hear their songs of peace in the valley," they said with glee. Her eyes glittered too, and in the morning she and Bar Adir fled on their way, carrying their pieces of sheepskin with their message on it.

I have read this message many times, a forlorn password, a sentence folded into pieces of sheepskin. Who could imagine that it would matter to Florus. His troops have already stepped over the holy vessels. From the time of Pilate I have seen nine procurators, and not one has differed by more than a hair from the others. If I were a Judean, I would make the best of it, but they quarrel as much with themselves as with us. They dig their own graves, and she will die in one of them. Yesterday thirty-six hundred were slaughtered because of the pranks of some children who wanted to embarrass Florus and took up a collection in a basket for him. Now the flies and the gnats suck their blood, and the sky smells bad again. Every day the streets smell bad, and every step in the city smells bad. No matter what they do, they make matters worse for themselves. By morning the Judeans had captured the fortress of Antonia and we could not stay any longer, but I had my revenge. I intercepted the woman and her son inside the gate. Even in the sour smelling blackness I knew who she was. There was no use for them to call out. The Judeans had taken the porticoes to the temple and cut the communications. Still I stuffed her mouth with stones. "Wise spy," I hissed, "now deliver your message," and dragged them outside the gate and hung them. Then we drew back to Caesarea in the dark, over roads wet with blood, through a night of delirium, every inch of the way stinking with blood. Only my native air, the blessed air of Ostia, finally cleansed my nostrils when I returned home.

The waves broke on the beach with muffled sound, as if heard from a great distance, but the foam crept persistently along the shoreline with its wash of flotsam. The debris angered Paolo--pieces of wood, shawl, sandals, nails. His hands were stiffening again with pain when he believed he would no longer suffer, and a knot of dread tightened in him. "I am an innocent man," he protested. But a wind blew up and the conviction blew away with it. It had given him no peace to say it, but what was he guilty of? Perhaps he should go back to his dreams. But neither was that reasonable. Nothing in the world was reasonable nor consonant with his thoughts anymore, not the sky nor the ocean, not the world about him and the people in it, certainly not the young boy and girl behind the dune, with their little pile of clothes settled against a bush. A tumult rose in his groin, a confusion of loathing and desire and wanton aging. It swept through him with unrelieved violence at the sight of their naked bodies, the pile of clothes neatly folded beside them, the anomalous glitter of a gold star on her adolescent neck, and his boyish head sleeping on her throat. He was fated to invade their lives and entwine them forever in his confusion.

They were fated to join him in this inexplicable destiny, for with one unexpected, swift and powerful movement, he bent over them before they knew what was happening, and tore the chain from the girl's neck. Astounded, they jumped to their feet. Humiliated, they screamed inarticulate phrases in the morning wind: "What're you crazy or something! Hey, you crazy old man!"

Of course Paolo did not answer. Or turn back. Or care. He had nothing to explain to them. The ocean was too big for explanations, the sky too vast, and the trip very long before he would reach home. The boy and the girl were left on the empty beach, naked and astonished forever while Paolo walked into the ocean.

Beloved and Endangered Species

I have been climbing this mountain for millennia to bring you my answer. You have been waiting for it for millennia. I have been climbing towards you all this time. It has not been easy for me, burdened as I am with age. It has not been easy to find you, surrounded as you are by these plightful mountains. Your desire for me has been confusing, conveyed in signals of immense complexity.

Between good and evil is often only a veil, a line, a gesture, the raised hand or the outstretched palm. We can capitulate with a turn of the head, chastity lost in the wink of an eye. Immense evil can be accomplished with very simple means. So we always viewed the holy water, the wafer, the wine: on the one hand, as merely objects; on the other hand as loss of being. Rabbis asked: can these drops of water erase history and psychology? Can any *thing* signify so much?

Through all these questions I have been climbing through cutting glass and up ponderous hillsides, under unkind suns and through devious pathways that made me weep with frustration and fear of duplicity. All this while you have waited for me, for my capitulation, to yank me once and for all off my mountain and into your valley. Up to now, I resisted from ignorance or from perversity, as you always said.

What was I defending? The indefensible, you always said. Psychology more than history prevailed in your answer, for what is so hard to brook as someone else's perversity. Your people became furious that their god was scorned. Why my yea? I asked them. You have millions of yeas. You have half the world now. Why my yea?

I have had to learn how to hide in rocks and crevices to escape detection, to live with the lizards. I have learned the ways of snakes and termites and stones, and how to slip between the shadows, how to live between the boots of soldiers. I have gone through cycles of being human and animal as I snatched at any means to stay alive. All unnecessary, you said. It all could have been prevented by my yea. I am the author, you said, of my own suffering, my own cause, my own effect. What so awkward in history as a man who eats himself to prevent others from eating him.

Perversity has its daring. This insight into the process of self cannibalism suspended me in the abyss of dark ages. Perhaps it was psychology and history more than faith, but what is faith but an historical process, religion an accumulation of insight? I am left alone with it now, standing in a plain of blasted vision. I am the last of my people. There are no more left. I cannot even mate. I am the last.

They put me in a huge enclosed area to protect me because I was the last. I had enough space to give me a sense of freedom. Nothing wanting. I was fed, pampered, cared for, watched over, and kept under observation. I was the last. I was precious.

Why me? I said through the bars? I am the last. You have all the others, about two billion by now. Your message of love has been carried to all the corners of the world. I am the last. Let me be.

They put me in a cage with the Przewalski, ancestor of the horse, and hung a sign on the bars:

WARNING: Irritable Nature, Bites.

I spent a century with them, hooving it over the hills, eating grass, sleeping under the stars and the sun. "So, you're it," I said to them, "all that's left, a living fossil." They weren't even the right shape for a horse. They did not resemble any horses I had ever known. You couldn't ride them or use them in any way. They were lost in the evolutionary scale, having gone backward in size and manners, a hangover from a wild Asian past, yet arrogant all the same, dangerous if teased. "Why don't you keel over and call it a day," I said to them.

"Clever man," their leader said, "always looking for an alibi to stay alive. Must have a reason to breathe. The unexamined life isn't worth living for you. Take it from me, it is. I don't care whether you think I should or I shouldn't, ought or ought not. I care nothing for Socrates. Me for Leviathan."

He looked at me narrow-eyed through the long hairs on his forehead, his eyes devious, his teeth large. To tell the truth, I resembled him in temperament.

"Guru," I said, "still what is the use?"

"The use of what?" he asked.

"The use of struggling. We are the last of the line. There are six of you and one of me. We'll never make a comeback."

His blubbery lips parted over his terrible teeth. "Die if you want to," he said. "As for me, whether I am the first or the last makes no difference to me. What do I care for reasons or lines or points. God created me. Let Him find a reason. Do I have to do His thinking? If you have to give yourself a reason for living, you're half dead. Keel over and finish it! Survival is my religion. It's my business. My genes work that way. They never refused the call. That's why I am still here after fifty thousand years. Talk when you reach my age. Take it from me, my seed still sings."

His words braced me, but my keepers beckoned to me.

Precious, they said. Brother, they called me. They caressed my cheek and said, Your yea is more precious to us than all the others.

Their friendship always weakened me, unhinged my knees, made me tremble. My temptation was so terrible, my tongue dried in my mouth. I could not even mate with the Przewalskis. What was the use of holding out? No one would walk in my footsteps after me.

They sent doctors to minister to me. They offered me a female egg to fertilize. They requested my seed to preserve. They serenaded me in the twilight. They admitted they had been cruel in the past. Mea culpa, a child lisped in a charming voice beneath my cage. Mea culpa, the wind whispered. The whole universe wept for the wrongs it had done me. I was ecstatic, expectant, then cautious. I remembered Ulysses and the sirens. The child, a dove in her mouth, a garland in her hair, her eyes shining with faith and love, held her hand out to me. Come, she said, I will lead the way.

My guru whinnied.

"Shut up," I said to him. I peered through the bars, blinking, stupid, unbelieving. I am the last, I said, sulking, what difference can I make? I am surrounded by the world, four billion souls, in every color and shape pray for me, wait for me. This human pressure taxes my heart; I tax their patience. They wait, even I wait for my answer.

A wasp settled on my nose and distracted me. My decision hung in the air. They watched it. I watched them. Their love was as inexplicable to me as their hatred.

"What do you want?" I said. I spoke carefully, in a controlled voice, not to alarm the wasp on my nose. My eyes centered and watched it carefully. "I am the last," I said breathlessly, waiting to be stung, "what can you possibly want of me?"

"We love you," they said.

The insect damaged my poise. Anxiety afflicted me. Sweat dripped in my armpits. Even I found myself intolerable. Why should anyone want me? I was perverse. But my perversity made sense to me, like a habit makes sense. Their love seemed more perverse to me than my perversity. Why should they love me? Why should they crave me? I had a motive for my perversity, grounded in accumulated reactions, a point of view. What was their motive? You, they said.

I said I'd think about it, and turned away from the bars. That was enough to cause the mood to change. I had been incautious. The wasp stung me. I jumped with surprise. The singing stopped. The dove changed into a toad. "Perverse," they snapped at me.

I laughed. "What have I been telling you all these years?" Still my bones ached. Not from bad treatment, just from the persistence of bad mood.

They let me alone. I wandered about in my cage with the Przewalski, thinking they had forgotten me. But they hadn't. My yea, my precious yes, they still wanted it. They filled my cage with mirrors, fed me with the illusion that I was one of many, several million perverse souls wandering about, each looking as morose as myself, skinnied down to a wire of willful resistance. They forgot they had hung the mirrors up and wondered where so many of my kind had come from. They fretted about my comeback and hung a thousand megaphones on every rock and tree to remind me that they waited for my yea, the world waited for my yea, for its redemption through my yea, for its salvation through my yea, for its final solution to everything through my yea, war, strife, unemployment, capitalism, racism, communism, slavery, bourgeoism and, most of all, to my perversity. It would all end when I ended. It was up to me to save the world. The wasp bit me on my nose with guilt. I alone held back all prophecies.

I gritted my teeth and shouted at them, Why me?

We need you, we want you, we love you, they said. Flattery was my weakness, but I was wary.

My guru looked in the mirrors with me and laughed. His pink horse lips curled over his big, brown teeth.

Can't you save the world without me? I shouted back.

You're the last, they said. Faith has to be complete. No loopholes. The flattery continued, persistent, cruel, cosmic.

To tell the truth, I could not stand it anymore, the implications, the persistence of guilt. One must do what one can to save the world.

O.K. I shouted at them, you have it. Let the Kingdom of God be ushered in.

They took me out of the cage and showed me the path through the mountain to the heart of the world.

If we let you free, don't go back on your word, they said.

Did I ever?

Yes, they said, you're a backslider.

Their distrust made me gloomy and thoughtful: what was the point of laboring up their mountain if they didn't believe me? We believe you, they sang. You've said that before, I said. It's different this time, they said. Now, go.

I started to climb, but where was I going? What was the top like? What could I see? Nothing when I looked back. The sun in their visors blinded out everything. I could only see the armor of their love shining with impeccable steel. I could not even see my gruffy Przewalski. I missed them. I swung out there on the mountainside all by myself, hanging on to an outcropping of rock, delirious. The wind whistled against my cheekbones. I thought of the Przewalski, safe, nibbling warm grass. Regrets at my decision mounted, but I continued to climb. They perceived my hesitation and stopped singing. I hung there, precarious, indecisive. They began to hiss. Backslider!

So what, I said, I still have the original idea. As ideas go, it's a good one: Thou shalt not worship idols, especially if they come in human form. It clings to me like a second skin, hard to take off without bleeding.

The wind whistled all around me and the stars glowed like flaming blue letters.